PRAISE

"A gritty, compelling, and altogether engrossing novel that reads as if ripped from the headlines. I couldn't turn the pages fast enough. Chad Zunker is the real deal."

—Christopher Reich, *New York Times* bestselling author of *Numbered Account* and *Rules of Deception*

"*Good Will Hunting* meets *The Bourne Identity.*"

—Fred Burton, *New York Times* bestselling author of *Under Fire*

HUNT THE LION

OTHER TITLES BY CHAD ZUNKER

The Tracker

Shadow Shepherd

HUNT THE LION

CHAD ZUNKER

This is a work of fiction. Names, characters, organizations, places, events, and incidents are either products of the author's imagination or are used fictitiously. Any resemblance to actual persons, living or dead, or actual events is purely coincidental.

Published by Thomas & Mercer, Seattle

www.apub.com

ISBN-13: 9781503903074
ISBN-10: 1503903079

Cover design by Jae Song

Printed in the United States of America

To Liz Pearsons and Gracie Doyle,
who saw something in the early pages
and took a chance on an unknown.

What was silent in the father speaks in the son, and often I found in the son the unveiled secret of the father.

—Friedrich Nietzsche

They are like a lion hungry for prey, like a fierce lion crouching in cover.

—Psalm 17:12

ONE

At two in the morning, a cold mist hung in the Moscow air, and the streets around Sam were all but still. Only a few isolated cars passed by every couple of minutes. A scattering of late-night wanderers, mostly vagrants who probably had nowhere else to go tonight, was out on the sidewalks along Chistye Prudy, a clean-water pond in Moscow's Basmanny District. Sam exhaled a nervous breath. He was five thousand miles away from his apartment back in DC. A million miles away from a life that had just started to make sense to him a month ago, then had *everything* flipped upside down on him within a twenty-four-hour period.

Nothing made sense to him now.

Sam Callahan, CIA agent?

Rushing across the street, Sam stepped up onto the opposite sidewalk and carefully approached the ten-foot-high white-stone wall that surrounded the block-wide town house property. As an extra measure of security, a decorative row of razor-sharp steel points lined the top of the wall. They weren't quite rolls of barbed wire, but Sam knew they conveyed the same message: *Stay the hell out!*

His heart racing, Sam paused, searched both ways up and down the sidewalk to make sure he was in the clear, and waited for further instructions. He knew there were usually guards at each corner of the property. Men dressed in military fatigues and holding black assault rifles. There were also guards roaming inside and outside the building. At least one guard was inside a small room on the ground floor at all times, where he monitored a dozen different security cameras. If that wasn't intimidating enough, Sam had also seen surveillance photos of several guard dogs. Highly trained black muscle-bound Dobermans ready to tear off his flesh. This gave him extra pause. Dogs had never been too kind to him. Of course, the only ones Sam had ever encountered while growing up on the streets had been trained guard dogs he had run into while breaking and entering somewhere.

He tried to swallow the thick knot that sat in the back of his throat. Although he'd been secretly training for countless hours with Marcus Pelini's clandestine CIA squad back in DC, Sam still found it hard to fathom that he'd suddenly been dropped into the center of this powerful foreign city. And with an intricate plan for him to carry out a covert intelligence operation that, if he was successful, was supposed to somehow make America a safer place. CIA? He was just a twenty-six-year-old rookie lawyer fresh from Georgetown Law and still wet behind the ears. Still the scared orphan boy who had lived for several years as a homeless teenager, where he'd survived the streets by stealing wallets, purses, and even cars, and who'd eventually done a three-month juvie stint.

Now, after only a few weeks of training, Sam was supposed to feel equipped enough to carry out a covert CIA operation? This was crazy.

"Get ready," Roger instructed in his earpiece.

Roger and four other members of the group, including Pelini, were inside a safe house a mile away, with all the windows blacked out, surrounded by computers and surveillance equipment. Sam had visited the safe house upon his arrival from London for a final equipment check. Two more agents, Luis and Mack, were supposed to be out on the streets somewhere, providing him with backup in case things went badly. Sam had been unable to spot either of the men.

Adjusting his black-framed glasses that sent a live video feed to the safe house, Sam stepped back to give himself some room to maneuver and set his own mental countdown clock. He had only thirty seconds, or he was toast. Jabber—a hacker on their team who ran their computers—would be freezing the security cameras temporarily, giving Sam the briefest of windows to pass undetected through the property. However, Jabber couldn't leave the cameras frozen for long, or the video guard might notice and place the property on full lockdown. It had to look like a momentary camera glitch, with everything going back to normal just seconds before the guard became concerned.

"Green! Go!" Roger ordered.

With more adrenaline racing through him, Sam ran straight for the stone wall and leaped, his gloved hands reaching up and clasping the very top of the wall. He quickly pulled himself up, carefully avoided being jabbed by the row of sharp steel points, flipped his legs over on the other side, then scaled down until his shoes met the wet grass. Pivoting, he surveyed a familiar scene—one he'd memorized in dozens of surveillance photos—a massive resort-style pool area, enveloped by well-landscaped grounds. A Russian tycoon named Vladimir Zolotov owned the property.

Tucking his head low, Sam sprinted toward the far corner of the town house property—the place with the most shadows. He hurdled a set of bushes, then dove up onto a stone ledge, where he rolled and regained his balance. Roger was in his ear, urgently counting down, "Eight, seven . . ." Sam took off again, praying he'd reach the corner of the building before a guard or a dog suddenly popped into his view. "Three, two . . ." He reached the back corner, grabbed on to the cream-colored edges of the stone building, pulled himself up off the grass, and began climbing just as Roger yelled, "One!" in his earpiece.

"Cameras are live again," Roger stated. "Keep moving, Callahan."

Sam tried to catch his breath, his heart pounding away. He stared a hundred feet straight up to the very top of the massive Moroccan-style town house. Using the architectural details to his advantage, Sam began climbing the back corner of the building, one careful reach of his hand and slide of his foot at a time. The wet mist in the air made the climb more difficult than his hundreds of practice sessions back in the dank warehouse in DC. With no rope harness or safety gear to protect him in a fall, he could rely only on the tacky grip of his special rock-climbing shoes, the strength of his gloved fingers, and his uncanny ability to steady his frantic mind.

About thirty feet up, Sam paused, heard a noise below him. Staring down, he silently cursed. He spotted the silhouette of a guard *and* a guard dog directly beneath him. The guard had stopped to light a cigarette. Sam could see the flame of the cigarette lighter and the flicker of the man's bearded face in the glow. The huge Doberman seemed at ease, sitting perfectly still right next to the guard, which was good. The dog wasn't yet tracking him, but Sam knew the dog's heightened hearing would likely pick up one false move. He'd be pumped with bullets and then fed to the canines. He held his breath for what felt like two minutes, his fingers trembling as they tightly gripped the edge of the building. Finally, the guard and dog both moved along, out of sight.

Sam exhaled, reached up again, continued to climb. Even though it was cold, beads of sweat were already pouring down his face and stinging his eyes.

"How you doing, Callahan?" Roger said in his ear.

"Hanging in there," he whispered back, only slightly amusing himself.

Roger chuckled. "Indeed."

Continuing to climb higher, Sam stopped every ten feet to calm himself. His shoulders throbbed. Although he'd practiced this climb nearly every day to exhaustion for the past month, nothing could truly prepare him for doing it live, inside Moscow, in the middle of the night, with guards and dogs below him, and his adrenaline spiking off the charts. Not even Pelini could manufacture that feeling in a warehouse. Sam's fingers felt like they were on fire.

When he reached the sixth floor, he paused again to catch his breath, steady himself. He pivoted his head around for a moment and looked out over the vast city. He could see the colorful Saint Basil's Cathedral glowing in bright lights inside Moscow's famous Red Square near the banks of the Moskva River. On his own, Sam had done his share of personal study on Moscow. Although he wasn't there as a tourist—he was planning on being there for only a few hours, after all—getting a certain lay of the land made him feel more comfortable.

"Need to get a move on, Sam," Pelini said in his ear.

"I'm working on it," he snapped.

He reached up again, pulled himself a few feet higher, and could now see a balcony edge right above him—the top level of the building. He was almost there. As he reached for the top of a stone railing, his right foot unexpectedly slipped off the edge, shooting a charge through him. He barely got a hand around a column to keep himself from dropping more than a hundred feet to his certain death. As both feet dangled beneath him, he swiftly reached up with his other hand and clasped the balcony column.

"Careful there, cowboy," Roger encouraged him.

His heart beating so fast that he thought he might pass out, Sam quickly pulled himself up and secured his feet again. Peeking up and over the stone railing, he made sure a guard with a gun wasn't standing there waiting to greet him. Then he pulled himself over the railing and dropped to the stone floor on the other side.

Already exhausted, Sam still had a long way to go.

He scanned the top level of the town house. As expected, he was in the very back corner of a massive open-air garden, with hundreds of plant features and three huge water fountains that were all currently running. Zolotov probably had some amazing parties on top of his home—it was as if he owned an oasis in the middle of an urban jungle.

Sam searched for any shadows of movement but spotted nothing. From Pelini's advanced surveillance, Sam knew the security guards didn't usually tour the very top of the building. The only way to the top was by heavily secured and camera-monitored stairs or elevator. Zolotov probably never thought anyone would be stupid enough to climb a hundred feet straight up the side of a building guarded by a squad of armed men and ruthless dogs in the dark of night.

He was wrong.

Sam *was* that stupid.

TWO

Sam quickly located his designated target. An eight-foot circular opening sat directly in the middle of the top-level garden, completely surrounded by a four-foot-high stone wall. Peeking over the stone wall, he stared down through thick metal safety netting deep inside the town house, finding exactly what the architectural plans and surveillance photos had suggested—an eight-foot-wide glass cylinder had been constructed in the very center of the home, stretching from the first floor all the way up to the top of the residential tower. Sam took in the massive hundred-foot-long green ivy hanging in the center of the glass cylinder interwoven with tens of thousands of colorful flowers.

Apparently fascinated with rain forests, Zolotov had decided to build his own version that he could view on every floor of his home. Although Sam knew bright lights usually lit the glass cylinder during daylight hours—showcasing its staggering beauty—the tube was currently dark. This was critical if he was to proceed to the next bold step in the operation. A step that was maybe even more dangerous than his climbing a hundred feet straight up the outside of the building.

"You're two minutes behind," Roger mentioned in his ear.

"Then how about we trade spots?" Sam countered.

"Just pick up the pace some, okay?"

Wearing a black jacket with numerous pockets holding all his special-ops gear, Sam unzipped a pocket on the left side and pulled out a pair of heavy-duty industrial metal cutters. He then carefully snipped away at the metal netting that protected anyone from falling inside the glass cylinder. When he'd cut out a square big enough to slip through, he set the heavy netting over to the side. From a larger jacket pocket, he located a small black metal box with a thick metal carabiner sticking out of one end. The carabiner was attached to a thin steel wire coiled inside the box—the strongest wire on the planet, he'd been told. The high-tech wire would definitely hold his six-foot, 175-pound frame; he'd done this drill with this very same equipment more than a hundred times already back in DC.

Still, that was just a drill.

This was live, with men with assault rifles nearby.

Pulling up on his jacket, Sam used straps to secure the black box to a vest that was tight to his body. Grabbing the carabiner from the metal box, he pulled out the coiled wire, wrapped the carabiner five times around one of the thick steel beams that held the hanging-plant feature in place, then clipped the carabiner and the wire securely to the beam. He tugged twice and felt safe.

He was set and ready.

Another deep breath filled with nerves.

Climbing up over the stone wall, he sat on the edge, dropped his legs through the eight-foot opening. He gripped one of the steel beams with both gloved hands and slowly lowered himself down inside the cylinder. Steadying himself, Sam let go of the steel beam and began floating in the air. When he made sure he had no sway, he reached down to his vest and pressed a button on the side of the fancy box. The wire began to uncoil slowly, and smoothly lowered him deeper into the cylinder. Hanging beside the flowered ivy, he was careful not to bump *it*, or the curved glass wall on the opposite side.

When he'd lowered himself to the sixth floor, Sam paused, suddenly feeling exposed and uneasy. It was dark both inside the glass cylinder and inside the interior of the town house. One flick of the lights in a hallway, and he'd be caught hanging there like a human piñata waiting to be clobbered.

The same thought kept flashing through his mind.

What the hell am I doing here?

Taking a moment to peer through the glass, he could make out a few night-lights on in the hallway that circled the tube but very little else. According to the floor plan, the sixth level was Zolotov's master bedroom suite. Nearly two thousand square feet with a bedroom, a changing room, a reading room, an exercise room, a meditation room, and a spalike bathroom. Zolotov's wife—his third in six years—had a closet that was bigger than Sam's entire apartment.

He waited a moment to see if he spotted any movement on the sixth floor. The town house remained quiet. Pushing the button again, Sam lowered himself deeper into the building, cruising past the fifth and fourth floors without pause. Again, he saw no signs of movement. Sam finally eased down to his target level—the third floor, which housed Zolotov's office suite. He unzipped a pocket along the right side of his jacket and pulled out a small handheld device that had a powerful fist-size suction cup on one side. Grabbing the handle, Sam carefully pushed the suction cup against the glass wall of the cylinder. He then pushed a button on the device's handle, and the suction cup gradually sucked tightly to the glass. He wiggled it several times to make sure it was securely in place.

From another jacket pocket, he extracted a second handheld device that with a push of a button revealed a sharp jagged blade on one end—a blade he'd been told could cut through dinosaur bone, if necessary. Sam had often wondered how they'd come to that conclusion but didn't ask. His heart was beating so fast, his hands were shaking. He looked away from his hands, hoping the team back in the safe house didn't notice his growing nerves. This was the next huge hurdle in completing the mission. It had to go perfectly. One false move, and he might as well stick the blade in his own gut to avoid the trouble of the guards and dogs.

Holding the device tightly in his right hand, he placed the blade against the thick glass. He then pushed a button on the device, which began to vibrate powerfully and cut straight through the glass. The cutting device was quiet but *not* silent. Sam thought it sounded a hell of a lot like a damn chainsaw churning. More beads of sweat poured down his face. He watched closely to see if any lights came on inside the home. Nothing happened. Working quickly, he guided the device in a large circle all the way around the suction cup. Before fully connecting the circle, he grabbed the suction-cup handle in his left hand, then finished the cutting job.

Holding the suction cup, Sam was able to push the glass cutout all the way through to the inside of the town house and gently set it on the carpeted floor. Using both gloved hands, he pulled himself up against the glass, stuck his feet through first, created some slack in the wire, then carefully wiggled his way inside the interior of the town house. Kneeling, he quickly released the metal black box from his vest and used a strap to secure it to the handle of the suction cup. He would need the high-tech pulley system again in a few minutes.

"I'm in," he whispered, his mouth completely dry.

"We can see that," said Roger. "Nice job."

From another pocket on his jacket, Sam grabbed a penlight. A powerful, narrow beam of light shot out in front of him. Getting to his feet, he began to make his way down a dark hallway, pulling up the building's memorized floor plan in his mind. Entry into Zolotov's office chambers should be just around the corner. If all went well, he'd be in and out within ten minutes. Then back to London.

Using the flashlight, Sam stepped catlike down the hallway. Easing around the corner, he suddenly froze when he spotted bare feet directly in front of him. The small beam of the flashlight shifted from the feet all the way up to a face, which was staring right back at him. Sam cursed.

THREE

Sam was shocked. A small boy of maybe five stood in front of him, looking half-asleep and disoriented. The boy wore Batman pajamas and had disheveled brown hair, as if he'd just rolled out of bed. He was rubbing both eyes with his small fists, bothered by the blinding beam of light that was shining directly in his face. Just the same, Sam kept the flashlight on him to guard the boy from seeing him. What the hell was the kid doing on the third floor? Was he sleepwalking?

"We've got company," Sam whispered into his collar.

"Get rid of him," Roger ordered. "Do it quickly."

Sam mentally scrolled through his thirty-day crash course in the Russian language. He never expected to use any of it.

"You okay, kid?" Sam quietly asked in Russian.

"Stop the light," the boy replied in Russian, squinting.

Sam lowered the light just a bit from the kid's eyes, asked, "What's your name?"

"Charlie."

"My name is Leo. One of the guards."

"You speak English?" the boy asked in English, gaining some of his sensibilities.

Sam was surprised, didn't respond. This was *not* good. Roger was in his ear again. "Get rid of him, Callahan! That kid is going to blow everything for us."

"I heard you speak English," the boy insisted. "I have an English tutor."

The boy spoke very good English.

Sam stuck with Russian. "Why are you down here?"

"My room," the boy said, in Russian, looking over his shoulder.

"Where's your room, Charlie?" Sam said.

Sleepily, the boy turned, pointed down the hallway right behind him, which didn't make any sense. There were two doors on the left, two more doors on the right. Why would the kid have a bedroom on three? According to the floor plan, all the kids' bedrooms were supposed to be up on the fourth floor.

Roger cursed. "They must have changed the layout or something."

"Fantastic," muttered Sam.

"What?" the boy said, confused.

"Come on, Charlie."

Placing a hand on the boy's frail shoulder, Sam guided him back to the first door on the right, which was open. Charlie walked over to a small race car–type bed pressed up against the wall. Sam did a quick scan with the flashlight. Definitely a little boy's bedroom. There were posters of sports figures all over the walls. Most looked like Russian hockey players, although there were a couple of American basketball players. LeBron James. Stephen Curry. The boy crawled back into his bed. Sam pulled up the covers and tucked in the kid. Charlie was already asleep again. Sam took a second look at the boy's young face, tilted his head. The boy reminded him a lot of himself when he was a five-year-old. Same scraggly brown hair. Of course, when he was five, Sam was living in a two-bedroom shack near loud railroad tracks with two angry foster parents who used to feed him a stale slice of bread covered in some kind of awful homemade jam every morning.

Charlie, on the other hand, lived in a $100 million tower.

"Get going," Roger urged him.

Easing out of the bedroom, Sam shut the door behind him. "Where?"

"Try the other rooms first," Roger instructed.

Sam stepped over to the door next to Charlie's bedroom. He turned the knob, cracked the door open. Another boy's bedroom. A night-light was on in the room. More sports memorabilia on walls and shelves. Large toy construction trucks all over the carpeted floor. A boy with blond hair, slightly older than Charlie, was asleep under the blankets of a twin bed. Sam was careful not to wake him with the flashlight.

Quietly shutting the door, Sam moved across the hallway and opened another door. The third bedroom was all pink. A chandelier hung from the ceiling. He poked the flashlight beam inside and found a small girl with long blonde hair, who looked Charlie's age, lying in a castle-type bed. When she stirred under the brightness of his flashlight beam, Sam quickly exited. He moved to the fourth bedroom, cracked the door. A purple bedroom. A huge dollhouse sat against the wall. A pile of stuffed animals in one corner. Yet another tiny girl, the smallest of the group, under the sheets. Sam cursed. The third floor was all children. Every single room.

"What the hell?" Sam whispered. "Where is the server room?"

Off microphone, Sam heard Roger say, "Where the hell did Marcus go?"

Sam then heard another voice respond in the background: "Said he needed to step out for a sec."

Roger cursed again, said, "Dammit! Go find him! Now!" Back online, Roger sighed, said, "Okay, Callahan, go up a flight."

"How? Using the wire?"

"No, we don't have time for that. Use the stairs."

"I thought the stairs were on security camera."

"They are, so be careful and be quick."

Sweating profusely, Sam moved farther down the hallway, peeked around the corner. No shadows, no movement. All looked clear. Still, he felt sick to his stomach. The original plan, one they'd practiced hundreds of times, was rapidly unraveling. This brought on a new level of stress. Even though he had a knack for getting himself out of tricky spots, he'd hoped he'd never have to use that skill tonight.

That hope had just been obliterated.

He'd have to use his free-form instincts now.

With the flashlight beam guiding him forward, he stepped into what looked like a huge game room, with all sorts of table games in the middle—ping-pong, air hockey, pool, table soccer—and then he noticed an entire wall lined with more than a dozen modern full-size arcade games. He carefully eased through the playroom and found a hallway leading toward what he believed was a secure door to the main stairwell. According to Pelini's surveillance, Zolotov's security squad monitored everything outside of the town house as well as the inside stairwell and the elevator. The guts of the house, however, where Zolotov lived and entertained guests day-to-day, was off-limits and private from the guards. Zolotov understandably didn't want his own men watching him walk around in his underwear.

Sam was about to step outside his safety zone and right into a highly secured area, something that had never even been discussed or considered.

He felt a surge of panic coming on again.

What the hell am I doing here?

Roger was back in his earpiece. "All right, Callahan, listen up. Jabber is about to give you a quick five-second pause with the stairwell camera. Don't hesitate. You understand me?"

"Yes."

"On my mark."

Sam took a deep breath, his hand tightly gripped on the doorknob.

Roger said, "Three, two, one . . . go!"

Sam turned the doorknob, pulled the door fully open, and raced straight up the private stairwell. He didn't even search for cameras. They were there somewhere. He hit the carpeted steps at full speed, made the turn at midlevel, and rushed upward again. He found a door to the fourth level. Quickly pulling it open, he stepped inside, hoping not to see another random face waiting for him.

"Good job, kid," Roger stated. "Cameras are live again."

Catching his breath, Sam stepped down the dark hallway, passed through a large sitting room with an impressive view of the glass cylinder, then turned a corner, where he was relieved to find Zolotov's expansive office. A huge glass desk the size of a Volvo sat on one side of the room with matching glass shelves behind it that covered the entire wall. Sam did a quick scan with the flashlight. The shelves were stuffed with books, artifacts, and hundreds of pictures showing Zolotov standing next to celebrities and powerful political figures from all over the world—Sam recognized several faces, including many prominent American leaders.

Next to the office door stood a massive eight-foot-tall bronze statue of Leo Tolstoy. In front of Tolstoy sat two luxurious brown sofas that both faced what Sam guessed was probably a hundred-inch flat-screen TV. However, what dazzled Sam the most was the floor-to-ceiling glass window that looked out over the streets of Moscow. An unbelievable $100 million view. He could see the bright lights of the Kremlin near Red Square, home to Russia's president, with its massive palaces, cathedrals, and towers.

Stepping through the office, Sam found a connecting hallway on the opposite side. If the floor plan was correct, even if the levels had flipped, Sam expected to find a highly secured server room behind the first door on his right.

When he got to the door, he put his flashlight beam on a digital touch pad on the wall. That was a good sign. Sam pulled a tightly sealed Ziploc bag from a jacket pocket. Inside, he extracted the thinnest of flesh-covered gloves and carefully tugged it onto his right hand. The glove felt like a second layer of skin. He pressed the touch pad with a finger, and it flickered to life. From memory, Sam quickly punched in an eight-digit code on the digital keypad, prayed that Jabber had given him correct information. The screen blinked and then switched from the keypad to a hand imprint. Sam lifted his gloved right hand, pressed it against the screen, held his breath.

A second later, the screen flashed **Access Granted**.

Exhaling, Sam opened the door and stepped inside a small room with black metal shelves that housed what looked like enough electronic boxes, cables, and touch pads to run a small town. Expensive computer equipment lined every wall. Sam unzipped a slim pocket on the inside of his jacket and pulled out a black pouch the size of a paperback book. Unsealing the protected pouch, he grabbed a small computer tablet. From another pocket, he found a tightly coiled computer cable. He quickly plugged the cable into the tablet, unwound the coil, and looked for his target port on one of the dozens of metal computer boxes that sat on a middle shelf. He finally found the supposed target port, labeled B12.

Sam whispered, “Confirming access point.”

“Hold,” Roger instructed. Five seconds later, the man said, “Access point confirmed.”

He pulled the current black cable out of the B12 port and immediately replaced it with the cable he'd brought with him. He paused again, waited. No alarms went off, no flashing lights, no dogs barking. So far, so good. He set the tablet on a shelf and quickly powered it up. Wiping moisture from his face, Sam watched the tablet screen begin to flash through all kinds of computer code—numbers and letters that he didn't really understand. However, he'd seen this kind of thing aplenty over the past year because of the invaluable assistance he'd received from his good friend Tommy Kucher, a brilliant twentysomething hacker who'd helped rescue him from the hands of certain death on more than one occasion.

To Sam, it looked like the tablet was possessed, with so many different screens pulling up and closing, all in rapid fashion. He had nothing to do with any of it. Jabber fully controlled the tablet from inside the safe house.

Closing his eyes, Sam took a moment to gather himself. He'd done his job to this point. Against incredible odds, he'd somehow navigated his way inside the interior confines of a heavily guarded fortress and given Pelini's team the necessary local access to Zolotov's private network—the only way, he'd been told, they could secure the object of this secret mission. He focused his mind solely on his pathway back out of the town house. Jabber would need to give him another free pass down the stairwell. Then he'd head back to the glass cylinder, gather his gear, and travel up to the top of the town house again with the high-tech pulley system, as previously planned.

Finally, he'd climb back down the outside of the building.

Sighing, Sam knew this wasn't even close to being over yet.

He checked his watch. Jabber seemed to be taking longer than he had expected.

"What's going on?" Sam whispered.

"Hold steady," Roger replied. "He's almost there."

Waiting impatiently, Sam thought of Natalie Foster, his fiancée. He was seven hours ahead of her, which meant Natalie was probably sitting inside her office cubicle. As an investigative reporter for *PowerPlay*, a popular online DC news site, she often worked deep into the night hours. Natalie lived and breathed to break the next big story. She was also damn good at her job. He could envision her right now, eyes locked in on her laptop, fingers pecking away, nibbling gently on her bottom lip like she always did when her mind was spinning. He was so ready to get this thing over with, get back to DC, and start his new life with her. It had really torn him up inside to keep this huge secret from her.

Pelini had insisted any mention would put a target on Natalie and immediately put her life in grave danger. Sam had been intentionally dragging his feet on setting an actual wedding date. Not because he was uncertain of being with her. Hell, he'd never been surer of Natalie. However, deep down inside, he'd been carrying around this small fear for the past month that he might not return from Russia. He knew he had to get through this first.

"He's got it!" Roger yelled into Sam's ear. "File secure!"

Sam actually heard some clapping in the background of the safe house, as several members of the team were openly cheering about operational success. That made Sam smile for a fleeting moment. Growing up mostly alone on the streets, he'd rarely had the chance to experience the thrill of a team victory. He'd never high-fived teammates after gridiron glory or celebrated a game-winning shot on the basketball court. He'd never been part of a dog pile on the mound after closing out a baseball championship. The cheering made him feel good.

But where was Pelini?

"Good job, Callahan," Roger said.

"Thanks. I can disconnect?"

"Yes, disengage. Let's get you out of there."

"Music to my ears."

Sam powered down the tablet and pulled the cable out of the black box.

Roger suddenly blurted, "What the hell . . . ?"

Sam paused. "What happened?"

"What's going on!" Roger demanded, even louder.

"Did I do something wrong?" Sam asked, getting concerned.

Sam realized Roger wasn't actually speaking to him. Instead, he was speaking to someone else inside the safe house. Then Sam heard sudden loud cursing in the background, coming from multiple voices. Something wasn't right. A second later, the audio in his right ear exploded with *Thump! Thump! Thump!* He recognized the terrifying sounds both from his political tracker assignment last year and from an infamous assassin hunting him just last month. It was the distinct sound of a gun firing with a silencer.

Someone was shooting inside the safe house?

More shots fired. *Thump! Thump!* He could hear crashing noises in the background.

A second later, Sam's earpiece went dead silent.

"Hello?" Sam said into his collar.

He tapped the earpiece. "Roger, you there?"

Nothing. No response. This brought on a new wave of panic.

What the hell was going on? Who was shooting?

Standing inside the server room, Sam didn't have much time to ponder what had just happened inside the safe house. Not with a piercing alarm suddenly going off inside Zolotov's fortress, shaking the damn walls.

FOUR

Grabbing the small computer tablet, Sam quickly placed it inside the protective pouch, sealed it up tight, shoved it into his jacket, and stepped outside of the server room. The alarm was even louder in the hallway, a repetitive high-pitched sound that punished his eardrums. Hustling back through the office space and down the hallway, Sam found the door to the stairwell locked. He wiggled the knob, but it wouldn't budge. He cursed. The guards had probably secured the building and were temporarily holding everyone in place, which meant they knew an intruder was on the inside. Did they know where, exactly?

He couldn't just stand there and wait to be discovered. He had to get out of the building as fast as possible. Kneeling, he studied the doorknob. There was no lock-and-key system. It was electronic, with thick dead bolts. There was no easy way for him to pick the lock and get into the stairwell. He had to find another way out. Pausing and listening, he suddenly heard voices on the other side of the stairwell door.

Spinning around, Sam raced back to Zolotov's office, shut the door behind him, and locked it. He then pushed the heavy bronze statue of Tolstoy over in front of the office door. Anything to buy him a few seconds. Turning, he stood still a second, closed his eyes, began to scroll through several escape maps that were now flashing through his mind. None of them seemed like good options. He opened his eyes and stared straight ahead at the glass wall. With guards likely on him at any moment, it was perhaps his only way to get out of the building. His only chance to survive. The only way he'd ever get back to Natalie.

He grabbed the handheld blade device he'd used earlier while hanging inside the glass cylinder. Stepping up to the glass wall, he knelt and pressed the blade against the thick glass at the bottom near the hardwood floor. He quickly cut a jagged line six feet straight up, then across three feet, and finally all the way back down toward the floor.

Sam paused when he heard a pounding behind him at the office door. The guards had arrived. He stepped back and kicked at the glass with the heel of his shoe. It took three strong kicks before the glass cutout broke free and toppled over to the outside. Poking his head through the opening, Sam watched as the glass pane shattered into a thousand pieces on the patio directly below him. He quickly calculated the distance from where the glass hit the patio to the edge of the massive resort-style pool. Maybe ten feet. He'd have to get a running start.

He heard gunshots outside the door, saw holes splintering around the doorknob. The guards were shooting their way inside. It was now or never. Rushing back over to Zolotov's desk, Sam turned, said a prayer. Then he sprinted toward the cutout in the glass wall and, like a long jumper at a track meet, took a flying leap out of the building. As he rapidly dropped toward the pool water below, he braced himself for impact, hoping the pool was deep enough so he wouldn't break his legs on impact.

He hit the water feetfirst and plunged into the pool. His entire body went under at an angle, shooting him forward like a torpedo, until his back collided painfully against the bottom of the pool, jarring his body and knocking out his breath.

Pushing himself off the bottom of the pool, he swiftly swam to the surface just in time to gulp in a breath of air and keep himself from swallowing gallons of pool water. He looked left, right, saw no guards in the immediate vicinity. He quickly made his way to the side of the pool, pulled himself out of the water. His right knee felt wobbly as he stumbled away behind a set of bushes and sprinted through the grass toward the ten-foot wall around the property.

He was only five feet from the wall when he felt the Doberman somewhere close behind him. He knew he couldn't even turn to look—the dog would be on him like a silent missile. Lunging for the wall, Sam reached up with his wet, gloved hands, grasped the top, began frantically pulling his body up. He swung his legs around just before the dog nearly ripped him to shreds.

Looking back down, he could see nothing but sharp teeth. Then he heard the familiar loud popping of an assault rifle from inside the compound. The wall directly beneath him began to spark with the impact of bullets. Sam didn't even try to get his grip; he didn't have time. He just jerked back, rolled, and allowed himself to fall off the wall onto freedom's side.

He landed hard on his right shoulder on the cold sidewalk. He could still hear the dog snarling on the other side of the wall, men yelling in Russian.

FIVE

Sam made it ten blocks before he finally collapsed to the pavement in a dark alley behind an old commercial building. He tried to catch his breath, examine himself, see if he'd been shot or badly injured. He could hear multiple sirens in the general area and figured the police were on their way to Zolotov's place. He wondered if he'd been caught on security camera during his escape. He had no time even to think about that; he just had to run his ass off. Would his picture soon be planted inside every Moscow police car?

His lungs on fire and his body still dripping wet, Sam could now feel sharp pains running up and down his right arm. Was it broken? The fall from the ten-foot wall had clearly done some damage. But how much? He squeezed his fist, slowly moved his arm back and forth. It hurt like hell, but he didn't think anything was broken. Although his knee throbbed, he could still move around on it. Everything else seemed to be in decent shape, all things considered. He was still alive—though he wasn't sure about the rest of his team.

The earpiece remained dead, so he'd tossed it while running away, along with the high-tech glasses. He took a moment to think again about what he'd heard before he'd lost complete contact and everything went dark. It sounded a hell of a lot like an ambush inside the safe house. There was a lot of suppressed gunfire and enough yelling and cursing to make Sam fear the worst. Was it one shooter? More than one shooter? He thought about Roger, Jabber, and the others. He didn't know any of them too well, but it was still shocking to think about the possibility that they might all be gone. Just like that.

His mind flashed on Marcus Pelini, and he felt a sudden catch in his throat. Was his father also dead? Was the man gone before Sam had ever had the opportunity to know *anything* more about him? Had this all been for nothing?

Shaking his head, Sam didn't even want to think about that just yet.

Gradually catching his breath, he began to wonder about Luis and Mack. His supposed backup men on the streets. Where the hell were they? Had both of them also been taken out? Was this apparent ambush more coordinated than he thought? If so, by whom? Zolotov's security assassins? Had the powerful Russian somehow discovered their secret operation? The Russian was well connected, both politically and militarily. He was also corrupt as hell, according to the CIA. Pelini said Zolotov liked to dabble in the illegal international arms trade. The CIA had also tied Zolotov to several terrorist organizations. The wealthy Russian was apparently willing to shed the blood of American intelligence agents for his own financial gain. A dangerous top-secret list had somehow fallen into Zolotov's possession—a list that could potentially jeopardize dozens of covert operations around the globe and expose hundreds of agents and informants. Their intel suggested that Zolotov was about to put the list up for sale on the black market. The CIA desperately wanted the list back.

Or was it someone else? Sam thought about the supposed intelligence mole. Was that a possibility? The recent discovery of a mole deep in their network had hamstrung the Agency's pursuit of the lethal list. That's why Pelini's unit had gone to extremes to recruit him from the outside. They needed someone with no official ties to the Agency. Someone who had never been in its system. An individual who not only possessed the rarest of skill sets but who could be trained quickly. Someone they felt they could trust to succeed against seemingly insurmountable odds because he'd already passed an incredibly daunting test.

Sam thought of the Gray Wolf, an infamous international assassin he'd somehow repeatedly evaded last month, and shook his head.

Sitting in the cold alley, Sam felt completely alone. Maybe more alone than he'd felt in his entire life, which was saying a hell of a lot, considering his tragic youth. He again thought of Natalie, grimaced, and cursed himself repeatedly. How could he have been so stupid as to jeopardize his future with her? For what? Pelini, his estranged father who may now already be dead?

Gritting his teeth, he pushed himself off the pavement. He couldn't let it end this way. Not tonight. Stepping toward the head of the alley, Sam tried to get his bearings. He felt like he had a good grasp of his current location. He could see a map of the city in his mind. If he was visualizing things the right way, the CIA safe house was four blocks to his left.

He needed to go there, see what had happened for himself, if possible. He peeked out both ways. Everything looked clear. There were no men with assault rifles running up the sidewalks, no sleek black dogs, no police cars with lights flashing. Hitting the sidewalk, Sam moved under the protection of as much night shadow as possible. Every hundred feet or so, he'd duck next to a building, check behind him, survey the landscape. When he felt safe again, he kept moving.

Crossing in front of an ornate building labeled the **EMBASSY OF THE REPUBLIC OF BELARUS**, Sam knew he was close. They'd passed the same building on the drive to the safe house earlier.

He cut through another alley and stepped out onto a quiet street lined with nearly identical redbrick one-story homes. The safe house was in the cul-de-sac at the very end of the block. He'd wondered if he'd find police or emergency services on the scene, but he saw no such thing. The house looked completely undisturbed. There were no cars of any sort on the curb.

Was anyone alive inside? What was he about to find?

Sam watched the house for several minutes, looking for anything suspicious. Any movement on the property. Anyone out on the sidewalks. Any approaching cars. Anyone who may be watching or waiting for him. He noticed nothing unusual. Finally, he stepped out of the shadows and hurried across the street. He hustled up the empty driveway to the side door, where he'd been ushered inside only a couple of hours ago. Before entering, he tried to peer through the square window in the door, but it was blacked out. He listened as closely as he could for any signs of life inside. Voices. Movement. But it was eerily quiet.

Putting a timid hand on the knob, he slowly cracked the door. The lights were still on inside the small kitchen. He listened again, heard nothing from deeper inside the house. Whoever had ambushed them either was sitting perfectly still or had already left. He stepped through the kitchen, poked his head around into the living room. He immediately felt nauseated and had to fight to keep himself from vomiting. Although Sam had seen dead bodies before—way more than he'd ever wanted—this horrific scene took his breath away. Multiple bodies lay haphazardly sprawled on the carpeted floor and in chairs where Pelini's team had set up their operations.

The first dead body belonged to Vita, a fiftysomething woman with brunette hair who was wearing a black windbreaker. Lying on the floor with one leg awkwardly cocked behind her, Vita had blood pooling around her body. She looked like she had a bullet hole in her head and several more in her chest area. Just awful. His heart racing wildly, Sam stepped around Vita, careful to avoid the blood on the floor, surveyed the other carnage. Juan, a man in his forties with black hair, was facedown on the floor, the rear of his head exploded and his back also bloodied with bullet holes. The young hacker, Jabber, was slumped over one of the foldout tables. Most of the computer surveillance equipment looked like it had also been shot up in the ambush.

Finally, Sam stepped over to Roger, who was still sitting in the same chair where Sam had last seen him in front of a wall of computer screens. The headphones and head mike were still on the man, only his head was now slumped all the way back, and blood was streaming down his neck. Sam cursed, feeling overwhelmed. He'd had the most rapport with Roger, since they'd spent so much time communicating through the earpiece during practice drills over the past month. Roger was both funny and kind. He seemed to appreciate that Sam had signed up to do this with them, even after everything they'd put him through last month.

Sam reached down and tugged Roger's right pant leg up, where he knew the man usually kept his cell phone in an ankle wrap. He'd learned these CIA types carried guns, phones, and other tech gadgets in odd places. He found the phone, pulled it out. It was locked. Taking Roger's right hand, careful not to get blood on himself, Sam placed the man's thumb on the Home button of the phone. The phone's thumb scanner read it and allowed Sam access. Sam went straight to the settings and turned off the security feature. He then shoved the phone into his pants pocket, took another look around the room. There was no movement from any of his team members. This wasn't some hocus-pocus the CIA had concocted to trick him again, like they had back in Mexico City. This was the real deal. No one was breathing. However, Sam was breathing so hard, he nearly hyperventilated.

He said a quick prayer for each of them. They all surely had families of some sort and people who would miss them. Parents. Children. Wives. Girlfriends. They all had someone out there who would grieve over this—*if* those people even found out what had actually happened to them. For all Sam knew, the CIA might simply make them vanish.

Sam went to each body and carefully checked pockets for cash or any other resources—*anything* that might help him survive the night.

Most of Pelini's team had been in Moscow for the past few days. They would have had to use *something* to meet their basic needs. However, he knew none of them would have their own wallets with personal credit cards or any other such legit IDs. The operation was completely clandestine. They'd all been given new aliases. They all had to be ghosts, with nothing that could legitimately tie them back to the CIA. Fortunately, Sam was able to gather a few hundred dollars' worth of Russian rubles, although he felt like a callous thief pilfering the dead on the battlefield.

Moving to the corner of the living room, he found his small black leather travel bag exactly where he'd left it earlier. He quickly swung the bag up over his shoulder, stepped back through the carnage. He hated leaving them all there, but what choice did he have? If he didn't keep moving, he could be next.

As he stepped out the side door, Sam could think of only one thing.

Where the hell was Marcus Pelini?

SIX

Sitting in her office cubicle, Natalie Foster squinted at the words on her laptop screen with the same intense focus of a heart surgeon who'd just opened up a chest in the operating room. After all, she believed her job was just as important, so she needed to get the words down as fast as possible. Not only was her potential story piping hot, she was close to nailing it and sending it out tonight. Timing was everything in her business. In a day when breaking news was measured by mere seconds, Natalie had to be ready to release her story at a moment's notice if she was going to win.

And Natalie *lived* to win. Losing just wasn't in her blood.

Natalie came from a family of winners. Her father had won a World Series while playing with the Cardinals in '82. Her mother had won an NCAA tennis championship while attending Ohio State. Growing up, Natalie had watched her four older brothers all win big in a variety of sports. Her own bedroom at Foster Farms, their homestead back in Glendale, Missouri, was chock-full of trophies. Soccer, tennis, track and field, and literally dozens of softball championships. Tonight, Natalie's adrenaline was pumping just like it had when she'd been an all-state second baseman at Glendale High. At four different points during her senior year, she'd come up to bat with the winning runners on base in the bottom of the last inning. All four times, her team had walked away in celebratory victory. She'd always thrived under the pressure of the moment.

Tonight was no different—except for the playing field.

Natalie had a trusted source who earlier that morning had claimed that Henry Dowerson, a new foreign policy adviser to the president, was about to go under official investigation by the FBI for a recent trip to Russia, where he'd given a Russia-friendly talk at the New Economic School. According to her source, several higher-ups at the FBI believed Dowerson—a former decorated navy veteran and now a successful investment banker—might have actually turned Russian spy. Apparently, there were surveillance photos and hidden recordings. Natalie was working desperately to get her hands on them. Because Dowerson was so well connected politically on both sides, the story was packed with firepower, and, if confirmed, it could set off a bomb that would seriously rattle DC. Natalie hoped to get that confirmation tonight.

Her eyes growing blurry, Natalie grabbed her empty coffee mug and walked over to the office's mini kitchen. It was a few minutes after eight, and most of *PowerPlay*'s news team had already headed home for the night. The only other reporter still with her inside their fourteenth-floor DC news office was Nelson, who exclusively covered the Hill. She could hear him arguing with a source on the phone four cubicles over, although she wasn't paying too much attention. After refilling her coffee mug, she stepped inside the large conference room, where the office had a splendid view. She took in the Capitol Building, smiled. She never grew tired of what it felt like working inside the power circles of this town. Her job had never felt more important. In an age where fake news had become so commonplace, Natalie considered her role as a legit investigative reporter willing to come hard at both sides more vital than ever.

She fiddled with the engagement ring on her left hand, like she'd been doing ever since Sam had placed it on her finger weeks ago. Her fiancé was currently in London on business for a few days. She hoped he was feeling better. When they'd talked earlier, he'd said he thought he might be coming down with a stomach bug and was going to crash in his hotel room for the rest of the night.

Staring at the engagement ring, she shook her head. It still felt surreal to be engaged to Sam, especially after the roller coaster of ups and downs they'd ridden over the past two years. Just a month ago, Natalie had been abducted in a DC parking garage, before she'd eventually escaped a remote warehouse, and Sam had barely survived an infamous international assassin hunting him.

In the aftermath of that ordeal, Natalie had strong suspicions that there was more to the story behind Sam's crazy trip to Mexico City. Something hadn't settled well with her. She was sure Sam was hiding *something*. She'd been digging around a little but still hadn't found anything. Because she'd made a promise to Sam that she wouldn't personally pull him into another one of her news stories, Natalie felt obligated not to stir up too much trouble. Besides, she loved Sam deeply and didn't want to do *anything* to put up new barriers between them. They'd both committed to a fresh start. Still, there was something there—she just couldn't put her finger on it yet. Something was still off between them. Was he cheating? She didn't want to believe that, but she'd overheard a few hushed phone calls in the middle of the night and noticed a couple of strange text messages from random numbers showing up on his phone when he'd left it sitting out. Sam had also acted unusually anxious about his travel plans to London. He'd seemed jumpy and distracted. When she'd pressed, he'd claimed it was simply stress from the drama of his last trip to Mexico City.

Hearing her cell phone ringing, Natalie rushed back over to her desk, feeling a new spike of energy. Michelle Blair, her trusted friend and her best source within the FBI, had been digging into Dowerson's situation for her all day. Natalie hoped she was about to get the confirmation she wanted.

"We need to meet, *right now*," Michelle said.

"What do you got?" Natalie asked.

"Not over the phone."

SEVEN

Natalie picked up Michelle in her silver Jeep Cherokee right outside the Metro station at Fourth and E Street near the FBI's office. Climbing into the passenger seat, Michelle looked serious as hell and instructed Natalie to simply drive. In her thirties, Michelle had short brown hair and an athletic build. The two of them had met several years ago, when Natalie was working a story where she'd first used Michelle as a source. They'd bonded quickly when they discovered both had tragically lost their mothers early in life and were basically raised by the men of their family. Natalie cruised past Lower Senate Park, waited for Michelle to speak. The intensity in the woman's face got her really excited. Natalie could tell she had something *big*.

"Talk to me, Michelle," Natalie begged.

"Pull over up here somewhere."

Natalie pulled into a near-empty lot next to the Hart Senate Office Building.

Michelle turned to her. "Where's Sam?"

Natalie tilted her head. The question caught her off guard. "He's in London."

"When was the last time you talked to him?"

"A few hours ago. Why?"

Michelle pulled out a small computer tablet from her purse. Natalie had an uneasy feeling growing in the pit of her stomach. Why was Michelle mentioning Sam? Was this meeting not about Dowerson? Opening up a video on the tablet's screen, Michelle handed it over to Natalie to view. She stared at the screen. The video looked like some kind of surveillance footage taken from inside a small house. What was this? The camera gave a wide-angle view of a small living room. Natalie could suddenly make out several people inside the room, only they weren't moving. Some of them were lying on the floor, and several of them looked like they were covered in something dark. Was it blood? A man, probably in his fifties, was sitting in a chair directly in front of the camera, his head cocked all the way back with what clearly looked like blood running down his neck. Natalie grimaced.

"Why're you showing me this?"

"Just keep watching."

A few seconds later, a man walked into the living room. Natalie stiffened. *Sam!* She felt her stomach coil up into a tight ball. Sam was wearing all black. Standing there, he looked around the living room for a few seconds, began carefully stepping around the bodies. He then moved directly in front of the surveillance camera. Natalie couldn't believe her eyes. It was definitely him, although he seemed oblivious to being recorded. She could see fear in his eyes, and he looked like he was all wet. Why? What was happening? Sam reached down and grabbed something from the man who was sitting in the chair. A cell phone? He took the dead man's hand and fiddled with the phone. He then began going to each of the bodies and digging in pockets. What was he doing? He moved offscreen for a moment. Seconds later, he came back on-screen again, then quickly left the room.

The video stopped. Natalie could barely breathe.

"We intercepted this from inside Moscow a few minutes ago. We believe the video was taken from a built-in computer camera. We don't have the whole thing—it looks like the recording was triggered after whatever happened had already gone down. We're not sure yet of the original source. Lamar, who handles our Russian affairs, thinks it's CIA. I was with Lamar tonight digging for you on Dowerson when another analyst sent this over to him. Lamar didn't make too much of it—he doesn't know Sam from Adam—but I immediately recognized him."

"Moscow?" Natalie whispered, her head spinning. "That's not possible."

"What's he doing there?" Michelle asked.

"He's *not* there," she insisted. "I just talked to him a few hours ago."

"He may have been in London earlier, Natalie, but he's definitely in Moscow right now."

"Are those people really dead?"

Michelle shrugged. "It certainly looks that way. Can't confirm it, of course."

"Who are they?"

"I don't know. Not sure I'll find out, either. If this video is tied to the CIA, we probably won't touch it. I actually had to sneak this from Lamar, and I need to get this tablet back to him ASAP. You had some suspicions about Sam a month ago, so I knew you'd want to see it."

"I did. But nothing like this."

"I'm sorry, Natalie. I don't know what to say."

"No . . . don't be . . . thanks for showing me. I just don't . . . I need to call him."

"Drop me first, okay? I don't want to get into hot water over this."

"Yeah, okay."

Natalie pulled out of the parking lot. How could Sam possibly be in Russia, standing in a room full of dead people? Had he really been in London? Had he lied to her about that? She shook her head. He'd sent her photos of himself in London. They'd even done FaceTime yesterday, where he'd shown her the view from his hotel room. It was London! None of this made any sense. Her mind was bouncing all over the place.

She couldn't think of anything but the images of the dead bodies. She had to talk to Sam, make sure he was okay.

Suddenly, the Dowerson story was the furthest thing from her thoughts.

Still in a fog, Natalie was driving briskly down D Street to get Michelle back to her FBI office when a black Suburban came speeding out of nowhere from a side street at an intersection. Natalie caught only a half-second glance at the driver before impact. Gray ball cap. Glasses. Black goatee.

Then metal crunched, and glass shattered.

Natalie flew forward just as her airbag exploded in her face, then violently whipped her head back again. Coming from the front right of her vehicle, the collision made her Jeep spin in a full circle in the middle of the intersection before it finally settled in a heap of smoke and debris. Her world went dark.

Seconds later, she was alert again, although her vision was fuzzy. The left side of her face throbbed from the impact of the airbag, and she could hear steady popping noises in both ears. But she couldn't feel any other specific pain in her body. No clear signs of broken bones or other injuries, unless her body was in shock. Thankfully, she had been wearing her seat belt.

She looked over at Michelle, who wasn't moving. Her friend's forehead was bleeding profusely. Although Michelle's airbag had also engaged, she hadn't worn her seat belt. She'd been tossed around inside the vehicle and now was slumped forward. Natalie tried to mutter Michelle's name, but she couldn't even tell if the words were actually coming out. The popping in her ears was so loud. She reached over, gently pushed on Michelle's arm, but her friend didn't respond to her touch. Natalie cursed. Michelle needed help. Natalie had to call someone. Where was her cell phone?

She suddenly heard the roar of a car engine nearby—it was loud enough for her to hear over the popping noises in her ears. Natalie tried to look around through all the shattered glass. What was happening? She stared out Michelle's broken window directly into bright headlights.

The driver of the Suburban wasn't finished with them yet. He'd backed up the large vehicle and was now racing forward for another round. Natalie braced for impact. The Suburban again crushed the right side of her car, this time pushing it completely across the intersection, until the tires of the Jeep collided with a sidewalk curb, and the vehicle flipped up onto its side.

More glass shattered and fell across Natalie's face and body. She tried to cover her eyes with her hands. She felt completely penned in, the concrete sidewalk just six inches from her bruised face. She could taste blood in her mouth. She could smell a terrible mix of gas, burned rubber, and lots of smoke. Michelle had been thrown all the way into the back seat of the Jeep. She still wasn't moving.

Why was this happening?

Who was doing this?

Hearing tires squeal again on the street, Natalie wondered if she was about to feel the impact of yet another collision. How much could she survive? But a third impact thankfully never happened. She was relieved to hear multiple sirens quickly approaching. Then she heard Michelle suddenly moan in agony.

At least her friend was still alive.

EIGHT

Fifteen minutes later, Natalie personally ushered Michelle's gurney over to the waiting ambulance. Although she could now feel a sharp pain in her side, as well as scrapes and bruises all over her face, Natalie had basically walked away clean—even though the medics wanted her to sit still so they could check her out more thoroughly. She refused further medical attention until they'd fully dealt with Michelle, who though now alert was clearly in a tremendous amount of pain. Natalie heard medics discussing multiple broken bones and the possibility of serious internal injuries. Natalie squeezed Michelle's hand and then stepped away as two medics lifted the gurney and slid it into the back of the ambulance.

Moments later, the siren blared, and the ambulance sped away.

Natalie said a prayer for her friend. Michelle would survive this. She was a fighter, just like Natalie. Sitting down on a street curb, Natalie finally allowed a medic to examine the extent of her injuries thoroughly. There were cops and emergency personnel everywhere, and a big crowd had gathered on the sidewalks to watch the chaos.

Across the street, her Jeep was a mangled mess. It was a miracle she was not in the back of an ambulance right now. She'd already given her version of events to two officers. The Suburban had been abandoned six blocks away. One of the officers mentioned it was an armored SUV reported stolen from one of the embassies, which explained how the vehicle had survived the impact of the two collisions. She also heard murmurs about a hit-and-run, but Natalie knew it was much more than that. The first hit could be categorized as an accident. The second was attempted murder.

Who had done this? Was it somehow related to her story on Dowerson and the Russian investigation? Did someone catch wind and aim to derail the story by completely derailing her? That kind of crazy thing had happened before in this morally bankrupt city. A fellow reporter's car had been torched just a few weeks ago. Fortunately, he wasn't inside the car. Or was Michelle the target? Did someone want to take out the FBI agent?

Natalie's mind switched gears. She thought of the video of Sam standing in a room full of dead bodies. Was this about something else? Somehow related to Sam? She desperately needed to call him, but she didn't even know where her cell phone was.

While the medic put a bandage on her forehead, Natalie scanned the growing crowd of onlookers. Had anyone else seen the guy behind the wheel? She searched the crowd, face by face. Then her eyes locked in on a man standing off by himself near the back. She cursed, bolted to her feet, shocking the medic who wasn't finished with her bandage. That was the guy! The driver. Gray ball cap. Glasses. Black goatee.

Natalie began to frantically point and yell at two nearby cops, when everything suddenly went dizzy and her legs fell limp. The medic caught her in midfall and slowly set her back down on the sidewalk, where he begged her to lie still so they could do a full concussion protocol. It took several minutes for her head to clear again.

When it did, she slowly sat up, again searched the crowd.

The goateed man was gone.

NINE

Spencer Lloyd sat in a booth in the back corner of Founding Farmers, a local dining favorite three blocks from the White House. He ate at the restaurant at least twice a week and often brought along Pop, his eighty-nine-year-old senile father, who lived with Lloyd in his cramped two-bedroom condo. As assistant director in charge of the FBI's DC field office, Lloyd had hit every dining hotspot in the city more than ten times over. In his opinion, this was the best meat loaf and gravy in town.

Lloyd checked his watch: 8:52 p.m.

Agent Michael Epps, his right-hand man, should be joining him any moment. Epps had texted earlier, claiming to have news. A manila folder open in front of him, Lloyd studied a stack of eight-by-ten-inch surveillance photos they'd captured earlier that week near the Washington Monument. Two men were prominently positioned in the photos. Lloyd knew the identity of one of the men: Samuel W. Callahan. A twenty-six-year-old rookie attorney with Benoltz & Associates. A young man who'd made headlines last year because his job as a political tracker had unwittingly pushed him into a firestorm of an election scandal. A man who just last month happened to somehow become intertwined with Lloyd's official hunt for an infamous German assassin named Alger Gerlach—also known as the Gray Wolf.

Regretfully, Lloyd had not captured Gerlach. The assassin had simply vanished on him. To Lloyd's further dismay, the boss man himself, Director Luther Stone, had shut down Lloyd's involvement with Callahan. He'd ordered Lloyd to stand down, leave it alone, and not ask any further questions. Later, Lloyd had discovered that Stone's orders had come at the specific request of CIA director Cliff Barton. This revelation had infuriated him. Normally one to stay in line and not rock the boat, Lloyd had a hard time letting this one go—especially when he believed the CIA was not only involved with Callahan but had also directly assisted somehow in the Gray Wolf's overnight disappearance.

In his mind, Lloyd had been played, then bullied, and he didn't like it one bit. With the help of Agent Epps, Lloyd had been running his own off-line investigation the past month and keeping loose tabs on the lawyer, Callahan. Lloyd knew he was playing with fire. If Stone caught wind of it, Lloyd's head would likely be on the chopping block. But he wanted answers so badly that it kept him up at night.

So far, Lloyd had been unable to identify the other man in the photos with Callahan. Sporting a gray beard, he looked to be in his midsixties, only a few years older than Lloyd. Their inability to ID this guy had completely baffled Lloyd. After all, they were the FBI. They had access to damn near everything. Yet every trail on this guy went cold, and *nothing* came up in their facial-recognition software.

By all accounts, the gray-bearded man was a living ghost.

Taking another bite of his meat loaf, he looked up when he spotted Epps navigating the restaurant. A tall black man in his late forties, Epps had been Lloyd's trusted colleague for more than a decade. And about his only friend. Epps slid his lanky body into the booth, set a brown leather satchel next to him.

"You ever get *anything* but meat loaf, chief?" Epps asked him, eyeballing Lloyd's plate.

"You ever get *anything* but the pork chop?" Lloyd countered.

Epps smiled. "Nope. Best in town."

"Then zip it," Lloyd replied. "Before I fire you."

Epps shook his head, kept grinning. A waiter came by, and Epps ordered his beloved pork chop and a beer.

"You mentioned news?" Lloyd inquired.

"I finally got him, boss."

"Who?"

Epps pointed at the surveillance photos on the table. "Our mystery man."

"You're kidding? How?"

"With all the failures on the high-tech front, I went the old-fashioned way. Tracked down an old friend of my father who did twenty-five years with the CIA. Retired ten years ago. Guy now spends nearly every day fishing over at Fletcher's Cove. On a hunch, I showed him the photos. Thought maybe an old-timer could piece it together for us. Sure enough, the fisherman says he believes he knows the guy. Or he *knew* him a long time ago—he said he hadn't spoken to the man in probably more than fifteen years."

"So who the hell is he?"

"His name is Marcus Pelini," Epps continued. "The fisherman said Pelini ran CIA missions in the Middle East for more than twenty years and then went way off the radar years ago to do covert ops. They called him the Lion."

"The Lion? Why?"

"He said Pelini was king of their intelligence jungle, a real badass, someone you did not want to mess around with. You did not ever want the Lion on your bad side."

"You ran his name up the channels?"

"Yes, sir. I can find nothing. He's a shadow."

"All right, so what the hell is the Lion doing with a guy like Sam Callahan?"

Epps shrugged. "Beats the hell out of me."

TEN

Sam stepped into a twenty-four-hour gas station near the Moskva River. At three in the morning, the store was empty except for a half-asleep young clerk who stood behind the front counter and casually eyeballed him while listening to headphones. Head tucked low, Sam took an aisle toward the back corner, where he locked himself inside a small but clean single-toilet bathroom. He set his black leather bag on the floor, quickly took off the black jacket and the black vest, set them to the side.

Standing bare-chested in front of the mirror, he stared at himself, took a few deep breaths, and slowly exhaled. A new wave of disbelief poured through him. How could he possibly be stranded in a random gas station in the middle of Moscow with the team of highly trained special agents who'd brought him here all slaughtered a mile away? He cursed himself. He could be with Natalie right now, safe and warm inside her apartment, watching a good movie on the sofa. He yearned to feel her touch right now, hear her laugh. Instead, he was cold, hurting, and once again running for his damn life. He could have sidestepped this entire ordeal a month ago, just walked away and never again spoken with Marcus Pelini.

Standing there, Sam thought about the gray-bearded man. A thirty-year CIA master spook who'd entered Sam's life only nine short months ago but who'd already twice toyed so cruelly with him. First, with the scandal involving Lucas McCallister and Redrock Security while Sam worked a low-paying job as a political tracker during election season; then again, just a month ago, with Sam's unorthodox trip to Mexico City, where he'd barely survived being hunted by hit men, the police, the FBI, and even an infamous assassin called the Gray Wolf. All because of a wicked script that Pelini had both written and directed to recruit him into this mission.

The wounds were still incredibly raw from that ordeal.

Sam knew it was only last month's shocking revelation that Marcus Pelini was his long-lost father that had ultimately put him in Moscow tonight. The still-scared orphan boy was so damn desperate to know his real father—even if the man had been willingly absent for Sam's entire tortured life—that he'd somehow allowed himself to be recruited into this dangerous situation while lying to everyone he cared about. Working directly with Pelini the past month had done little so far to release him from a lifelong emotional prison cell. The gray-bearded man seemed to have zero interest in building an actual father-son relationship with him. Pelini had been *only* about the mission at hand. Sam and Pelini hadn't spent any time tossing the football around or grabbing beers. The gray-bearded man had said *nothing* about his twenty-six-year absence. They'd talked only about the operation. This had made Sam angrier by the day. There had been several moments during the final days leading up to the execution of this critical mission where he'd felt like bolting. It was just too damn painful.

However, he never did.

He just kept showing up for training the next day.

Hope was a powerful drug.

Although false hope could ultimately prove to be his demise.

He sighed, tried to shake off the pity party. There was no time for it. He'd made his own bed; now he had to get out of it all by himself. He would never get back to Natalie by standing there and whining about his stupid mistakes. He had to keep moving forward. He had to stay alive.

In the mirror, he examined his face more closely. His bottom lip was busted up good. He had a small cut along his left eyebrow. A few scrapes on his right cheek and chin. He scanned the rest of his body. He could already see a lot of dark bruising forming down his right arm. He was in decent shape, considering what he'd put himself through the past hour. He washed his face in the sink, ran his hands through his short brown hair. His hair had just started to grow back after he'd shaved his head completely bald last month to escape from a federal police building in Mexico City. Should he shave it again? Or dye it another color? Black? Blond?

For now, he decided against all those options. He'd been wearing a black knit cap inside the compound. Grabbing a stack of paper towels, he began to dry himself. He reached down, unzipped his black travel bag, found the same clothes and shoes he'd worn on the private plane over from London: blue jeans, gray T-shirt, dark-blue hoodie, running shoes. He took off his black climbing shoes and black pants and changed back into the dry clothes from the bag. He'd brought nothing else with him from London—no phone, no wallet, no cash. Pelini had instructed him to carry *nothing* on him during the mission. He also hadn't brought along any toiletries or extra clothes in the travel bag, as he hadn't planned on being away from his hotel room for very long. He regretted that now. He should have prepared for the absolute worst.

Thankfully, he had one important item that could prove to be highly valuable right now: the alias passport given to him by Pelini before the mission as a precautionary measure. Every team member had received new aliases at the same sitting. They'd all had good laughs while comparing new fictitious names. Taking the alias passport out of the back pocket of his blue jeans, he stared at the name: Dean Alexander. Someone on Pelini's team had even stamped the passport appropriately for his Russian travels *before* he'd ever left the United States.

Putting the toilet seat down, Sam sat and held Roger's phone in front of him. Scrolling through the contact list, he looked for Pelini's name, found "MP," placed the call, and prayed that the gray-bearded man would simply answer his phone, be hiding out in a hotel somewhere nearby, and they'd begin working out a plan to get Sam out of this mess. The phone rang four times and then went to an automated voice mail. Cursing, Sam hung up, pressed an option to send a text message instead.

Are you out there?—Sam

Then he continued to search the phone's contacts for Luis and Mack, his backup men on the streets. He easily found them both and sent them the exact same text message he'd just sent to Pelini. Hopefully, one of these men was still alive and would be able to help.

Setting the phone on the counter, he shoved all the excess clothes back into his travel bag and zipped it up. He kept the small sealed pouch with the computer tablet on his body, just in case, by tucking it into the back of his blue jeans. The tablet might prove to be valuable at some point.

He was about to leave the restroom when the phone suddenly buzzed. A text message had arrived back from Luis, sending a charge through him.

Red Square. Saint Basil's Cathedral. 15 minutes.

ELEVEN

Sam tossed his travel bag into a dumpster behind the gas station. He needed to be as nimble as possible. With his hood up over his head, he made his way through Moscow's empty streets as swiftly as possible, his eyes on a swivel the entire time. He was not sure who might be out there searching for him at the moment. Russian police? Zolotov's kill squad? Those who ambushed the safe house? Were they one and the same?

Red Square was only a few blocks west of the gas station, sitting along the Moskva River. He jogged most of the distance, in and out of dark alleys, trying to stay off the main roads. Arriving, he slowed, caught his breath, and pulled up a mental map from his personal study of Russia. As the centerpiece of Moscow, Red Square was surrounded on all sides by prominent Russian historical buildings—the massive Kremlin, Lenin's Mausoleum, the Kazan Cathedral, and Saint Basil's Cathedral, among others. At three thirty in the morning, the vast square was eerily empty. Sam tried to hug the edges and stay out of the center, where he felt the most vulnerable.

He made his way toward Saint Basil's Cathedral, which sat impressively aglow in bright lights. With its colorful towers with domes at the top, all wrapped in vibrant reds, greens, blues, and yellows, the old church looked like it had flames reaching up into Russia's night sky.

He paused, pulled out Roger's phone, typed a message.

I'm here.

The reply was immediate.

Monument to Minin and Pozharsky.

Luis was referring to the statue of two historical Russian men in togas that stood directly in front of the cathedral. Sam hesitantly approached it, searching in every direction for the fortysomething man he'd called Desperado a month ago because of his likeness to the actor Antonio Banderas. Sam turned sharply when three men around his age suddenly crossed through the square behind him. They all looked like normal guys in casual clothes who might be returning home from a late night at the bars. None of them even glanced in his direction. Still, they sent a shiver through him.

Seconds later, Luis stepped out of the shadows from the other side of the monument. He was wearing all black—jacket, pants, shoes—much like Sam had been wearing earlier. He hobbled over to Sam as if he were injured, their eyes connecting in recognition. Before speaking, Luis did a quick visual sweep of the square and then returned his focus to Sam.

"You really are alive, man," Luis said, as if both surprised and pleased.

"Barely. What the hell happened?"

"I was hoping you could tell me. I lost all communication while you were inside Zolotov's place, right after you ran into that damn kid. Everything just went dark on my end. Then I heard all the chaos from the compound."

"Everyone is dead."

Luis's brow dipped. "How do you know that?"

"When I escaped the residence, I managed to make my way back to the safe house. They were ambushed. That's how I got Roger's phone."

Luis cursed. "Marcus?"

Sam shook his head. "He wasn't there. I don't know if he's alive or dead. Where the hell were you? You were supposed to be providing me backup. I had to jump out a fourth-story window into the pool and nearly got sprayed with bullets."

"Sorry, man. I was a block south. Near the park. When I first heard the alarm go off, I rushed forward but nearly was taken out myself. Two men were waiting. I don't know how they found me. I got clipped in the leg but managed to get away from them."

"Who did this, Luis?"

Luis shook his head. "I don't know."

"Have you heard from Mack?" asked Sam.

Another shake of the head. "Nothing. You're my first communication in the aftermath. No one else is responding, which makes sense now." He cursed again, as if reality was sinking in. "I can't believe they're all dead."

Sam could see the genuine emotion in the man's face. While the group was still mostly strangers to Sam, they were clearly Luis's friends.

"I'm sorry," Sam offered. It felt empty.

Luis shook it off. "I'm glad you're still alive, Callahan. Pretty damn impressive, under the circumstances. You were definitely the right man for this job. None of us could have gotten out of that building like you did."

"Well, I'd like to stay alive. What the hell do we do now?"

"Get out of Moscow ASAP. Reestablish secure contact."

"Secure contact with who? Everyone appears to be dead. Marcus is missing and probably dead, too."

"I'll figure that out later. You still have your new passport?"

Sam nodded.

"Good. Let's get going."

Sam followed behind Luis, who limped along at a steady gait as they moved away from Saint Basil's Cathedral. He was grateful to find the guy. In no way, shape, or form did Sam want to go at this alone right now.

Unfortunately, fate had other plans. The first bullet hit Luis square in the chest. He spun around from the impact. A quick second bullet hit him in the back and dropped him to the ground. Sam stared fifty feet straight ahead of them, spotted a man charging forward, gun in hand. He immediately reminded Sam of the massive Russian boxer, Ivan Drago, who'd battled Sylvester Stallone's character in *Rocky IV*.

Pivoting, Sam dashed back toward Saint Basil's Cathedral, head ducked low, his legs propelling him forward in a full-on sprint. He again heard the familiar *thump* of the gun, saw something ricochet right in front of him. He circled the cathedral, created a path away from Red Square, where he chased a main street straight toward the Moskva River. Two more *thumps* behind him. He hunkered down, braced for impact, but nothing came. The Russian had missed again. But how many bullets could Sam possibly dodge? He had to break free of the Russian somehow, and quickly.

Reaching the Moskva River, Sam sprinted up onto the Bolshoy Moskvoretsky Bridge until he was straight over the water. For the first time, he took a glance behind him. Although he was easily outpacing the assassin, the man was still in pursuit. If he could just somehow get across the bridge, Sam felt he could lose the guy entirely. He turned, kept sprinting forward on the bridge's walking path. A few isolated cars passed beside him on the bridge. Suddenly, one of the cars veered up onto the bridge's walking path, thirty feet in front of him. Sam saw two men jump out of the car, stare straight at him, looking like they were holding guns. He jerked to a stop, felt caught in the crosshairs. One man behind, two men in front, all intent on killing.

There was only one thing for Sam to do. Get wet again.

Climbing up over the top of the bridge's concrete wall, he stared down into the water. When he heard another *thump*, he immediately jumped. Dropping maybe fifty feet, he plunged feetfirst into the ice-cold river water, which made his chest tighten on impact. Still, he knew he couldn't immediately resurface. He swam deeper when he could tell the men were shooting into the water all around him. As fast as he could, he made his way back underneath the bridge to create a sight barrier. When his lungs threatened to give way, Sam finally surfaced, gasped for breath. He was safe beneath the bridge. But he had no intention of remaining there for long. He had to get out of the water or his body would go into hypothermia.

Dipping beneath the water again, he swam with every ounce of energy he had left, his arms and legs growing numb, as far away as possible from the side of the bridge where he'd jumped. He surfaced only when he thought he might drown. Treading water, he looked back, could still see at least two of the men up on top, frantically searching, but their focus was too close. Sam had created more space than they'd expected. He went under again, swam even farther, until he finally made his way over to the border of the river and pulled himself up onto the dirt bank.

He lay still on his back, sucking in the night air.

When his mind thawed, he thought of Luis and cursed.

He was alone again. Unsure of his next move.

TWELVE

A firefighter recovered Natalie's cell phone in all the wreckage. Thankfully, the phone was still in good working condition. After being dropped off on the sidewalk in front of her brownstone by a police officer, Natalie immediately called Sam. She sat on the outside steps, closed her eyes, and prayed that he would answer. That he would then explain how that wasn't him in Moscow, that he was still in London, and this was all a big misunderstanding. But Natalie wasn't naive—her gut told her otherwise. Her shoulders sagged when the phone call went to Sam's familiar voice mail greeting. At the beep, she begged him to call her back immediately. She then called his number three more times, still hoping he might answer, thinking the repeated buzzing might wake him from sleep if that was the case. No luck. Finally, she hung up and sent him a text with the same message she'd left in her voice mail: Call me back ASAP!

She climbed the stairs of the brownstone and entered her third-story apartment. Inside, she called David Benoltz's cell phone, knowing Sam's boss was also in London with him. Again, the phone rang four times and went to voice mail. She cursed, dialed David three more times. Still no answer—it was one thirty in the morning in London. Natalie refused to give up. She searched Google on her phone for the

Amba Hotel in London. Calling the front desk, she paced in a nervous circle around her living room. When a man answered, Natalie explained that her fiancé was staying in the hotel, and she was afraid for his safety. She hadn't been able to get ahold of him and had reason to believe something may have happened to him. Could he please check the room? Along with the room of her fiancé's boss, who was also staying in the hotel? The hotel staffer collected all the pertinent information and told Natalie he would call her back as soon as he was able to pursue proper hotel protocol.

Hanging up, Natalie went into the bathroom. She stared at herself in the mirror, examined the scrapes and bruises on the left side of her face. She'd probably end up with two black eyes. Her jaw felt sore. And she ached something fierce in her midsection. The medic thought she might have bruised ribs and had given her some pain meds. She refused to take them—she needed to be clearheaded right now. She couldn't afford to be numb or knocked out by pain medication, no matter how much it hurt. She set her cell phone on full volume so she could hear the ring, then jumped into the shower to clean herself up. The hot beads of water felt good against her hurting body, but she didn't stay under the water long. She wanted to answer the phone at first ring and be ready to respond in whatever way necessary—even if it meant getting on a damn plane to London.

After rinsing off, she dried herself with a towel and quickly put on a pair of blue jeans and a worn Saint Louis Cardinals sweatshirt. She checked her phone every thirty seconds, her impatience growing. What was taking the hotel people so damn long? While waiting for the hotel to call her back, she called Sam's number four more times. Still no answer. She called David again. No answer. She was ready to pull out her hair.

Walking into her kitchen, she quickly made a hot cup of tea, hoping it would somehow help calm her nerves. While letting the tea bag saturate the hot water, she set her mind back on the driver of the

Suburban, the man with the gray ball cap, glasses, and goatee. Natalie thought the crash had to be in response to her meeting with Michelle. It felt like too big of a coincidence for it to happen only minutes after Michelle had wanted to meet privately. Who was he? She'd given a full description to the police and told them she thought she'd spotted him in the crowd in the aftermath, but they'd been unable to locate him.

When her cell phone rang, she nearly spilled her hot tea. David Benoltz.

"What's going on, Natalie?" David asked, his voice groggy. "Hotel security just banged on my door and woke me up. They said you called the front desk all frantic. Then I see all these missed calls from you in the past fifteen minutes."

"Where's Sam?"

"In his room, I presume."

"Has hotel security gone inside his room yet?"

"Well, no, they said they knocked repeatedly, then came over to my door when he didn't answer. I told them I figured he had taken some meds because he was feeling ill earlier and was probably knocked out cold."

"You need to go inside his hotel room right now," Natalie demanded.

"What's going on, Natalie? You sound panicked."

"I think Sam's in trouble. I just need you to check on him. Please, David."

"Okay, calm down. Give me a second. The guy from hotel security is still at my door, waiting to sort this all out with me. Stay on the phone."

Natalie again paced in a circle in her living room, the anxiety growing with each passing moment. She listened as David had a brief conversation with hotel security, where he insisted they enter the hotel room and check on his employee. She heard four firm raps on a door, and David told her over the phone they were knocking on Sam's door again. When there was no answer, David said they were unlocking the door and going inside. Natalie sat on the sofa, her breathing heavy. She waited several seconds for the next update from David.

"He's not here, Natalie," David said, concern now growing in his voice.

Natalie exhaled deeply, her faint hope crushed. "Is any of his stuff in the room?"

"Yes, everything is here. His luggage, his clothes. All his toiletries are still in the bathroom. His phone and wallet are even sitting here on the dresser. Maybe he just went for a late-night walk? Jet lag and all that. Why do you think something happened? Because he's not answering his cell phone?"

Natalie paused. *Sam left his phone in the room? Why?*

"Wait a second," David suddenly announced.

"What is it?"

"There's an envelope sitting here on the desk with your name written on it."

Natalie felt the heavy weight of fear collapse on her. "Open it and read it."

"Are you sure?"

"Yes!"

She heard the tear of paper, and then David began to read.

Natalie, if you're reading this, I fear the worst has happened to me. Although I'm unable to explain anything in this letter, for your own safety, please know that I never wanted to lie to you. I only wanted to protect you. I'm sorry. I love you with all my heart.

Yours always, Sam

THIRTEEN

Lloyd exited the elevator on the fourth floor of his building, eager to grab a shower and catch the end of the Nationals game. When he turned the hallway corner toward his condo, he bumped right into a man in a black leather jacket. The midthirties man had short black hair and was in a real hurry. Lloyd offered an apology, but the man said nothing in return. He just kept moving at a brisk pace toward the elevator. Frustrated by the lack of returned courtesy, Lloyd thought of chasing him down, shoving his FBI credentials in the man's face, and making a few veiled threats about arresting him; instead, he wisely took a deep breath, collected himself, and let it pass. He was already dead tired. The jerk wasn't worth the hassle.

Lloyd pulled out his keys, then stared down at the doorknob. There were scuff marks in the wood near the knob that hadn't been there before. That was odd. What had his pop gone and done now? His father wasn't supposed to leave the condo anymore without calling Lloyd. Twice already, Lloyd had received calls from random people who had found his father out wandering the damn streets, still in his bathrobe, unable to tell anyone who he was or where he was going. Lloyd put the key in the lock and then realized the door was already unlocked. Another sigh, shake of the head. *Come on, Pop!*

However, when Lloyd opened the door, all frustration with his father disappeared, and he immediately reached for his gun. His condo had been ransacked. The sofa cushions were tossed about, the coffee table knocked over, the old recliner flipped up on its side, stacks of FBI papers from the small kitchen table splayed everywhere. Was that someone still there? Where was Pop? His heart raced.

Stepping around the ruckus in the living room, Lloyd rushed into the short hallway that led to the two bedrooms. He stopped in his tracks. His father was lying flat on his back, still wearing his bathrobe, but he wasn't moving. Pop's eyes were closed. Lloyd dropped to a knee over his father, then noticed the old man's head was bleeding. A small puddle had started to form on the carpet. Lloyd stood again, his gun squeezed in his fist, moved to the bedrooms. Both had been destroyed. But no sign of a perp still inside the condo. He hurried back to his father, knelt again.

Lloyd swallowed, put his hands on Pop's shoulder, shook gently, said his name twice. His father never moved. Lloyd checked his neck for a pulse. He had a heartbeat. Lloyd then looked down and noticed that a handgun was lying on the carpet near his father's right hand. Pop's old Smith & Wesson revolver. The same one he'd used during his last ten years on the police force. Lloyd cursed. His father must've heard the destruction going on, gotten his gun, and walked in on it. The head wound looked like blunt-force trauma.

He thought of the guy in the hallway, someone he'd never seen in the building before, and raced for the door. On his way to the elevator, he dialed 911 and frantically asked for an ambulance. He hung up, pounded the Down button for the elevators. When one didn't immediately arrive, Lloyd took the stairs, his tired legs bounding down three steps at a time, four flights, until he poured out into the small lobby near the wall of mailboxes. There was no one else inside the lobby. Lloyd hit the glass door and spilled out onto the sidewalk in front of his building. His head whipped left, right, searching everywhere for the man with black hair wearing the black leather jacket. He raced up to the street corner, stared down the long sidewalk on the side street in both directions. Others were out and about, but he couldn't locate the guy.

Lloyd heard a siren approaching. He had to get back to Pop.

He dialed Epps. "Get to my place right now!"

FOURTEEN

Soaking wet, Sam hobbled through Moscow a half mile from where he'd finally surfaced from his swim in the Moskva River. Roger's cell phone was no longer working—a result of the dip in the ice-cold river water—so he'd tossed it. Fortunately, the computer tablet was still at his back and remained sealed tight in the waterproof pouch. Sam didn't currently have access to the tablet's contents—it was locked down by security—but he hoped to find someone soon who could get him inside. He was working that plan out in his mind right now.

Wandering the streets for a half hour, hypothermia nearly setting in, he finally found what he was searching for—a place to get some dry clothes. The redbrick four-story building said SUIT SUPPLY on the front sign and had mannequins wearing men's clothing displayed in a few windows. Obviously, the shop was closed at four in the morning.

Skipping the front door, Sam circled the building and found a back entrance near a loading dock and half a dozen dirty dumpsters. The black metal door had an old lock-and-key system. Sam began searching for a tool. He could pick a standard lock with any variety of options—a skill he'd established early in life to survive out on the streets—but he couldn't do it with his bare hands.

He found a box of metal clothes hangers in the third dumpster, pulled two of them out, and returned to the back door. Straightening the hangers, he dropped to a knee, stared at the lock. He carefully put the end of one hanger into the lock's slot, felt it bump up against the familiar machinery. He then put in a second hanger end above it. This would've been an easy job if not for the fact that his hands were numb and shaking uncontrollably. He tried to steady his fingers, but it was impossible. They were like frozen Popsicles at the ends of his arms. He put his right ear close to the lock to help guide himself by sound and not feel. As he moved his hands and guided the two hangers, he could hear the necessary scraping inside the lock. Seconds later, he heard the click. He turned the knob, and the door opened.

He listened for an alarm system, something he was willing to risk since he was probably going to die in an alley if he didn't get out of the wet clothes. He didn't hear anything or see a keypad on the wall. Still, he needed to be quick. Moving inside a dark hallway, he shut the door behind him, immediately felt the warmth of the building's heating system. He hadn't been this cold since he'd barely survived one of the worst blizzards Denver had ever produced while a homeless teenager. That blizzard had pushed him to break into Zion Baptist Church, where he'd thawed out and had his first encounter with Pastor Isaiah, a man who would save him from juvie six months later. Sam thought of Pastor Isaiah. He'd give anything to have that man with him now. He needed a little divine intervention.

Without turning on any lights, Sam moved deeper into the building. He finally located two swinging doors that led into the retail shop on the first floor. He could see better inside the shop, as the front windows allowed some light in from the street. Sam nearly shouted hallelujah when he found himself surrounded by racks upon racks of men's shirts, pants, jackets. He quickly grabbed a long-sleeved flannel number off one rack and a pair of gray jeans off another rack. Against a wall, he found a shelf loaded with men's underwear and socks. Right in the middle of the clothing shop, he peeled out of the frozen clothes and quickly put on his dry replacements. He then went to the racks of jackets and grabbed a gray cold-weather number with a hood. After putting on the new clothing items, he crossed the store until he found a section for men's shoes. Searching two racks of shoes that were all on sale, Sam located a pair of Nike running shoes that looked like his size, slipped them on his feet, and tied them up tight. He felt like a new man.

A beam of light suddenly crossed his face.

Sam dropped flat to his stomach.

He cursed, rolled over behind a rack of clothes. He could tell now that the beam was from a high-powered flashlight. Was someone else inside the shop with him? He listened but didn't hear anything. Getting to a knee, he peered around the clothing rack, searched for the origination of the light beam. The front of the store. When it crossed over him again, he spotted a shadowed figure wearing a uniform with a flashlight standing right outside the glass front doors of the old building. A policeman. Sam thought he must've triggered a silent alarm, because he highly doubted anyone actually spotted him breaking into the building.

He had to get out ASAP. He didn't need the extra trouble.

As quietly as possible, Sam made his way back to the swinging doors that led to the rear of the store and returned to the dark hallway. Along the way, he noticed a small tool kit sitting on the concrete floor beside two metal ladders and some paint cans. Sam did a quick search through the tools, pulled out an Allen wrench and two small screwdrivers, stuffed them in his coat pocket, trying to think two steps ahead. He inched the black metal back door open, peered into the darkness behind the building. When he didn't spot anyone, he stepped out, carefully closed the door, and hustled down the alley.

FIFTEEN

With her Jeep completely totaled, Natalie took the Metrorail across town to Sam's apartment. He lived on the fourth floor of Capitol Plaza, an aged yellow brick building two blocks from the Georgetown University Law Center, where he'd spent the past three years studying to become a lawyer. Something had told her his unexpected presence in Russia had *nothing* to do with his new legal career. Her mind kept flashing back to the finale of his trip to Mexico City, when they'd all sat down to answer questions with so-called FBI agents, only for Natalie to discover later through Michelle they were actually CIA agents. Natalie felt it was no coincidence that only a month later, Sam was caught on video in Moscow, standing in a room full of dead bodies, while everyone, including his fiancé and his boss, thought he was still asleep in a swank hotel room in London.

Natalie focused on answering two initial questions. First, how could Sam have walked into his London hotel room earlier and then ended up in Moscow only a few hours later? That kind of travel didn't happen by commercial flight. Had he privately flown to Russia? How? The CIA? Or someone else? Second, what did Sam mean in his brief letter to her? *I fear the worst has happened to me . . . I never wanted to lie to you . . . only wanted to protect you.* He clearly knew he was involved in something dangerous—something that could possibly bring harm to both of them if revealed. Protect her from whom? And from what? Had someone forced Sam to go to Moscow? Was that why he was there? Was it blackmail? Or had he gone voluntarily? She had a difficult time wrapping her mind around that last thought.

Riding the Metro, Natalie's heart kept steadily pounding, the same way it did right after she finished a strenuous run. She couldn't seem to calm herself down no matter how many deep breaths she took. Sam was in grave danger. That was clear. He seemed to know that he might not return to her. Was he already dead? She refused to allow her mind to go there. If anything, Sam was a survivor. He'd proved that time and again. Natalie refused to believe he wouldn't survive. Not with the engagement ring he'd recently placed on her finger.

Still, she was furious with Sam. He'd lied to her. Why? He'd sworn to her he'd never shut her out again. And yet right away, he'd chosen to deceive her and had already owned up to it in his letter. That really pissed her off. Did he not trust her? Natalie was not some princess who needed to be sheltered. She was also a fighter and a survivor. She'd overcome the tragic death of her own mother. She'd repeatedly faced down direct threats from all sorts of DC political forces while doing her job at *PowerPlay*. A year ago, she'd driven the getaway car for Sam while they'd dodged bullets from swarming helicopters. She'd even escaped from a group of men who wanted to keep her tied to a damn chair in an isolated warehouse with a black hood over her head. Why the hell would she need Sam's protection? They were in this life together—or so she thought.

Taking a deep breath, she exhaled slowly. Natalie knew she couldn't continue to ride this changing tide of emotional waves. It would only exhaust her. She had to focus on the task at hand—finding the truth. She just had to get Sam home. She'd tar and feather him to no end later.

When she reached her stop, Natalie hurried off the train, made her way up to the streets. Sam's apartment was a block south. They didn't spend much time together inside his studio; however, she did have her own key. Entering the lobby, she grabbed the elevator to the fourth floor. Reaching his door, she put the key in the knob, stepped inside, and felt another wave of emotion push through her. She could immediately smell Sam's fragrance, and it gave her pause. She swallowed, flipped on the lights. The studio apartment was barely four hundred square feet. A half kitchen with a two-person folding table to her right, the living area with the brown foldout couch in front of her, a small bathroom on the other side. It was a mess, as usual. Dirty dishes on the counters, pizza boxes stacked on the kitchen table, piles of legal books and papers spread across the coffee table and covering the carpeted floor in the living area.

Stepping farther inside, she stared at a small glass shelf near the door that held four framed pictures of the two of them together. A charity softball game. Serving at a homeless shelter. A friend's wedding. One picture was from their trip to Saint Martin earlier in the year. That made her think of Sam's mother, a woman she'd grown to love so dearly. Sam had found out his mother was on a swift decline the moment they'd stepped off the plane. Soon after, she would be tragically gone, sending Sam into another tailspin. Again, Natalie had to force back the emotions, which seemed to be coming at her from every direction.

She scanned the apartment. There had to be something that might give her a clue as to what he was involved in. She rummaged through the stacks of papers and the books on the coffee table. Most of the papers looked like law-firm matters. She recognized several names from their recent dinner conversations. Still, she carefully reviewed every page, looking for bread crumbs—*anything* that might point her in a direction.

It took her more than thirty minutes to pore through the various stacks on the coffee table. Still, she found *nothing*. Sitting on the sofa, she began picking up the legal books spread all about. They were the standard variety, mostly focused on the practice of criminal law. Nothing grabbed her as suspicious. She entered the tiny bathroom, spotted a white card key to the offices of Benoltz & Associates sitting in a pile of wadded cash and crumpled receipts next to the sink. She grabbed the card key, headed for the door. Striking out at his apartment, she would search his law office next.

Benoltz & Associates was on the eighth floor of a high-rise near Union Station. It was late, so Natalie didn't expect anyone to be working—especially with the boss in London. She took the elevator up and then swiped the card key at the pad beside the glass doors to the office suite. Seconds later, she was inside the lobby. There were a few lights on down the hallway, but Natalie didn't hear any voices or movement. Not that she'd feel uncomfortable if discovered in the office. She'd visited several times, and she was familiar with most of the staff. She could simply tell someone she was grabbing a file for Sam.

She quickly took the hallway and then dipped into Sam's small outer office, where he had a decent view of the city. Natalie hit the light switch. Sam had an L-shaped wooden desk with a desktop computer in the corner of the unit. One wall had wooden shelves that mostly held various sets of legal books. There was a framed photo of Sam with Pastor Isaiah and his family. Several more framed photos of Natalie. Unlike his apartment, Sam kept his office tidy. The desk was well organized. Natalie circled the desk, sat in his leather office chair. She did a quick search of the stacks of paperwork on the desk, found nothing interesting. Then she began rummaging through his desk drawers and still came up empty-handed.

Finally, she scooted up to the desktop computer, grabbed the mouse, and moved it. The screen came to life. She knew Sam's password—he used the same one for just about everything. She typed it into the password box and gained access to his office computer. Opening his email, she began to scroll down the list. Again, nothing stood out. They were mostly work related. Several of the emails were from Natalie. She scanned the email folders he'd set up, opening each of them, searching intently, but still found nothing helpful. Next, she went to all the file folders that were set up on his desktop. She again recognized several of the titles from their conversations about his work the past couple of months. Still, she searched inside each file folder and grew more frustrated with all the dead ends.

She paused on a folder in the bottom corner of his desktop screen simply titled BH. When she clicked on it, another password box popped up on the screen. She tilted her head. Sam had put extra security on this particular file. Why? She typed in his usual password, but it didn't work out. She typed in another password he'd used while in law school. Blocked again. She sat back in the chair for a second, thinking. Easing forward again, she typed in the day they got engaged—a date Sam had called the most important of his life. She was inside the folder!

There were several file folders inside the BH folder. The first one that grabbed her attention was labeled MOSCOW. She felt a chill rush through her. Opening it, she scanned the different documents, most of which seemed like basic tourist information. She jumped out of that folder and quickly reviewed the others, labeled LANGUAGE TRAINING, CLIMBING, SELF-DEFENSE, LOGISTICAL PREP. *What the hell?* She searched through each folder, finding extensive course work on LEARNING RUSSIAN 101, as well as all kinds of training material on rock climbing and self-defense. Inside the folder for LOGISTICAL PREP, she discovered a document that listed a physical address and showed a weekly schedule for the past month. Each afternoon was segmented hourly with the same tags that were on the file folders: LANGUAGE TRAINING, CLIMBING, SELF-DEFENSE, LOGISTICAL PREP. The schedule covered the same time that Sam was supposedly involved in a legal intensive at the American Law Institute. It was all a lie? He was constantly carrying around that thick notebook with the American Law Institute logo on the cover.

Natalie's eyes returned to the top of the document, settled on three words.

Operation Black Heron.

SIXTEEN

Natalie left Sam's office in a rush, with plans to head straight back to her cubicle at *PowerPlay*. She now had a solid lead and was eager to run with it. Sam was clearly involved in something much more complex than she'd even imagined. Operation Black Heron? She was convinced it had somehow rolled right out of the finale of his trip to Mexico City. Language training? Climbing? Self-defense? Logistical prep? She shook her head. What the hell was Sam doing, and why?

She briskly made her way back to the underground Metro terminal. She swiped her Metro card at the gate, descended the escalator in a small crowd of other travelers, and waited in the tube for her designated train. While she waited, she tried to call her editor at home, the man she trusted the most in this town, to see if he could start tackling different sides of this story with her. Unfortunately, he didn't answer. She left an urgent message to call her back ASAP.

When her train arrived, she climbed into a half-full car and made her way to an empty seat near the back. The doors shut; the train began moving at its usual swift pace. Pulling her phone out again, Natalie typed the physical address she'd found on Sam's document into her maps app. The digital pin dropped onto a location over in Fort Lincoln, northeast DC. She clicked on the map and pulled up a street view of the exact location. Squinting at the screen, there was really not much to it. It looked like an old block-wide, redbrick warehouse. There were no business names or any other identifiable markers on the building. And yet it seemed clear that Sam had spent part of the past month doing something inside that warehouse. She'd have to go see for herself.

As the train made a few stops and the back of the car grew more crowded, Natalie continued her investigation. She did a quick Google search on Operation Black Heron. As expected, nothing popped up other than a few bars and restaurants that had the words *Black Heron* in their names. Out of curiosity, Natalie did a quick search on the animal itself and found a picture of a medium-size black bird found mostly in Africa. She kept reading, wondering why someone had chosen that specific animal as the name of an operation. She discovered the black heron was one of the most clever hunting animals in the world and used a method called canopy feeding—it spread its wings like an umbrella over the water, creating the illusion of night—that helped to draw out unsuspecting fish.

Sitting back in her seat, Natalie pondered the title. Sam was part of a secret hunt? Using an illusion? A hunt for what? Who pulled him into this hunt? And why would Sam agree to it if it was dangerous enough where he might not return to her? So many questions, but the last one continued to baffle her the most. How could *anything* have been more important than their future together? She could feel her anger with him steadily growing. And for the first time since they'd gotten engaged, Natalie let some doubt creep back into her thoughts.

Could Sam ever truly commit to her?

Is that why he'd been delaying setting a wedding date?

Sighing, Natalie tried to distract herself from that line of thought by haphazardly scanning the other travelers. As usual, there was a mixed bag of old and young, couples and singles, clean and dirty. She stiffened when she found one specific traveler staring right back at her from across the pack, standing maybe twenty feet away. His eyes never moved—they locked on her. The man was probably in his thirties. Serious scowl. Black jacket and blue jeans. The gray ball cap was now missing, but he still had the glasses and the black goatee. Natalie cursed. The driver of the Suburban. The same man who'd tried to take her out completely on a DC street just two hours ago and who'd put Michelle in the hospital in critical condition. Her heart started pounding furiously again. The man looked like a younger version of Walter White, the character played by Bryan Cranston in the TV series *Breaking Bad*. Natalie now had an answer to her question from earlier.

Michelle was *not* the target—at least not the *only* target.

Natalie was also the target.

She tried to glance away casually, pretending she didn't see him. But it was too late for that. The man had clearly recognized she'd become alert to him, as he began shifting his way through the crowded train carriage toward her. Natalie frantically pondered her next move. Should she call 911? Should she start screaming like a crazy woman that a psychopath was on the train?

The train slowed. They were nearing the next stop. At that moment, the man placed himself midway between two door openings. If she was quick, she had a chance. She was only five feet from the nearest door, although still blocked by a half dozen travelers. When the train completely stopped and the doors swooshed open, Natalie made a dash. Elbowing her way past two men, she jumped up over the top of a row of seats and all but dived out the train doors into the terminal. She took a glance back and could see the goateed man also making an aggressive move to get off the train. Another muscular guy took exception, made some threats, and that's when all hell broke loose—the goateed man pulled out a handgun. Screams and panic suddenly filled the entire platform.

Clutching her small brown purse in her fist, Natalie bolted through the terminal. She cut through other travelers, caught the stairs up, did her best to maneuver her way in and around those who were content with a more casual climb. Behind her, she could hear a growing wave of screams catching up to her. The goateed man was probably running after her with his gun on full display. Who the hell was this guy? Who wanted her dead?

There was no time to think about it.

Right now, she simply had to get away.

Natalie exited onto the sidewalk near Chinatown and Capital One Arena. Spotting a big crowd on the street in front of the center, she sprinted in that direction, hoping somehow to get lost in the mass of people. Another quick glance over her shoulder. The goateed man had already cleared the terminal and was still in pursuit. He was much faster than he looked for such a stocky guy, just thirty feet behind and seeming to gain ground. She needed another plan of escape.

Glancing up at the sign on the arena, she noted that a WWE event was going on tonight, which gave her an idea. She threaded the thickening crowd on the sidewalk right outside the venue, searching for the right help. She found a group of three hulking men, all looking like they could've been wrestlers themselves, raced straight up to them.

"Please help me!" she screamed into their faces. "A man is chasing me!"

All three men turned, stared behind her, just in time to see the goateed man burst free from the crowd. The wrestling fans quickly formed a testosterone-driven protective barrier. Natalie moved in behind them, continued to navigate away from her pursuer, while monitoring what was happening to the goateed man. He flashed the handgun, but it didn't deter the wrestlers, who quickly jumped at him and displaced the gun. Natalie watched enough to see that the goateed man could defend himself well, as he swung fists and kicked at knees, immediately knocking down two wrestlers. Fortunately for her, more testosterone-driven men decided to jump into the fray, probably still juiced up from some cage match going on inside.

Natalie did not stay to watch.

She tucked her head and kept running.

SEVENTEEN

Lloyd stood inside a media room at the FBI office, a wall of digital screens up in front of him, several of his agents at computer stations pecking away on keyboards. He'd driven straight over from Sibley Memorial, where his father had been stabilized in ICU. Pop had not woken up yet. Lloyd had held the old man's hand and ridden to the hospital in the back of the racing ambulance. It was not proper protocol, but the medics weren't going to argue with his FBI credentials. The damage to his father's head was indeed blunt-force trauma. Someone had used a hard object—Lloyd thought probably the butt of a handgun. His father had lost *a lot* of blood. With a man his father's age, the ER doctors were very concerned. Pop needed to somehow survive the night if he was to ever recover from such a serious head injury.

The whole situation was touch and go. His father had always been a stubborn fighter, once getting into a fistfight with Lloyd's high school baseball coach when they'd had a disagreement. Lloyd and Pop had even come to blows a couple of times themselves when Lloyd was in college and had done something the old man had disapproved of. Back then, his father had usually gotten the better of him. Pop had constantly fought with Lloyd's mother about church, politics, and how to raise their children. He'd lost most of those battles—Lloyd's mother was even more stubborn than his father. Lloyd just hoped Pop had one last good fight in him. Although the old man drove him crazy these days, he wasn't ready to let his father go just yet.

Realizing there was nothing he could do by standing around the hospital and twiddling his damn thumbs, Lloyd said a prayer, left, and distracted himself by flipping back into full-on investigative mode. He was determined to catch the bastard who'd done this to his father *and* find out why. *Nothing* had been stolen from inside Lloyd's condo. There was still a wad of cash on the kitchen counter, probably a hundred dollars, left completely untouched. He was clearly searching for something else. What? Although Lloyd had a hunch, he needed confirmation to run with his theory.

Epps had been busy rounding up security-video feeds from local businesses that surrounded the front of Lloyd's condo building. Unfortunately, Lloyd's dumpy building had no such video-monitoring system. The building was not high on luxury or security, which made it more affordable than others—something Lloyd needed more than bells and whistles, since he'd lost nearly all his life savings in a bad real estate investment several years ago.

"This was taken from right outside Barney's," Epps said, nodding toward the middle screen on the wall.

Lloyd squinted. Barney's was a men's shoe store right next to his building. The security camera was at an angle above the front door and showed people walking back and forth in front of the store. A man and a woman casually strolled past, then a man with a dog on a leash, and finally the back of a man who looked to be in a real hurry. Krieger, their tech expert, paused it with the back of this man in video view. Lloyd studied the image. Black leather jacket. Medium build. Short black hair.

"I think it's him," Lloyd said, nodding.

"Pull up the next one," Epps told Krieger, who began typing.

A second video appeared on the digital wall.

"Two doors down," Epps mentioned. "Corner bakery."

The video was similar to the first one, with a view at an angle above the front door. Several people walked past in both directions, then Krieger paused it when the man in the black leather jacket was right under camera, his face in full view. Lloyd recognized the scowl on the face of the midthirties man. He felt his blood boil.

"Yeah, it's definitely him," Lloyd confirmed.

Epps cursed.

Lloyd turned to him. "What?"

Epps shook his head. "I thought this might be the guy, so I had Krieger run it through our facial-recognition software. It's not good, chief. He doesn't exist."

Lloyd shared an uneasy glance with Epps, knowing what that likely meant. If the guy was truly a ghost, he could only work for one organization: the CIA.

"Take this all down," Epps ordered Krieger. "Pull it off-line. Don't leave any threads back to it, you understand me, Krieger?"

"Yes, sir," said Krieger, immediately pulling everything off the big screens.

Epps huddled closely with Lloyd, talking in whispers.

"You think this is connected to our investigation of Callahan and the Lion guy?" Epps asked Lloyd.

Lloyd nodded. Which put his stomach into a tight ball.

"We've got to find this guy, Michael. And we've got to go even deeper underground."

EIGHTEEN

Sam finally found much-needed asylum five blocks from where he'd stolen his new wardrobe. He needed a safe place to hide out for the next hour or so—to think, and to plan, and to somehow figure out how the hell he was going to survive this catastrophe. He didn't want to aimlessly roam the city the rest of the night. But finding a warm hideout had been no small task at this hour. He couldn't just walk into a hotel—especially with only a wad of Russian cash on him—and draw suspicion to himself. He thought of the Russian assassins. Cold-blooded killers were out there on the hunt for him. He still had no idea if the Russian police were also involved. Either way, he needed complete anonymity.

The Church of Saint Nicholas looked promising, with its small gold domes and unassuming property. For one, as he knew from his past, old church buildings weren't usually placed under heightened security. After all, they had been built to let people in and not keep them out. So they didn't often have high-tech alarm systems or hire security guards to patrol the property. Second, Sam had always been drawn to old churches, especially during times of crisis—which had been most of his life, actually. He had always found something comforting about them.

Sam pushed a creaky gate open along a wrought-iron fence that surrounded the church property. There were different monuments and statues on the grounds. Although the church building was smaller than the other colossal cathedrals he'd seen around Moscow, it was still designed with the same vibrant colors and ornate construction. He found a heavy wooden door at the side of the building, one that looked like it had been installed more than five hundred years ago. Although the lock system on the door was massive and imposing, Sam knew it would be simple to access. They didn't have complex lock-and-key machinery in the 1500s.

Kneeling, he took out one of the screwdrivers he'd stolen from inside the clothing store, inserted it into the heavy lock. He wiggled it a bit, scraped a mechanism he knew was inside, heard the familiar click of a heavy lock opening. He stood, slowly opened the door. The hallway was dark. Sam quickly shut the wooden door behind him, once again felt embraced by the warmth of a heated building. Listening, he didn't hear a peep inside. Only the rumble of the old heating unit.

He made his way forward, passed by what looked like two church offices and a small conference room. He then poked his head inside a kitchen. Flipping on a light switch, he began searching for something to eat to keep his energy level up. He found a loaf of bread on the counter, pulled it out of its plastic wrap, ripped off a huge chunk, and shoved it into his mouth. He opened a small white refrigerator. Grabbing a half-full carton of milk, he finished it off in two aggressive gulps.

He moved deeper into the old building until he found the main sanctuary with its massive gold altar up front and huge stained-glass windows on both sides. The pews were wooden and ornate and looked rather new compared to the rest of the building. He sat in the first pew, tried to make himself comfortable. He stared up at the massive gold crucifix of Jesus, built in the center of everything, with a huge wall of artistic paintings of all the saints behind it. He studied the paintings. Saint Peter, Saint Paul, and many of Jesus's disciples. Men he knew from study had endured much suffering for their faith. He'd always been most drawn to Thomas, one of the original twelve who had walked with

Jesus. Doubting Thomas, as he was often called, because the man had refused to believe that Christ had risen from the tomb after suffering death on the cross unless he saw the wounds with his own eyes. Only later, when Thomas had physically touched the wounds, did he truly believe, saying, "My Lord and My God."

Sam had often pondered if that's what it would take for him to believe fully. It had always come much easier to Natalie. She'd often told Sam he had to get out of his own way, that faith was not about the head but the heart. Pastor Isaiah, his mentor, had always said the same thing. Unfortunately, Sam had a history of getting in his own way—clearly, a hard habit for him to break, considering tonight.

He again thought of Natalie, probably curled up with her Kindle in the warmth of her sofa right now. Damn, he missed her so much. He so desperately wanted to be with her instead of sitting here five thousand miles away, alone in an old church building in the heart of Moscow, hiding out from assassins.

Why couldn't he have just walked away from Pelini?

NINETEEN

Natalie paid cash for a twenty-minute cab ride into Virginia, where she was dropped in front of a brand-new strip mall. After barely escaping a ruthless killer with a gun—the same man who'd tried to crush the life out of her with a speeding armored Suburban—she was paranoid as hell. Did the man follow the police car that took her home from the scene of the crash? Was he waiting in the wings to take another shot? Or was he able to track her down in other ways? Who the hell was this guy?

Natalie felt one thing for sure. She couldn't go back to her place right now. Someone could be waiting for her there. Nor could she keep using her credit cards or cell phone. She couldn't chance being tracked. She had no idea how far all this reached or the level of the players involved. She had to play it safe. And she wasn't going to pull any of her friends or colleagues into the danger zone with her. Not when she had another option—an option that Sam had set up for them a month ago that she never thought she'd use.

At the end of the redbrick strip mall, she found her destination: Commonwealth Vault. A private security company that offered twenty-four-hour access to safe-deposit boxes. The parking lot out front was nearly empty. All the other businesses were closed. She took another cautious glance behind her, looking around for other suspicious vehicles in the parking lot; then she opened a glass door at the front of Commonwealth Vault. There was nothing inside the small lobby but a windowless secure door. Following instructions listed on a small sign posted on the wall, Natalie stepped up to the door, placed her finger on a scanner, and looked up into a camera above the door. Through a lobby speaker, a male voice asked for her full name. Natalie Elizabeth Foster. The door clicked open.

A guy wearing a nice brown sport coat with the Commonwealth logo sewn on the front met Natalie inside, and he ushered her over to a desk with a computer. He quickly confirmed more of her security information and then disappeared around a corner. Seconds later, he was back with a set of keys. She followed him down a clean hallway, where he unlocked a huge vault door and led her inside a room lined with metal safe-deposit boxes of various sizes. He located hers near the middle and asked her to put in her key. Natalie pulled her key out of her purse, stuck it in the lock, turned. The vault guy did the same with his key, and she now had access to the metal box inside. He handed it to her, guided her to a private viewing room, then asked her to hit the buzzer at the door when she was done.

Alone in the room, Natalie couldn't believe she was sitting there. Did Sam know this was coming? Is that why he'd set this up in the first place? It was only under the most dire of circumstances that either of them were to use the contents of the metal box. It felt surreal to be the one doing it. Natalie exhaled, opened the box. She found two sealed manila envelopes inside—one marked *Sam*, the other marked *Natalie*, both in Sam's familiar handwriting. Tearing open her envelope, she poured the contents on the white table in front of her. There was a thin rubber-banded stack of hundred-dollar bills totaling $2,000 in cash. Another rubber band was wrapped around a DC driver's license and a credit card, both with the name Sarah Dearborn—a name she'd dreamed up while sitting at the kitchen table with Sam and sharing laughs, as if this were something fun to do. It wasn't fun now. Natalie's profile picture was next to the strange name. There was also a passport for Sarah Dearborn. And, finally, a burner cell phone.

Unsealing the other manila envelope, Natalie poured out a second set with the exact same items, only for Sam. His name was David Doyle. Driver's license, credit card, passport, cash, and burner phone. She exhaled, shook her head. They were two people able and prepared to disappear at a moment's notice. What kind of life was this? However, after last month's ordeal involving assassins, abductors, and a crazy oilman named Lex Hester, Sam had insisted they have Tommy Kucher create these packages for both of them. In case something unusual happened and the FBI couldn't find Hester, he'd suggested, and they somehow found themselves in sudden peril.

Staring at his face on his alias, Natalie felt anger rise up in her again. Sam had known something was going to happen. That's why he'd had Tommy pull all this together. Sam had been aware that he was walking straight into a perilous situation and had prepared in advance. Stuffing the IDs, cash, and the burner phones into her purse, Natalie shut the metal box and buzzed the sport-coat guy. After returning the box to its secure spot, she signed out and asked the guy to call her a cab. A few minutes later, she was on her way back to DC proper.

She stared down at the new driver's license in her fingers.

Natalie Foster, meet Sarah Dearborn.

TWENTY

At about five in the morning, Sam left the safe confines of the church and again hit the cold streets of Moscow. The sun was already rising, and the streets were growing busier with traffic. Hands tucked in pockets, he managed to locate an Aeroexpress station a few blocks south of the Moskva River, where he used some of his rubles to pay for a ticket at a machine and waited with a crowd of commuters. Sam pressed his back against a cool gray wall, making sure he could monitor every single person who passed in front of him. Two Russian police officers strolled in his direction. Sam turned to avoid any direct eye contact. When his train finally arrived, he boarded with a crowd of others, found a seat in the very corner, kept his eyes mostly at his feet. In his peripheral vision, he didn't feel any suspicious stares back at him. Most of the other travelers looked just as weary as he—although he doubted any of them had had a night quite like his.

The Aeroexpress train took twenty minutes to drop him at the Sheremetyevo International Airport. Sam felt uneasy walking into a place with so much security—like a gazelle walking into a crowded lion's den. The men in uniforms were trained to seek out suspicious people, so he did his best to walk with an unsuspecting gait. He had no choice. He had to get the hell out of Moscow as quickly as possible. He found a digital board for exiting flights and located a 6:30 a.m. Aeroflot flight to Munich. He checked the time, needed to hurry. He walked briskly through the terminal until he found a counter for Aeroflot, a Russian airline, waited five minutes in a short line, then asked the attendant if there were any seats open for the early flight to Munich. Fortunately, she spoke good English, smiled in a flirting kind of way, and told Sam she still had five seats available. Sam handed her the alias passport Pelini had given him, along with the fake travel visa in the back, and a stack of rubles to pay for the seat. The attendant typed everything in with no apparent issues, as he received no second glances, and she handed back his passport and a newly printed boarding pass.

"Enjoy your flight, Mr. Alexander," she said with a thick Russian accent.

With the last few rubles he had left, Sam purchased a pair of dark aviator sunglasses and a gray knit cap inside an airport store, put them both on, then moved deeper into the bowels of the airport. He was now flat broke. Five thousand miles from home without a dime in his pocket. The line for security was long and slow. Sam kept looking at the time on the digital board nearby, hoping he wouldn't miss his flight. When he finally reached the front, he immediately felt eyeballs on him from the older security guard. While waiting, Sam had wondered if it would seem odd to security for him to pass through with no bag—not a briefcase, satchel, or even a backpack—as he noted that every other person in the line around him carried some kind of travel bag. It was too late to do anything about it.

To Sam, the old man in uniform behind the kiosk looked like the stereotypical old KGB agent from an eighties cold-war movie, his face wrinkled and set with a permanent scowl. Swallowing, Sam handed him the boarding pass and his passport, reflecting stupidly for a moment on his trip to Mexico City last month, where he'd had to bolt out of the airport line at the very last minute to avoid being captured by Mexican security personnel. He never wanted to do that again.

"Glasses," the guard demanded in Russian, eyes slits.

Sam apologized, slipping off the sunglasses.

Three or four more stern looks back and forth between them. Sam begged his own face to stay relaxed. The KGB agent finally grunted, stamped his passport, and allowed Sam to pass through to the other side. However, it wasn't until Sam had made his way through a body scanner, got a full-on pat down by a husky security guard, then retrieved the sealed pouch with the computer tablet from the conveyor belt that he finally exhaled.

Checking the time on one of the flight boards, Sam had only a few minutes to board the plane before the doors closed. If he missed the flight, he had no other way to purchase another ticket. And no intention of openly hassling with a Russian airline agent to try to get on another plane. He threaded the other travelers in the large terminal hallway, hoping his best walk-run wouldn't draw any extra eyes to him. Approaching, he noticed the seating area at his gate was completely empty, and the airline attendant was just about to shut the doors leading out the walkway to the plane. He held out his boarding pass. She smiled, told him he'd just barely made it, scanned the boarding pass, and allowed him down the walkway.

Sam took several deep breaths—he was the last person to board the plane. A flight attendant inside welcomed him and sealed the door behind him. Sunglasses on, Sam made his way down the aisle, found his seat near the very back, next to an older couple. He buckled himself, slouched down, and made sure his posture told the older couple he wasn't at all interested in any small talk.

When the plane finally lifted off Russian ground, Sam felt a measure of relief pour through him. Closing his eyes, he eased even deeper into the seat cushions. He had somehow survived Moscow. No small feat considering the catastrophic circumstances of last night. He couldn't say the same for those who were there with him. As the plane climbed into the sky, he again reflected on the faces of his team members, nearly all of them dead. His heart felt heavy. They had all treated him with dignity and respect—like he was truly one of them.

Three team members were still unconfirmed.

Lucinda—who had remained in London.

Mack—his second backup man on the streets.

Marcus Pelini—his long-lost father and the man who had lured him into this death trap in the first place.

TWENTY-ONE

The cab dropped Natalie two blocks from the warehouse facility she'd discovered in Sam's file. She didn't want to be let out right in front, just in case there were other eyes watching the building. She had no idea what to expect. She hoped to be able to piece together a clue or two on Operation Black Heron. The rusted red warehouse sat in an industrial part of east DC, situated among several other run-down warehouse-type buildings of similar size. At nearly midnight, there was not much activity going on in and around the buildings. The warehouse sat in near darkness.

Natalie paused at a street corner, gave another sweep of the area. She double-checked the address again. This was the right place. She had no clue what she was about to find inside the warehouse, *if* she could even gain access.

Crossing the street, she sidled up next to the massive four-story warehouse building, which had several huge garage-type doors in front probably big enough to fit eighteen-wheelers. There were no windows anywhere in the front. The place wasn't big on aesthetics. Between two oversize garage doors, she found a normal black office door. Locked. She moved farther down and found another similar door. Also locked. Where was Sam when she needed him to pick a damn lock? She tried the metal handles on the massive garage doors, seeing if she could somehow manually lift them, but they were secure to the concrete. The place was locked down.

Circling around to the side of the warehouse, she spotted a square window about fifteen feet up. There was no easy way to reach it. No emergency stairs, ladder, or anything of the sort. She'd have to be creative if she was going to get inside. Next to the building were several metal dumpsters, all stuffed full of trash bags, boxes, and dozens of empty wooden storage crates. Natalie dug through the trash and found five crates that were still in decent shape. One by one, she tugged them out of the dumpster and stacked them directly beneath the window. When she had a shaky crate tower built, she began to climb carefully. The tower shifted a bit back and forth against the metal warehouse but held steady enough for her to reach the window.

Peering inside, she couldn't make out much. The warehouse was pitch-dark. Natalie grabbed the edge of the window, tugged, found it locked. Looking away from the window, she balled her fist and thrust her sleeve-covered right elbow into the glass as hard as she could, hoping she didn't break a bone in the effort. She didn't climb up these crates for nothing. The glass easily shattered. Leaning in, she listened but heard nothing. She took a moment to knock all the jagged glass away so she didn't cut herself. Then she pulled herself up over the window ledge. There was nothing for her to scale down on the inside. She'd have to jump for it. She dropped to the concrete floor and immediately rolled to absorb the direct impact on her legs, banging her shoulder hard in the process.

Getting up, she rubbed the ache in her shoulder. She pulled out her burner phone, turned on the flashlight, began to investigate the huge facility. In the middle, she discovered what looked like movie-production sets, each with makeshift rooms—bedrooms, hallways, offices, living spaces, and even bathrooms—every kind of room she could think of inside a house. Most of them were fully furnished. Beds, chairs, tables, sofas. On the exterior walls of the sets, she found pieces of white paper taped up, marking the different sections: Floor One, Floor Two, Floor Three, all the way up through Floor Six. Were they filming something? She snapped dozens of pictures with her phone.

Moving farther into the warehouse, she discovered another massive construction project. She allowed her flashlight to shine over the full height of it. Built floor to ceiling, it looked like the side of a tall building. There were several ropes hanging from the top all the way to the bottom. She found climbing harnesses sitting in a pile on the dusty concrete floor. Her eyes went back up to the wall. Climbing was listed on Sam's schedule, but she'd never even heard him talk about such a thing. Although she'd noticed his hands were more calloused than normal the past few weeks. When she'd mentioned it to him, Sam had claimed he'd started lifting weights at the gym inside his law firm building.

Was that a lie, too?

If so, why would he need to practice climbing the side of a tall building?

Behind the climbing apparatus, she found several tables surrounded by metal folding chairs. The tables were covered with fast-food paper bags, foam cups, and other assorted trash. Clearly, people had sat around them, eating, and discussing whatever was going on inside the warehouse. She found a binder sitting at the end of one of the tables. Russian Language 101. Inside, she flipped through full sections of completed grammar worksheets in what she recognized as Sam's handwriting. Sam had received a crash course in Russian. She paused at the back pocket of the binder, where she found a news clipping from a Russian publication.

Pulling it out, she stared at the face of a midforties man with a neatly trimmed brown beard, wearing a sleek gray suit. She recognized the name.

Vladimir Zolotov.

TWENTY-TWO

The Aeroflot plane touched down in Munich around eight thirty in the morning. Exiting with the crowd, Sam thankfully passed through the appropriate immigration and customs checkpoints without incident. No second looks, no suspicious stares. His alias passport seemed to be working out just fine; he was grateful to have it right now. What he didn't have were any resources to catch a cab or rent a car. No cash, no credit card, nothing but the stolen clothes on his back. He doubted he could hitchhike his way out of the airport, nor did he intend to try. To get to Salzburg, he'd have to resort back to the street skills that had landed him in juvie as a teenager. For someone who'd long wanted to put his life of crime behind him, life had sure forced him to steal a lot of cars over the past year.

Following the airport signs, Sam made his way outside to the busy pickup lane, where dozens of family members and friends had pulled up in their cars to welcome tired travelers and load luggage into car trunks. Sam had no luggage. At least that kept him agile. Standing on the curb, he peered in both directions, spotted several airport security guards situated up and down the sidewalk. He would need to be careful and quick. Fortunately, it was chaotic and loud. Dozens of cars were constantly pulling in and out of open spots, all up and down the long pickup lane, horns honking everywhere. At different places, the vehicles were even stacked two deep.

Sam patiently waited. He couldn't foul this one up. Not when surrounded by an army of security personnel. After five minutes, he spotted a potential target—a young man, midtwenties, left a black Nissan Rogue idling. The man didn't even wait for an open spot. He just parked in the second lane and temporarily boxed in two other cars. He obviously couldn't wait a second longer to see his young girlfriend. She stood by a bench holding a small dog in her arms, and there were several large designer bags of luggage at her feet. Smiling with glee, the man went in for a hug and a kiss. The woman set the dog down and wrapped her arms fully around him.

During their extended embrace, Sam made his move. This was not the first time he'd stolen an idling car with the driver nearby. He'd done this kind of job more than a dozen times as a teen, casually dropping inside a Mercedes or a Lexus at various gas stations where wealthy drivers were ignorant or arrogant enough to keep their cars running outside, pumping that cold AC while they rushed inside to grab their Snickers bars and Diet Cokes. Sam would slip in, pull out, and calmly drive away. He barely needed more than thirty seconds.

Trying to move with the same brash confidence of his youth, Sam stepped off the curb and circled the front of a waiting BMW sedan, where it looked like a grandfather was loading luggage for three teenage grandkids. The group created a nice sight barrier between Sam and the Nissan Rogue driver. Sam briskly moved to the driver's door of the idling Nissan, climbed inside, put the car in drive, then eased into exiting traffic. He closely watched his rearview mirror. As expected, the young man and woman were still in a full-on embrace on the sidewalk, in no real hurry to take their hands off each other. The dog was now running around at their feet, which was perfect. Every extra second of distraction mattered. Sam figured he probably had a full three minutes before the couple realized something was going on. That was damn near an eternity with car theft.

Pressing the gas pedal down even farther, Sam accelerated up the exit lane. When he noticed a cell phone sitting in the cup holder, he lowered the window and dropped it out onto the pavement. He didn't need police using GPS to track him. He kept his speed under control, left the airport, and drove into the city.

He stopped at the first gas station in sight, searched the Nissan for any loose cash. Finding a few euros in the middle console, he hurried inside the station. There were maps by the front counter. Sam grabbed one, paid the clerk, and rushed back to the SUV. Opening the map, he identified the most direct path to get him to Salzburg. He estimated it would take him just under two hours.

Jumping back on the highway, Sam said a prayer, punched the gas.

Tommy Kucher had better be there.

TWENTY-THREE

By midmorning, Sam ditched the Nissan Rogue in a parking lot near the Salzach River in the heart of Salzburg. With the Eastern Alps set in the distance over his shoulder and a massive castle sitting high up on a hillside right in front of him, he surveyed the picturesque city. The sky was clear, the sun out, and Salzburg was already bustling with activity as throngs of people strolled along the sidewalks next to the river. How would he find Tommy?

Although Salzburg was no booming metropolis, Sam would still be searching for one guy among a couple hundred thousand people. Even though he had his own unique style that stood out—tattoos, funky hair, piercings nearly everywhere on his body—Tommy really didn't want *anyone* to find him right now.

After things had gone haywire last month during Sam's trip to Mexico City—a trip where he'd pulled Tommy in for much-needed help—the brilliant hacker who'd played such a pivotal role in saving Sam's life on another occasion in the past year had decided he needed to uproot. Tommy talked about heading overseas, going off the map, and reestablishing his online crusade somewhere more obscure. It didn't sit well with Tommy that an outside party had so easily infiltrated and manipulated his private online network—one he'd spent years insulating. Unfortunately, Tommy didn't have full disclosure on that; Sam had been unable to tell him the truth about Marcus Pelini, the CIA, and Operation Shadow Shepherd. He regretted that now. He needed his hacker friend more than ever, but he could no longer simply contact Tommy by logging in to the secure website they'd used to interact regularly. Tommy was no longer there. He told Sam he needed to go into a dark hole for a long while.

When they'd last spoken, four weeks ago in DC, Tommy had told Sam—with his usual goofy grin—not to go and get himself into any trouble over the next few months. Tommy Boy would not be around to help bail him out this time.

Famous last words, Sam thought.

However, a week ago, Sam had received a postcard in the mail with a picture on the front of the sun rising up over beautiful Salzburg, along with a few simple words scribbled in black pen on the back: *Don't say it's a fine morning, or I'll shoot ya.* There was a smiley face drawn next to those scrawled words. The postcard had made Sam laugh. Although there was no name listed, he knew it was from Tommy. The quote on the postcard was from John Wayne in the classic western *McLintock!*, a film they'd watched together at Tommy's favorite old DC movie house—one of dozens of such films Tommy had insisted Sam come watch with him. When Tommy wasn't hacking, he spent the rest of his time obsessed with these films. He'd even given Sam the nickname Duke early on in their friendship, the same one John Wayne had carried throughout his legendary film career.

A few blocks from the river, Sam grabbed a chair in front of an open computer station inside a copy shop near Alter Markt, a wide-open market with huge water fountains surrounded on all sides by medieval-looking buildings. To locate Tommy—a true needle in a haystack—Sam needed to be able to pinpoint every tattoo parlor, video arcade, and movie house he could find in the city. Tommy must have been to one of them. He began a Google search, printed out a two-page list, paid for the cheap copy job with the money he took from the stolen car, and hit the streets again. Unfortunately, he did not have a photo of Tommy. If you typed his name into Google, you'd find *nothing*. Not his photo, not his name. Tommy always made sure of that.

Most of the locations on Sam's Google list were within walking distance. He had doubted Tommy would choose to live on the outskirts of the city. He liked to be in the center of the action. Sam hit four tattoo parlors, three video arcades, and two movie houses within the first hour. No one at any of the places was able to identify the man Sam had tried to describe in vivid detail. Just a bunch of blank stares and shakes of heads. Last he'd seen Tommy, he'd had a black Mohawk, a dozen rings in both ears, and tattoos everywhere—including his most identifiable one: a blue-and-gray one wrapped around his skinny neck that read *Tommy Cool*, the name of his onetime punk band. Sam led his search with that tattoo.

Just when he was about to get desperate, Sam caught a solid lead at the third movie house, a classic theater called Mozartkino. He wasn't surprised when he spotted several advertisements for upcoming shows of a few classic westerns he recognized. The young woman working the concession nodded at the mention of Tommy Cool. She told Sam that he'd been a regular; she'd even seen him yesterday, and she usually spotted him hanging out at 220 Grad, a small café just a block over from the theater.

Sam hustled up the street, put eyes on 220 Grad, which was housed in a yellow building with orange umbrellas on the patio out front. Several people were sitting in orange chairs around tables and enjoying a variety of menu items. Sam didn't recognize Tommy as being one of them. He pushed through the doors and stepped inside the café. A short line was at the counter. Most of the tables inside were also taken—the place was popular. Again, Sam surveyed the faces of the patrons. A couple smiling and laughing together. A gray-haired man reading a newspaper. A mom corralling two small children. A bald young man with square black glasses working on a laptop. Two men in suits with papers spread between them. A young woman with headphones on, watching something on her phone.

No Tommy. He cursed to himself. He hoped that the guy at the counter could offer some assistance. Sam waited in the short line. He began to read the menu, feeling hungry. He felt a tap on the shoulder, turned. The young woman wearing the headphones handed him a folded piece of paper.

"That guy over there asked me to hand this to you," she said.

"What guy?"

She turned, shrugged. "Oh, he's gone, I guess. Weird."

Unfolding the paper, Sam read it: *Meet me in the alley.*

Sam took another quick look around the café. One table was now empty that had been occupied only a minute ago. The bald guy with the square black glasses. *What the hell?* He stepped out of line, hurried outside. His eyes went left, right. He caught the back of the bald guy just as he was circling the building to his right.

Sam rushed after him, turned the corner, then stopped in his tracks. The bald guy had removed his eyeglasses and was now staring right at him with the biggest grin on his face. A very familiar grin. Sam couldn't believe it. Tommy Kucher. Only not like he'd ever seen him before. Completely bald. No facial hair. All the earrings were gone. He wore a pair of normal blue jeans, running shoes, and a neat blue button-down shirt with the sleeves rolled up. Tommy looked like a brand-new guy.

"You miss me that much *already*?" Tommy asked.

"More than you know," Sam confirmed, giving his buddy a quick hug. "I don't even recognize you."

"That's kind of the point, dude. I needed to reinvent myself."

"You did a helluva job."

"Clearly not good enough. You found me. What the hell are you doing in Salzburg?"

Sam sighed, his smile disappearing. "Can we go somewhere private to talk?"

Tommy eyeballed him curiously.

"It's important," Sam said.

"What the hell did you do now?"

TWENTY-FOUR

Tommy had set up his new residence on the top level of an old four-story apartment building that sat in a long row of other apartment buildings near the center of Salzburg. The apartment was about the same size as Sam's place back in DC. A tiny kitchenette. A miniature fridge. A futon. A beanbag. Not much else. Not even moving boxes stacked in a corner. Tommy had brought next to nothing with him from the States. Everything was makeshift except a decent metal L-shaped desk that already housed four giant computer screens. The tiny apartment wasn't much for design, but it did have a little balcony with a peek of the river. Shutting the apartment door behind them, Tommy took time to latch four different lock systems—he'd clearly added extra security measures. Sam walked over to the open balcony, peered down into a good-size marketplace below.

"You know Mozart was from Salzburg?" Tommy mentioned.

"I'd heard that. And something about *The Sound of Music* being filmed here."

"The hills are alive, dude," Tommy said with a smirk.

Tommy had begun to play the role of tour guide on their five-block walk from the café over to his apartment building. He seemed happy to have made his new home here in Austria, and he had already fully embraced the change of scenery. Sam hoped to hell he wasn't about to torpedo that for him in some way.

"I like what you've done with the place," Sam said, eyes on the room.

"Whatever. It works. I don't do much entertaining, as you know." He plopped down into the black office chair behind his desk. "I'd invite you to have a seat, but I don't really have an extra one, unless you want to use the beanbag."

"Thanks, I think I'll stand."

Tommy leaned back in his chair, studied Sam. For the first time, a silence hung in the air between them. The playful banter was over. It was time for Sam to get down to business. He almost didn't know where to start. He had a lot to tell his friend, most of which was probably going to really piss him off.

"Listen, I'm sorry to barge in here . . . ," Sam began.

"Just tell me what's happened already."

"All right."

Sticking his hands in his pockets, Sam proceeded to tell Tommy *everything* that had really happened in Mexico City, New Orleans, and DC last month.

Tommy cursed several times. "You've got to be kidding me, Sam! You mean I was played like a second-rate fiddle all the way to the end? Even by *you*?" Tommy asked, looking betrayed. "I thought you and me were like brothers or something. Hell, I put my life on the line for you. Why, man?"

"Because Marcus Pelini is my *real* father."

Tommy's eyes widened. "Whoa. I did *not* see that coming."

"Me neither, believe me."

Sam told him everything he knew about Marcus Pelini—the revelation about him being his real father, then the invitation to join him on a covert CIA mission. Something Sam stupidly had agreed to do to grow closer to him.

"I trained relentlessly for the last month," Sam said, pacing the room.

"Does Natalie know?"

Another sad hang of the head. "No, she doesn't. No one could know. That was all part of the deal."

"Brutal. But I'd have probably done the same thing as you. The wounds of the father and all, you know. Something tells me everything did not go as planned while in Moscow last night, or you wouldn't be standing here with me right now."

"*Nothing* went as planned."

Sam detailed the chaos of the previous evening—his delicate escape from Zolotov's compound, discovering all the dead bodies inside the safe house, the still-missing members of the team, including Pelini, and his night on the run. During the middle of this explanation, Tommy turned his attention to the computer screens and began typing away, pulling up stories and images of Vladimir Zolotov.

"You still have the tablet?" Tommy asked.

"Yeah." Sam pulled it out from under the back of his jacket, handed it to him. "Can you get into it?"

"Only one way to find out."

Tommy plugged a cord into the tablet, set it beside his keyboard, continued to peck away. His eyes bounced from screen to screen.

"Listen, you really don't have to do this, Tommy," Sam said, trying to mean it. "You don't owe me anything. Hell, it's the other way around. I'm the one that owes you big-time. You've just created a new safe haven here. I promise I'll understand if you'd rather not get involved. Just say the word and I'll walk out of here."

Tommy looked up, rolled his eyes at Sam. "How long you been practicing that little speech?"

"The whole drive from Munich."

Tommy grinned. "It wasn't bad. You delivered it well."

"I really mean it."

"No, you don't. But it's duly noted. Now come over here and take a look at this."

Sam circled in behind Tommy and looked at one of the screens.

"This it?" Tommy asked.

Sam stared at a digital folder entitled Black Heron. He nodded. Tommy continued to hack his way deeper into the file, his fingers pecking away at a hundred miles per hour. It took him a few minutes—there was a lot of strange code flashing across the screen—and then another digital folder appeared entitled The List.

"We've got it," Tommy confirmed.

"Can you open it?"

"You sure you want to see it? Sounds like this list is *nothing* but trouble."

"I want to see why people are shooting at me."

"Give me a second. It's encrypted, as well."

Tommy clicked away for a few more minutes.

"Voilà," he announced, finally opening the folder. "Well, that's interesting."

"It's empty?" Sam asked, squinting at the screen.

"Yep. It's an empty folder."

"Could the file have been moved?"

Tommy kept working his keyboard, shook his head. "I don't know. You sure they actually secured the list?"

"Yes . . . I think . . . everyone celebrated like we had it." Sam stood straight, pondered the events of the previous night. "Right after we secured the list is when all hell broke loose and I heard shots being fired in the safe house."

Tommy shrugged. "I don't know, Duke. Maybe your guy only thought he had the list. Maybe Zolotov became privy to your operation and pulled the list from his server at the last second. Or someone else did."

"Can you tell if that's true?"

"I can't verify anything without being inside Zolotov's server."

Sam cursed, shook his head. "I really need to find someone else from the crew."

"How many are still unaccounted for?"

"Pelini, Lucinda, and Mack. Everyone else is dead."

"Any way you can think of to track them down? Were they also using new CIA aliases like you?"

Sam's eyes lit up. "Yes! And I know everyone's names except for Pelini. He wasn't part of our group discussion."

"Give them to me. Maybe I can find a hit somewhere."

Sam gave him the alias names of Rod Luger for Mack and Clarice Nelson for Lucinda. Tommy went back to typing while Sam continued to pace the room. He shook his head, sighed. All that work to get inside the building, only to download an empty file? What the hell? At least five people were dead because of it.

He looked at a digital clock Tommy had on the kitchenette counter. Almost noon. London was only an hour earlier. He wondered if his boss had tried to check in on him this morning. Or would David let him sleep, since he'd feigned illness the night before? At some point, David would become concerned about his absence. Sam didn't want that concern somehow making its way back to Natalie and freaking her out.

It was only six in the morning back in DC. Within the next thirty minutes, Natalie would likely be rolling out of bed, making her coffee, getting ready for the day. She would call him and not get an answer. Should he call her first? Act like everything was okay?

Tommy snapped him away from his thoughts.

"What time did you say you entered Zolotov's property last night?"

Sam turned. "Exactly two thirty. Why?"

"Come check this out."

Sam circled in behind Tommy again. He was shocked to see one of the screens showing what looked like security-camera footage coming from Zolotov's town house. Six different video boxes from six different security cameras were on Tommy's screen. Three of the boxes were from cameras on the grounds of the property. Two from inside the stairwell. One from inside the elevator.

"Look familiar?" Tommy asked.

Sam nodded. "That's the place. You're tapped into their security?"

"Yeah, man, wanted to get the lay of the land and see if you could be seen on video anywhere breaking into and out of the property."

"Can you?"

"Not on the way inside. Your guy did a good job of minimizing the views. There's some footage of you leaving the property. But nothing where you can be identified. However, that's not what I really wanted to show you. Take a look here."

Tommy pressed Play. Sam watched the center video box on the screen. It was a camera on the grounds on the opposite side of the town house from where Sam had entered. The time stamp on the footage read 2:57 a.m. By that time, Sam would've already made his way inside the building. So what was Tommy trying to show him?

"There," Tommy announced, freezing the video.

Leaning in closer, Sam spotted a shadowy figure on the screen, and it wasn't a security guard or a dog. It was a man on the property. He was wearing all black—the same outfit Sam had been wearing.

"Can you enhance it?" Sam asked.

Tommy punched in a few keys, enlarged the video box, but it was impossible to see the man's face. As if he knew how to avoid the cameras. But Sam didn't need to see his face. He'd recognize that gait anywhere. The gray-bearded man.

Marcus Pelini.

TWENTY-FIVE

Alger Gerlach sat by himself at a café table near Maya Bay in the Phi Phi islands. The most beautiful spot on the planet, Gerlach thought, with its silky-soft white sand, vibrant fish, and colorful underwater coral. Southern Thailand had always suited him well. The man known as the Gray Wolf owned a bungalow nearby—one of a dozen homes he'd purchased in exotic locations across the globe with the more than $30 million he'd earned through his assassination efforts over the past decade. Money that was carefully laundered and hidden in several different offshore accounts.

The skin of his five-foot-ten, 160-pound slender body was quite tan. He wore a blue short-sleeve shirt, white shorts, flip-flops, and aviator shades. His gun was at the back of his shorts. It was never too far away from his reach. He sipped from a cold bottle of Blanche de Namur, a refreshing Belgian beer, and watched the sun begin its slow descent over the tranquil water. He'd spent the past month at the bungalow, flying different girlfriends in and out, going out on his boat every day, fishing, drinking, sunbathing, and basically living it up.

He was not eager to take on another job, but he could not turn down this requested meeting. He watched the front of the open-air café from behind his aviator shades. The man was right on time. He looked the part of a tourist—flowery shirt, straw hat, sunglasses, long yellow swim trunks, and sandals. Only he carried a stupid black briefcase. A waitress near the front pointed toward Gerlach's table. Gerlach shifted his weight, making sure his gun felt right at his back. These were always anxious moments for him, meeting a client. He never knew when someone would infiltrate his network and use a job as a way of taking out the Gray Wolf, the greatest assassin on the planet. Understandably, he had more enemies than friends.

Gerlach didn't even acknowledge the man as he sat in a chair on the opposite side of the table, setting his briefcase at his sandaled feet. He was in his midforties with a goofy thin mustache. The pretty waitress came by, and the American ordered a fruity cocktail. She returned from the bar with it a minute later.

"Quite the view," the man said, sipping, gazing out toward the water.

Gerlach didn't say anything, just sipped his cold Belgian beer.

"Thanks for taking this meeting," the man continued.

"As if I had a choice," Gerlach finally replied, his German accent prevalent. Although he could speak a dozen languages fluently, in every known tone and accent, he always went back to his natural tongue between jobs. He had to have some sense of normalcy in life.

"Just the same," the man countered. "We appreciate it."

The man opened his briefcase, took out a manila envelope, dropped it on the table next to Gerlach's beer bottle. "Everything's in the envelope. My number is on the back. Call if you need anything."

Gerlach didn't touch it. "What if I say no this time?"

The tourist actually grinned, which nearly set Gerlach off. He had half a mind to whip his gun out right there and put two bullets through the man's forehead.

"My number is on the back," the man repeated.

With that, the mustached man left some cash on the table, grabbed his briefcase, and walked out of the café. Gerlach eyeballed the envelope, still seething at the exchange. He finished off his beer, flagged the waitress for another, then opened the manila envelope. Three eight-by-ten color photos slid out. He examined them one at a time. The first photo was a midthirties black-haired woman. He flipped the photo over to find a name written on the back: *Clarice Nelson*. Below the name, a last-known location: *Le Tréport*. The second photo was a man in his fifties with a thick mustache and balding on top: *Rod Luger. Milan.* The third photo made Gerlach sit up straight in his seat. A very familiar man, one who'd haunted Gerlach's dreams every night for the past month. A job left unfinished.

The only unfinished job of his legendary career.

Dean Alexander, also known as Sam Callahan. *Salzburg.*

Gerlach smiled, thrilled he hadn't said no to the tourist.

TWENTY-SIX

Sam paced in an even tighter circle inside Tommy's apartment.

"I don't get it!" he exclaimed. "Why was Pelini entering the property?"

"I take it that wasn't part of the plan?" Tommy asked.

Sam adamantly shook his head. "Not even close."

"Could Pelini have sensed trouble?"

Sam stopped pacing, looked over at Tommy. "What was the time stamp again?"

"Two fifty-seven."

Running the scene back through his brain, Sam tried to place his *exact* location inside the building. It was easy to recall, since his every move had been clocked by the second. "This took place a few minutes after I'd just discovered that the kids' bedrooms and Zolotov's office were on opposite floors. That was unexpected and troubling but not a rescue situation. Nothing had tripped the alarm. So I highly doubt Pelini was coming to get me, especially without a single word of it to anyone else."

"Could he have somehow gotten into the server room before you?"

Sam peered over at Tommy with a furrowed brow.

Tommy shrugged. "Your guy may have downloaded an empty file."

Sam pondered the thought. "I don't see how he would've gotten there before me. Hell, I had to scale the outside of the building and then drop in from the top while hanging from a damn wire. Something we had to practice for a month. And somehow Pelini walked right in and grabbed the file off the server?"

"I'm not saying it adds up. Just looking for answers."

"If that was even possible, why would Pelini do it?"

Tommy cursed suddenly, his eyes locked in on a computer screen.

"What?" asked Sam.

"We have uninvited guests at my door right now."

Rushing around to view the computer screen, Sam spotted two men standing right outside—Tommy had installed a hidden security camera above the door. The door was also miked. Tommy punched a button on his keypad and increased the volume. The men were whispering to each other as if they didn't want anyone inside the apartment to hear them. They weren't speaking German or English, either. They were speaking in Russian. That's when Sam suddenly put it together. One of the men was the Russian assassin who had chased him out of Red Square and onto the bridge in Moscow.

"You recognize them?" Tommy whispered.

"They're here for me," Sam announced, feeling a chill run up his back.

Tommy looked nervous. "What do we do?"

A second chill knocked Sam sideways when both men withdrew guns from their jackets and pointed them at the door. They weren't even going to knock—they were just going to shoot their way inside. As a string of muffled bullets hit the apartment door, blasting apart the locks, Sam grabbed Tommy, flung him to the floor, and shielded him with his body. There was no way in hell he was going to get Tommy killed because he'd unwittingly brought these assassins along with him.

Tommy let loose a string of frightened expletives, his face completely pale. Sam was trying to get his attention, but panic had set in as the two men outside were working their way toward busting the door open. Even with the four different heavy-duty locks, it wouldn't hold for long.

Grabbing Tommy by the shirtsleeve, Sam dragged him toward the small balcony opening. Sam peered down, looking for a quick escape route. Like a video game in his head, his mind quickly diagrammed his options. A drop to the stone walkway of the market below would definitely break a bone or two—hell, it might break all of Tommy's bones, since he had no extra muscle to cushion the blow. Sam turned when he heard a loud bang on the apartment door behind him. It was coming down within seconds.

Scooting to the edge of the balcony, Sam peered up, knowing they were on the top level of the old building. He noticed the wrought-iron trim on top of the building. A bracket hung down low enough where he might be able to get them both up onto the flat roof. According to his mind mapping, it was their *only* chance. He spun around, grabbed Tommy, shoved him toward the balcony wall.

"We're going to the roof."

Tommy kept cursing but did as Sam said. Sam helped him up on the balcony ledge. Tommy leaned over, looked up, then stared back over at Sam.

"Seriously?" he asked.

"Go!"

There was no time to question the decision. The door to the apartment broke open. Turning, Tommy reached up, grabbed the bracket, began pulling his skinny body up. Below him, Sam helped shove the kid up as fast as possible while trying not to fall four stories and splatter on the stone below. He heard the Russians inside the apartment, one yelling. *Balcony!*

Hopping up on the balcony wall, Sam nearly climbed over Tommy as they both reached the flat rooftop simultaneously. Sam could already hear one of the Russians climbing up the bracket after them. He helped

Tommy to his feet, and they raced over to the opposite edge of the building. Sam calculated about a ten-foot gap between Tommy's building and the four-story building next to it. He cursed. There had to be an easier way. Sam searched all sides for any emergency stairs that might lead them down to safety but found nothing.

"What do we do?" Tommy asked him.

Sam turned. The Russians were almost on the rooftop. He could see a head pop up. Turning back to Tommy, Sam said, "We jump. I'll go first to catch you."

Not even waiting for a response, Sam sprinted toward the edge of the building. When he got there, he leaped, his arms and legs spinning furiously in the air. Reaching out, he was able to grab the stone edge of the flat rooftop next door with both hands as his body slammed hard against the side of the building. He quickly pulled himself up and over, spun around, and begged Tommy to get moving.

Shaking his head, the kid did as he said and ran as fast as he could before jumping for it. Sam could immediately tell that his weaker friend wasn't going to clear the full distance. Leaning over as far as he could, Sam reached out with both hands to try to cover the gap. Tommy's hands slapped against his, and Sam did everything he could to grab hold of him. One hand slipped out, but Sam's right hand held on to Tommy's wrist like a vise as his friend dangled. Fortunately, Tommy was a lightweight. Sam was able to hold him steady with one hand while reaching down with his other and grabbing his shirtsleeve. He quickly yanked his skinny friend up over the stone railing and onto the rooftop with him—just before a spray of bullets came at them from the other side.

On hands and knees, hidden behind the short roof wall, Sam and Tommy skirted the edge of the rooftop until they reached an inner door leading back inside the building. The gunfire had ceased. Sam wondered if one of the men would try to make the jump. He poked his head up, glared in the bright sunlight over at the other rooftop. Neither man was still standing there. They'd clearly decided not to jump; they were most likely racing down the stairs inside Tommy's building to intercept them from the ground.

"Come on!" Sam yelled, pulling Tommy inside the rooftop door behind him.

They took the stairs down two and three steps at a time, passing a bewildered older woman carrying groceries on the way up. They were racing the clock. Which group could descend the stairs the fastest? Although Tommy was slowing him down, Sam would never leave the guy. He'd take a bullet himself before allowing something to happen to him. Reaching the ground level, Sam searched for a back door to the building instead of the front, where the Russians likely would be. They burst into a rear alley without pausing. Sam's head whipped left, right, trying to figure out which way to flee while also anticipating the Russians' next move.

"My moped!" Tommy yelled, gasping for breath.

Sam turned to him. "Where?"

"A block over from here."

They hustled down the alley, circled the building, and raced out into the open air of the busy marketplace. They both stood out because they were the only two guys in a full-on panicked sprint among the shoppers and café patrons. Until seconds later, when Sam spotted the two Russians also race into the marketplace behind them.

"Where, Tommy?"

Tommy pointed. "There!"

A hundred feet in front of them sat a row of mopeds. Sam and Tommy splintered the crowd in the marketplace and made a beeline straight toward them. Tommy kept yelling that the blue one belonged to him. When they got to it, Sam tossed another look over his shoulder while Tommy scrambled to get his keys out of his pocket. The Russians were closing in on them. Would they shoot at them in the middle of everyone? Sam didn't care to find out.

When Tommy pulled out his keys, Sam snatched them from his shaky hands, jumped onto the moped, and started it. Tommy had barely boarded behind him when Sam revved the small engine, jerked into the street, and nearly took out a guy walking two dogs. Zipping around them, Sam put it full throttle and listened to the small moped engine whine. He watched his mirror, noticed the two men in black jackets stumble into the street behind them. Sam had quickly put distance between them.

Turning another street corner, Sam again revved the moped engine, Tommy clutching both hands tightly around his waist like a scared child.

Hell, they were both scared.

TWENTY-SEVEN

Using her new alias, Natalie spent the night at the Sofitel hotel, a few blocks north of the White House, thinking it might make her feel safer to be in close proximity to a building under such tight security. But it didn't work—she hardly slept. It was impossible to drift off with visions of a man with a gun chasing after her through the Metro, or of him crashing his speeding Suburban directly into her Jeep, battering her body, and putting Michelle in the ICU. Every time she closed her eyes, she relived the glass shattering, heard the metal crunching, smelled the gas and smoke, and she could see Michelle lying motionless in the seat next to her. As if that wasn't enough, Natalie's mind kept spinning out of control about her discovery inside the warehouse, where Sam had likely been the past month, secretly preparing for his trip to Russia.

She spent most of her night searching Google on her phone for *everything* she could possibly find on Vladimir Zolotov, the man in the photo from the back of Sam's Russian-language binder. There was plenty of online info out there on Zolotov. The successful Russian businessman was incredibly wealthy and seemed to know prominent political figures from all over the world. There were dozens of online pictures of Zolotov with Russian leaders, where he seemed to have measurable influence, as well as many American leaders. Natalie found pictures of

Zolotov standing with a host of congresspeople—he seemed to visit the United States regularly on business. There were also conspiracy theories galore about Zolotov's connection to funding different rebel and terrorist groups.

Natalie was stunned most by her discovery of Zolotov's recent purchase of a seven-story town house in the heart of Moscow for nearly $100 million. There were different pictures posted of the outside of the compound property, as well as several taken by a Russian magazine from the inside of the town house during the time of the sale. Natalie was mesmerized. The pictures of the interior of the town house nearly matched what she'd found in the warehouse—six different elaborate sets, labeled floors one through six. And the four-story climbing apparatus resembled the outside of the ornate Moroccan-style architecture of Zolotov's building. *Everything* matched up. Which blew her mind. Someone had clearly trained Sam to go to Moscow and get inside Zolotov's town house. Why?

She flashed on the scene of Sam standing inside the room with dead bodies. Had that been taken from inside Zolotov's town house? She didn't think so—the room was simple and small. So what happened? Who were those people? Furthermore, who was trying to cover this thing up? Considering the multiple attempts on her life during the past twelve hours, Natalie felt certain someone wanted to eliminate any ties with whoever could possibly know what Sam was doing. Was it the CIA?

She gritted her teeth, her anger with Sam growing. Why hadn't he said a word to her about any of this? At first, she thought Sam must've been blackmailed into engaging in something like this and concealing it all from her. Running with that initial theory had made her less pissed at him. But the letter he'd left for her in his London hotel room, and all her discovery in the aftermath, now made her feel otherwise—it looked like he'd signed up on his own. She didn't need any protection. She'd rather just have the truth from the man she was supposed to lock arms with for the rest of her life. Would she ever feel safe with a guy like Sam?

She walked over to the window, peered down on quiet H Street below. The sun had just started to rise on DC. She'd at least made it through the night without an unwelcome guest knocking on her hotel room door. That was her first order of business. Walking back over to her phone, she again dialed into her office voice mail. She'd been checking it regularly, just in case Sam had used it to try to get in touch with her. As pissed as she was at him right now, she so desperately longed to hear his voice and know he was okay.

There was no message from Sam; however, there was a new message from David Benoltz in London. David said he'd been trying to get in touch with her, but her cell phone was off. He told her he'd still heard nothing from Sam and wanted to know if she'd found out anything more on her end. Then he'd said something interesting. The client they'd flown to meet with in London, Liz Fields from Caldwell & Meyer, had also seemed to disappear. They were scheduled to meet for brunch, but he'd heard nothing from her all day. She was not answering her cell phone. She had not checked out of the hotel. Hotel security found her luggage and personal items still inside her hotel room. David wondered if it could somehow be connected to Sam. David urged her to call him back ASAP.

Natalie decided she'd call David back using another phone. She didn't want to do *anything* right now that might somehow expose her. Using Google on her phone again, Natalie immediately searched for Caldwell & Meyer, discovering it to be one of the UK's bigger financial firms. She added Liz Fields's name to her search and found a few mentions of a female partner by that same name, along with a photo from the company's online profiles. A heavyset red-haired woman in her fifties. She dialed the main number listed on the firm's website, paced, listened to the phone ring. When an administrator answered, she asked to speak with Liz Fields. Three rings later a strong female voice picked up.

"Liz Fields speaking."

Natalie was shocked. She didn't expect an answer from the woman. Had David not simply tried to reach her at her office?

"Ms. Fields, this is Molly from the Amba Hotel. There's been some confusion here, so I just wanted to confirm that you'll be staying with us for another night?"

"Excuse me? I'm not staying at the Amba Hotel."

Natalie tilted her head. "You mean, staying again tonight? Because we still have your personal items inside your hotel room."

"I don't understand. I haven't been staying at your hotel. There must be a mistake. Those items aren't mine."

Natalie couldn't tell yet if she was being played. So she kept on pushing. "Your associates, Mr. Callahan and Mr. Benoltz, have been trying to reach you."

The woman started to sound agitated. "Who? Look, Molly, I don't know who you're talking about. Those names mean nothing to me. And I'm not staying at your hotel. I think you've got some wires crossed, dear."

"My apologies, Ms. Fields. Good day to you."

Natalie hung up, stared at her phone. *What the hell?*

Needing to call back David ASAP to get some more clarity on the situation, she decided to grab an elevator down to the lobby. She took a careful peek around, found no one suspicious awaiting her arrival, and located a courtesy phone in the corner. She sat in the chair beside it, called David's cell phone. He promptly answered.

"It's Natalie," she said in hushed tones.

"Why're you whispering?"

"I'm in a public place. What does Liz Fields look like, David?"

"What?"

"Your client from Caldwell & Meyer. She a heavyset redhead in her fifties?"

"No, not even close. She's a thin black-haired woman in her thirties. Why're you asking? Have you heard anything from Sam yet?"

"Not yet." She continued to redirect. She had no desire to give David any details about what she'd discovered. She didn't want to pull him into this any deeper than necessary. It was clearly in his best interest. "How did you find this client?"

"Sam found her. He set up the meetings. I guess you got my message that she's also missing. What's with all the questions about her?"

"Sorry to be abrupt, David, but I've got to run," Natalie insisted. "Leave a voice mail at my office if you hear *anything* from Sam."

She hung up before David could utter another word.

The client, Liz Fields, was clearly a setup to get Sam to London.

And Sam was leading the setup.

TWENTY-EIGHT

They hid out in a corner of the busy Salzburg train station. Sam stood with his back to the wall, arms crossed, eyes on high alert. Tommy sat cross-legged on the floor with a laptop, pecking away. He kept a backup laptop hidden inside a safe-deposit box ten blocks from his new apartment in case of a moment of crisis, he'd said. Unfortunately, that moment had *already* come—thanks to Sam, who felt horrible about it. He'd led Russian assassins straight to Tommy's doorstep. Sam thought Tommy's hands might never stop shaking. Tommy kept muttering how he *really needed a damn cigarette*, and Sam was shocked to find out that Tommy had quit smoking recently. His friend really had reinvented himself. No spiky hair with purple streaks, no earrings, no new tattoos, and now he was no longer even a smoker.

"I'm *really* sorry, Mav," Sam said for the fifth time, shaking his head. *Maverick* had been the nickname Tommy had used online with Sam for years.

"Let it go already," Tommy urged him. "I'm fine, I swear."

Sam stiffened suddenly when he spotted two figures down the walkway. As they approached, he exhaled. The two men were much older than the Russians. Still, those two killers were nearby somewhere—Sam was ready to bolt town. He just wasn't sure where he was going next. And he needed help to get there. Tommy had been working on that.

"You really think they tracked my CIA alias?" he asked Tommy.

Tommy shrugged. "Can you think of another way?"

Sam shook his head. "But that brings up more questions."

"Like who has inside access to the details of your covert CIA operation and would then use them to wipe you out?"

Sam thought of Pelini, kept wondering.

"Yes!" Tommy blurted out. "Let's go ask Rod Luger."

"Where?"

"He's in Milan," Tommy declared, turning his laptop to show Sam.

Sam knelt, examined the information. The name Rod Luger, Mack's CIA alias, had checked into Hotel Berna in Milan just two hours ago.

"That's our guy," Sam confirmed.

A surge of energy rushed through Sam, as he was already calculating his next move. He had to find Mack ASAP. He could only hope the man he'd first met inside a Mexico City hotel suite last month had some answers for him. Either way, it was so good to confirm that at least one other person from his crew was still alive.

Sam's eyes narrowed in on Tommy. "Listen, you really should go somewhere and hide out for a bit. Let the dust settle."

Tommy shook his head. "No way, man. I'm staying with you."

Sam was more adamant. "Staying with me puts you right in the crosshairs."

"It might also keep you alive, so drop it." Tommy shoved his laptop inside a gray backpack, slung it over his skinny shoulder. "Come on, the train will be here in twenty minutes, and we need to get two tickets to Milan."

TWENTY-NINE

Her hair tucked beneath a newly purchased Washington Redskins ball cap, Natalie took a cab ride ten blocks over to Metrorail headquarters. She wore dark sunglasses even though the early-morning sky was heavily overcast. Sitting low in the back seat, she asked the driver to watch his mirrors for any followers. The old driver didn't even give her a second look. Natalie guessed her request was not altogether unusual for this ridiculous town. Arriving at a nondescript building, she handed cash to the driver and darted inside the building.

Squeezing into a full elevator, she tucked into the corner and rode up to the third floor. She still wore the sunglasses. No one paid much attention. Everyone looked dog-tired and seemed to be dragging their way into a new workday, waiting for their coffee to kick in. Exiting, she followed a drab hallway, turned a corner, and found the door for her contact at Metro. She knocked twice, waited. The door clicked open a second later, and a balding man of fifty, with thick glasses and an unusually short tie, allowed her inside. He shut the door behind them.

"I really appreciate this, Max," Natalie said.

"Of course," Max replied.

Max Graham worked in a small office by himself in front of a wall of TV monitors as part of Metro's security division. The ten monitors on the wall in front of his desk all showed live security-camera footage from various points across DC's Metrorail system. Natalie had enjoyed several dealings with Max over the years while working different stories. He was always pleasant and helpful, if a bit awkward. There were four small framed pictures of Max sitting with his five beloved cats on the cluttered desk in front of her. A bachelor his whole life, Max said the cats were his kids.

"Crazy scene last night," Max suggested, sitting in his squeaky chair, pulling up security footage from the tube as Natalie stood behind him.

Natalie had called Max first thing, told him she was working a story, and asked if she could possibly see what Metro's cameras had caught of the man who'd run through the terminal last night with a gun. She did not mention that she was the one chased through the terminal, and Max had not seemed to put it together yet. Natalie had no desire to give more details than necessary. She just wanted to see if she could find out any more info on her hunter.

"Here it is," Max said, pressing Play.

Natalie watched the monitor in the middle. She shivered at the sight of the goateed man aggressively pushing his way out of a train car. The same car she'd just bolted from herself, although, thankfully, she was not in the camera shot. Gun in hand, the man raced into the terminal as people panicked all around him. Max switched cameras to keep tabs on the man as he moved all the way through the terminal, up the stairs, and out of Metro's final camera shot. Natalie knew the rest of the story and still felt grateful for the group of muscle-bound men who'd stepped in to save her.

"Any ID on the guy yet?" Natalie asked.

Max shook his head. "Nothing yet. Not sure we're searching too hard, since no one got hurt. We don't really have a clue what the guy was doing. We think he may have been chasing after someone, but it's too hard to tell because everyone in sight is running away from him. Although there's a report of an encounter with a girl outside the Capital

One Arena. Eyewitnesses place this same guy at the scene, where he apparently got into a brawl with several other men before fleeing."

"Can you go back to the second camera, in the stairwell?"

"Sure thing."

Max typed onto his keyboard, pulled up the footage of the man racing up the stairwell. It was the closest camera shot Natalie had of the guy. Max let the footage roll, and Natalie asked him to pause it right in the middle. She leaned in close. She spotted a marking on top of the man's right hand—the one holding the gun.

"Can you enhance that?" Natalie asked, pointing at the man's hand.

Max kept pecking away until they had a close-up of the hand. The marking was a small black-and-white tattoo of a creepy skull with dog tags that said *Hell Dogs*.

THIRTY

Lloyd slept overnight in a stiff chair next to his father's ICU hospital bed. He wouldn't really call it sleep, as not much of that actually happened. Not while sitting in a chair that felt more like a medieval torture device, with the machines in the room beeping annoyingly every thirty seconds and a carousel of nurses coming in and out all night long. Still, Pop had survived the night. Although still in a coma with no real signs of coming out of it anytime soon, his father was at least still with him. That mattered much more to him than his sleep right now. *Keep on fighting, Pop!*

Rubbing his face, Lloyd looked over at his father. It was hard as hell to see him lying in that hospital bed, white as a ghost, his body looking so damn fragile. His old man used to lift weights in their garage when Lloyd was a kid, and he'd always marveled at the superior strength of his father. Pop could throw up 250 pounds on the bench press as if he were lifting pillows. Lloyd used to brag about him relentlessly to his group of neighborhood buddies. *My dad can beat up your dad,* and all that jazz—except it was true. His pop was by far the toughest and strongest SOB any of them knew.

All of that onetime strength had now completely vanished.

Agent Epps arrived, handed Lloyd a huge cup of coffee.

"Thanks," Lloyd said, rolling his head around his tight neck.

"Any change?" Epps asked him.

Lloyd shook his head. "Not yet."

"He'll push through," Epps offered. "He's not done bossing you around just yet, Chief."

"I hope you're right." Lloyd took a sip of hot coffee. "What do you got?"

"Hard to find this guy. Took me working several different channels with the few friends I have over at the Agency, but I finally got someone to give me a name. Mike Madrone. Ex–Special Forces. I was told he now works with a unit doing covert activity. I was also told in no uncertain terms that it would be in my best interest to stop asking about him."

"You get an address?"

"Yeah, already went by there. No one was home. A neighbor recognized him from the surveillance video but said she hadn't seen him in probably six months."

"We need to find out who pulled Madrone off the grid."

THIRTY-ONE

The train ride to Milan would take them seven long hours. They tried to get comfortable in their seats. Sam sat by the window, Tommy in the seat right next to him, pecking furiously away on his laptop. He told Sam a guy from one of the rogue hacker groups he regularly associated with had shipped him one of the most secure and high-powered mobile internet devices on the planet, one used only by Chinese intelligence. The computer was like an extension of Tommy's hands. He rarely let go of it, as if his body might not function without it.

Their passenger car was half-full. Sam had taken extra time to study every other face in the car. None stood out as potential killers. No second glances. No suspicious stares. Still, he watched them all carefully for the first hour, seeing if someone would make a move. When the hour finally passed and no one sprang up and pulled a gun on them, Sam started to relax. At least as much as he could under the current conditions.

Staring out the glass, Sam marveled at the beauty of the passing Austrian landscape. The mountains, the rivers, the trees. Under different circumstances, this would've been an enjoyable train ride through a majestic setting. He would rather be sitting there with Natalie curled up next to him. She would've loved this train ride. But it was difficult to enjoy much of anything right now with Russian assassins still hot on his tail.

With the addition of a new burner phone Tommy had secured for him in Salzburg, Sam had considered calling Natalie, pretending he was still sick in bed inside his London hotel room, and telling her he would probably be there sleeping all day. Just to keep things normal. He knew with each passing hour that she didn't hear from him today, she would grow more concerned. He also considered calling his boss, David, who was probably already wondering if Sam was dead in his hotel room right now.

But he decided against making either call. It was just too dangerous. Even with a burner phone, he didn't want to risk unwittingly pulling either Natalie or David into this dangerous situation. He also couldn't stand the thought of lying to Natalie anymore. Every time he'd been with her the past month after returning from training at the warehouse, the lies had rippled right off his tongue. *The class is good. Learning a lot. Glad I signed up for it.* A full month of these lies had burned a big hole in his gut and had given him a perpetual stomachache.

He was so damn tired of the lies.

And so damn angry with himself for agreeing to do it.

Assuming he could survive this, he could only hope Natalie would find the strength to forgive him—again. He certainly didn't deserve it.

His mind again drifted to Marcus Pelini, his father, the man who'd asked him to lie to Natalie in the first place. Pelini was a man of lies. They came fast and furious from the gray-bearded man. Which is why Sam kept wondering why Pelini had left the confines of the safe house and entered Zolotov's sprawling property last night. What the hell was his father doing? Could Pelini have possibly been behind the disappearance of the CIA list from Zolotov's server? Could the man have sold out his own team? Could Pelini have willingly sacrificed his own son?

Tommy interrupted Sam's dark thoughts.

"They used to call your father *the Lion*."

Sam looked over. "Who did?"

"The CIA. Back when Pelini was doing more aboveground operations. The nickname is mentioned throughout all the classified files I'm finding on him. Pelini has been all over the world running top-secret missions the past thirty years, although most everything about him went officially dark around fifteen years ago."

"You can't find anything on the past fifteen years?"

"Oh, I can find it, but I doubt too many others can. It's clear that the CIA has reserved intel on Pelini's operations for only those eyes with the highest level of clearance. The blackest of black ops. We're talking assassinations of prominent foreign dignitaries, kidnappings, creating civil wars. It's crazy stuff, Sam."

"Great. My father, the master spook." Sam shook his head. "What about Black Heron? Was it even a legit CIA operation?"

Tommy nodded. "Yeah, it's legit. Everything you've told me rings true. Only the top brass knew details, and few at that. But it's clear that the list was the real target."

"That's oddly comforting to know. Can you find out *anything* from Zolotov's side? Something that might tell us what really happened last night?"

Tommy sighed. "I'm trying. But you're talking a needle in a big-ass haystack."

As Tommy went back to typing away, Sam stared out the window again, his thoughts once more on Natalie. Desperate to get back to her, he prayed they would somehow find Mack in Milan and finally get some real answers.

Then figure out how he could get his life back.

THIRTY-TWO

Still wearing her Redskins cap pulled low on her forehead, Natalie sidled up to a crowded bar. When the bartender came over, she ordered a pint of Bold Rock and the Rachel—a roasted turkey sandwich with spicy kraut on rye bread. She'd barely eaten a thing since before the car wreck last night. Even though hungry, she wasn't sure her stomach could handle much of anything. It had been tied up in so many knots. She casually glanced around the Ugly Mug, a popular sports bar near the Marine Barracks at Eighth and I, thus a local favorite for the military crowd. There were dozens of strapping buzz-cut young men sitting at the bar and crowding the tables, where they dined on burgers, wings, and other typical bar food. Even at the early lunch hour, the place was busy.

Natalie had been to the bar often the past few years, as it was a convenient meet-up location for many of her military sources. She had to admit she felt a bit safer with so many chivalrous young marines sitting all around her. Even if found, she doubted her mystery man with the goatee would make any serious moves in such a place. Still, there were a lot of second looks from several men. She didn't like being this exposed or staying in one place for too long right now. With dangerous people out there clearly looking for her, she needed to stay unpredictable and constantly on the move.

She kept her eyes straight ahead, where she could spot anyone approaching in a mirror behind the bar. She was specifically looking for one man. She took a gulp of the Bold Rock, the hard cider tasting good as it went down her throat. Staring in the mirror, her eyes looked puffy and tired. It had been a difficult night. She knew there would be little to no sleep until she got to the bottom of this and somehow had Sam home with her. If he didn't come home, she might never sleep soundly again.

A few minutes later, a man in his thirties with a buzz cut like the others and wearing a tan polo shirt with jeans made his way through the bar to an open stool next to her. His name was Levi Connor. After fifteen years of active duty in the marines, he now worked for an organization that lobbied on the Hill on various veterans' matters. Natalie had met with Levi several times over the past two years when she needed a military perspective or insight on different stories. And sometimes when she needed help finding someone. Levi was a wealth of knowledge and connections. Something she sometimes exploited, since she knew Levi had a thing for her.

"Didn't figure you for a Redskins fan," Levi said, glancing at the cap.

"I'm actually not," Natalie said. "The Chiefs are my team, but I needed the cap. Buy you a beer?"

"Sure." Levi ordered a pint of Pacifico from the bartender. He turned back to Natalie, glanced down at her left hand with wide eyes, and cursed. "What's that diamond ring doing on your finger, Ms. Foster?"

She gave him a tight grin. "I'm engaged."

"The Callahan guy?"

She nodded.

"Lucky fellow." Levi sighed, clearly disappointed. "Guess I was too damn slow."

The bartender returned with Levi's beer. He took a big gulp, drowning his sorrows, turned back to her. "So what's on your mind? You sounded cryptic in your message."

She pulled a glossy eight-by-ten photo from her purse, set it down on the bar top in front of Levi. It was an up-close picture of the Hell Dogs tattoo from the security video inside Max's Metro office. Max had printed off several photos for Natalie. So far, she'd been unable to find anything online that identified the tattoo or its potential association with the military. She was now hoping Levi could help.

"Hell Dogs, huh?" Levi said, eyebrows pinched, studying the photo.

"You recognize it?"

He pressed his lips together. "Maybe. Looks vaguely familiar. I think it's a platoon mascot, but I'd need to check around to confirm that."

"Can you do that for me?"

He looked over at her. "What's this about?"

She pulled out a second photo, one that showed the face of her attacker. "I'm trying to ID this guy. The tattoo is on top of his right hand."

"This taken from a security camera?"

Natalie nodded but didn't elaborate. The less Levi knew, the better for both of them. She'd wrestled with even contacting him in the first place.

"He has a gun in his hand, Natalie," Levi stated.

"Yes, I know. I need to find him ASAP."

Levi eyeballed her curiously for a long moment, clearly waiting for her to explain. She didn't.

"I can't say any more, Levi," Natalie said, putting a hand on his arm. "Can you please just trust me on this? I really need your help."

"Yeah, sure, of course. Anything else?"

"Can I borrow your car?"

THIRTY-THREE

The Gulfstream landed on a private strip at Milan Linate airport just as the sun was setting over Italy. Alger Gerlach was the only passenger on board. While he was usually fine traveling commercial first class, the swift time line for this new job made it necessary for him to contract a private flight. After the plane finally settled on the tarmac, near a private hangar, a pilot appeared in the cabin and lowered the stairs.

Stepping out, Gerlach breathed in the warm air. A car and driver were already waiting for him. Moving down the stairs, Gerlach quickly climbed into the back seat of a black BMW sedan. He turned down the driver's offer to help him load his travel bag into the trunk. With what he had inside, Gerlach was not interested in the bag ever leaving his side. The driver sat behind the wheel and eased the BMW out of the airport.

The drive to Milan's city center took a brief fifteen minutes. After arriving at the luxurious Armani Hotel Milano, Gerlach generously tipped the driver, grabbed his bag, and checked in at the front desk. He found the elevator and ascended to the fourth floor, where he opened the door to a plush but simple hotel room. There was no need for him to book a suite. He wasn't even sure he'd actually be spending the night at the hotel—that all depended on the success of the evening.

Walking to the window, Gerlach pulled back the curtains. Night was now upon the city. The room had a spectacular view of the Duomo, the city's ancient Gothic cathedral that was currently lit up in bright lights. Gerlach had been to Milan many times, although it was usually with excitable girlfriends who loved to shop, eat, and spend obnoxious amounts of his money. Few places drained the bank account like Milan.

There would be no shopping or fine dining this go-round.

He checked his watch, sat on the bed. Unzipping his travel bag, he pulled out a compact silver metal case. Opening it, he removed the black gun, screwed on the silencer, and carefully checked the calibrations.

Another glance at his watch.

He returned to the window, waited. The hours before a kill always required a bit of meditation, reflection, the exercise of calming his adrenaline. He closed his eyes, slowly rolled his head around his neck, and did a few breathing exercises. He didn't have the luxury of a sniper shot with this job. He'd first have to find the target and then approach with the utmost caution—much like an animal stalking its unwitting prey.

His cell phone finally buzzed. Gerlach stared at the screen. The trap had been set. Everything was in place. He quickly put on his skintight vest holster, inserted the gun, and slipped a black sport coat over it. He did one more inspection in the mirror; then he headed for the door.

Time for the Gray Wolf to go hunting.

THIRTY-FOUR

Around 10:00 p.m., the train dropped Sam and Tommy at Milano Centrale, a quick five-minute walk to Hotel Berna. Standing on the sidewalk across the street from the hotel, Sam considered their options for finding Mack. He studied the hotel's front entrance—which showcased dozens of colorful flags representing different countries—and looked around to see if he could spot anyone else who might also be watching the hotel for the same reason. It was impossible to tell. The street was busy with cars, the sidewalks thick with people. Sitting on a bench beside him, Tommy was pecking away on his laptop as usual, the bright screen illuminating his face against the backdrop of night.

"Any changes?" Sam asked Tommy.

"Doesn't look like it," Tommy replied. "He hasn't checked out of the hotel or used his alias anywhere else just yet. He's got to be here in Milan somewhere."

Sam pulled out his burner phone, placed the call. When the hotel operator answered, he asked for Rod Luger's room. Sam listened to the phone ring and wondered if Mack would actually pick up. He highly doubted it—even if he was inside his hotel room. But it was worth a try. When the phone call went to an automated hotel answering service, Sam hung up.

He turned back to Tommy. "You got a room number?"

Tommy nodded. "Room 513."

"Let's go pay a visit."

Waiting for street traffic to clear, Sam and Tommy walked into the main lobby of Hotel Berna. Sam kept his eyes on high alert the entire time. He had no idea who else might also be out there trying to find Mack. The Russians? Others? He didn't notice anyone suspicious hanging out in the small lobby. They headed straight for the elevators, where a young couple was already waiting. When the elevator arrived, they ascended along with the couple, who got out on three. Sam and Tommy went all the way up to the fifth floor.

Room 513 was located near the end of the hallway.

Standing in front of the door, Sam turned to Tommy. "Wait down the hallway a bit, okay? If he's here, I don't want to spook him. Mack likely has a gun."

Tommy did as told and waited halfway down the hallway toward the elevator.

Sam swallowed, knocked. *Come on, be there!*

He didn't hear any movement from inside. He knocked a little more firmly.

"Mack, it's Sam!" he said, just loud enough to be heard through the door.

Still no answer. *Damn.* Sam looked down at the door handle, noted it was an electronic card-key lock system. Impossible for him to pick the lock. But he had to get inside Mack's room somehow. Tommy rejoined him a moment later.

"No luck?" Tommy asked.

"No, but we have to get inside."

"Maybe I can somehow unlock it online," Tommy suggested.

"Not everything can be solved with a computer, Mav. I'll be right back."

Returning to the lobby, Sam stepped up to the female attendant behind the front desk, who looked up and gave him a friendly smile. He read her name tag, matched her smile.

"Hi, Martina, I can't find my wallet with my room key. I need to get back inside to see if I left it in my room. Can you help me out?"

"Certainly. Name?"

Sam knew the only thing that could blow this was if Martina happened to be working the front desk shift ten hours ago when Mack had checked into the hotel. He had to risk it.

"Rod Luger."

He received no second looks. That was good.

"Room number?" she asked.

"513."

"Do you have any ID on you, Mr. Luger?"

"I'm afraid it's all in my missing wallet."

Martina considered that for only a moment and then handed him a new card key. He quickly returned to the fifth floor, found Tommy hanging down the hallway from 513. They met up again at Mack's hotel room door. Sam swiped the card key, and the door clicked open.

"Nice work," Tommy admitted. "But my way would've been more fun."

Slowly cracking the door open, Sam poked his head inside. He noticed the bathroom light was on, and so was a lamp in the corner of the hotel room. Listening, he still didn't hear any noise coming from anywhere. Pushing the door farther open, he stepped fully into the room, Tommy behind him. They were alone. Sam checked out the bathroom first, finding a toothbrush, toothpaste, deodorant, and other assorted toiletries. A wet towel was hanging on the back of the door, as if someone had just taken a shower. They walked into the main room, which held a disheveled king-size bed. The dresser top near the TV held a dozen different empty mini liquor bottles. Empty bags of chips, crackers, and candies stuffed the trash can. It looked like Mack had already completely emptied the minibar.

Sam found a gray duffel bag sitting on the carpet and began sifting through it, finding nothing but wadded-up clothes that looked like they could be Mack's size. Tommy was checking the drawers of the dresser but wasn't finding anything helpful, either. Walking over to the small desk in the room, Sam spotted a computer tablet sitting among a variety of magazines. He pressed a button on the side, and the screen lit up. It was a generic screen front—nothing that identified it as belonging to Mack. The tablet was locked by a security password.

"Tommy?" Sam said, holding up the tablet.

Rushing over, Tommy took the tablet from him, sat in the desk chair, and immediately got to work. Sam walked to the window, pulled the curtains back. The view looked directly into other buildings across the street. Based on their findings, Sam felt certain that Mack planned to return to the hotel at some point. Should they just sit there and wait for him to come back? He didn't really see any alternative. Milan was a city with more than a million people. And Mack was a person who probably didn't want to be found right now.

He turned back to Tommy, who said he'd already bypassed security.

"Find anything?" Sam asked.

"Maybe. Looks like he did a news search for Moscow and Zolotov, probably trying to see if he could find out any more information about the events of last night. But as we both know, nothing has been put out there yet. I'm now retracing the very last steps he took with the tablet. Mack had logged into a highly secure private website, one much like Leia's Lounge, where you and I used to interact."

"Can you get in?"

"Working on it."

A sudden knock on the door startled Sam. He locked eyes with Tommy and gave him the universal, one-finger-to-the-lips, "Stay the hell quiet" sign. Looking around the room, Sam searched for a reasonable weapon to use, if necessary. Mack wouldn't have knocked. He'd just use his card key and walk right into the room. The best Sam could do was grab a blow-dryer from the bathroom counter. Could he take out a Russian assassin that way?

Moving to the door, Sam cautiously let his eye settle in on the peephole, then exhaled. A woman in a hotel uniform stood with a cleaning cart. Some kind of hotel turndown service. He chose not to answer the door, as he didn't want anyone, even a hotel maid, to put eyes on him inside the room.

Another knock, followed by *"Faccende domestiche."*

"No, grazie," Sam said, just loud enough to be heard in the hallway.

She moved on to the next room.

"Just a maid," Sam told Tommy, the blood returning to his friend's face.

Tommy went back to work on the tablet. Sam continued to poke around the room to see if he'd missed anything.

Seconds later, Tommy excitedly announced, "Dude, I got him!"

Sam circled in behind Tommy for a better look. "What is it?"

"Looks like your guy reached out to someone through this secure website this afternoon. He got a reply just an hour ago. Mack is MX889."

Sam read the brief message exchange between the user names MX889 and YX001.

MX889: Contact needed ASAP. Black Heron dead. Team in disarray.

YX001: Confirmed. Location?

MX889: Milan.

YX001: Anema e Cozze. Patio. 10:40.

MX889: Confirmed.

Sam looked at Tommy. "Can you find the ID of the other party?"

"If I had time, I could probably piece it together. But we only have twenty minutes before Mack is set to meet with *someone*."

THIRTY-FIVE

Sam spotted Mack sitting by himself at a small table in the back of the crowded patio of Anema e Cozze, a restaurant that sat along one of the city's popular canals. The sidewalks on both sides of the waterway were lively this evening, with hundreds of patrons out for dinner and drinking at the dozens of different restaurants and bars. Standing on a bridge, fifty feet from Mack, Sam watched as various boats floated back and forth in the water below him. Tommy had gladly agreed to wait in a café much farther up the canal, where Sam could make sure his friend remained safe from any danger that might come their way.

Sam still had no idea what he was about to walk into with Mack, although he felt his first real glimmer of hope since before Luis had been shot dead right in front of him. Mack wore a casual black jumpsuit with a matching black cap that both carried the logo of an Italian soccer team. Although the cap was pulled low on the man's balding head, Sam clearly recognized him upon his initial pass of the restaurant just a few minutes ago. Other than his new clothes, the fiftysomething man hadn't altered his appearance in any other dramatic way.

Sam's initial plan was to wait to see whom Mack met. He didn't want to unwittingly step into a potentially bad situation. He needed to show patience and choose his moment wisely. Checking the time on his phone, Sam noted that it was already 10:45 p.m., and still no one had joined Mack on the patio. Who and where was YX001?

Casually moving in behind a small crowd of people, Sam got even closer to the patio before standing in the shadows directly across the walkway, with his gray jacket hood up over his head. Another peek at the time: 10:50. Whoever was supposed to meet with Mack was running late. Sam surveyed the area all around him, trying to see if he could spot anyone else who, like him, might also be watching Mack. Maybe YX001 was also standing in the wings, waiting. He shook his head. There were way too many lingerers out to tell much.

By eleven, Mack was done waiting. He got up from the table, left the restaurant, and headed down a street corridor away from the busy canal. Sam stepped out of the shadows, carefully followed him at twenty feet. Where was Mack going? Had the meeting location changed? Or did he get spooked?

The farther they moved away from the canal, the less busy the sidewalk traffic. Feeling too exposed, even with the hood over his head, Sam dropped even farther back. However, when Mack suddenly turned sharply into an alley between two old buildings and Sam temporarily lost sight, he rushed forward to keep up with the man. He couldn't afford to lose Mack at this point. Blindly turning the corner into the same alley, Sam felt an arm suddenly whip around his neck, choking him and yanking him backward into the shadows, followed by a gun pressed to his temple.

"Mack! Wait!" Sam pleaded. "It's me! Sam!"

Mack spun him around, gun still aimed, eyes slits.

"Callahan?"

THIRTY-SIX

Mack looked like he was staring at a ghost.

"Surprise," Sam offered with a tight grin, pulling off his jacket hood.

The man cursed. "What the hell are you doing here?"

"Looking for you."

"Are you crazy trying to trail me like that? I could have killed you."

"Yeah, thanks for not doing that. How long did you know I was back there?"

"Spotted you on the bridge fifteen minutes ago. Just didn't recognize it was you." He exhaled a deep breath, tried to gather himself. "How the hell did you find me?"

Sam explained tracking his CIA alias to his hotel room with a friend's help.

"The Kucher kid?" Mack asked, obviously very aware of Sam's relationship with Tommy from their engagement in Mexico City last month.

Sam nodded. "He's sitting in a café across the way."

Mack peeked out from the alley to the sidewalk, then turned back. "Anyone else with you?"

"No, just the two of us."

"What about the others? Roger? Luis?"

Sam cocked his head. "Don't you know? They're all dead. Nearly every member of our team is dead."

Mack's eyes went wide. "How do you know that?"

Sam explained the tail end of his misadventures from the previous night—his escape from Zolotov's compound, the bloody carnage he discovered inside the CIA safe house, the meet-up with Luis in Red Square that nearly got them both gunned down, and his fleeing Russia altogether this morning.

"Besides you and me," Sam continued, "the only ones that are still unaccounted for are Marcus and Lucinda."

"Lucinda is alive," Mack verified. "We made contact today. She's hiding out in Le Tréport."

"France?"

Mack nodded. Then he shook his head, cursed, as if the weight of the devastating news suddenly hit him all at once. "I feared they were dead, since I'd been unable to connect with anyone but Lucinda, but I hate to hear it."

"What the hell happened? We totally got ambushed."

"We did," Mack agreed, telling Sam about how an assassin had come close to taking him out on the sidewalks outside of Zolotov's residence the previous night. Right before all hell broke loose on the inside. "I'm still trying to figure this out. Honestly, I thought you were for sure dead. I couldn't see *anyone* getting out of that place. So, nice work."

"Thanks, I guess. But none of it makes sense. The file turned up empty. No list."

Mack's eyes narrowed. "What? How do you know that?"

Sam told him about the tablet he'd kept with him and how Tommy had pulled out its contents. "There was nothing in the folder. The list was gone."

"You're right. That doesn't make any sense."

"There's more," Sam added. He went on to explain about the security footage that clearly showed Marcus Pelini entering Zolotov's property.

"Are you sure it was him?" Mack asked, dismayed.

"I can show you the damn video. It was him."

"What was he doing?"

"Hell if I know. It doesn't look good, if you ask me."

"Wait . . . You think Marcus is somehow behind all of this?"

"You tell me. You're closest to him. Could he have stolen the list out from under us? With plans to sell it for himself?"

Mack took his cap off, ran a hand over his balding head. He seemed to wrestle with his thoughts for a long moment before sighing, saying, "I hate to admit it, but it's possible."

Sam felt like someone had just punched him hard in the gut. It was one thing for him to make crazy accusations. It was another thing altogether to have someone close to Pelini confirm there could be truth behind the accusations.

"Why do you say that?" Sam asked.

"Just some offhanded things Marcus said to me in the weeks leading up to the operation. Like this might finally be it for him. The end. How he might disappear, where no one, including the Agency, could ever find him again. Go lie on a private beach for the next twenty years. We've said some crazy things like that over the last few years, as we've both gotten older, only it's usually just fantasy talk. Neither of us have gotten rich in the spy game. We can't just go buy our own private island."

"You could if you sold a list like this on the black market."

"That's true. And I'll admit that Marcus sounded a bit different this time around. But I still have a hard time believing he'd sacrifice his own team to do it."

"And his own son," Sam added.

"Right." Mack studied him a moment, shook his head. "Damn, Callahan, we've really screwed with your life here, haven't we? First Mexico, now Russia. I promise it wasn't supposed to go down this way. I'm really sorry."

"Don't be sorry. Just get me the hell out of this, okay?"

"I'll try my best."

"Who were you supposed to be meeting with tonight at the restaurant?"

"A CIA asset. Someone local who was supposed to be able to help."

"Why didn't anyone show up?"

"I don't know."

THIRTY-SEVEN

Alger Gerlach stood in the shadows a half block away from where his target had just unexpectedly ducked into a dark alley. Normally, Gerlach would've slipped into the alley right behind the man, to go for the quick and silent kill, but he'd been surprised by his target's unexpected encounter with a second man. Who was it? What was being discussed? Gerlach had been unable to get a good look at the second figure—the man had a hood up over his head—although it didn't really matter. The Gray Wolf only had one job tonight. Put a bullet into his target's head. So he patiently waited.

His client's trap had worked to perfection. His target had shown up, as expected, and allowed Gerlach to lock in on him. Even the man leaving the restaurant when his contact didn't show up for the meeting was part of the plan. Gerlach preferred not to kill his target in a public setting and cause a spectacle. He wanted to do it quietly.

Standing there, waiting, Gerlach shook his head. These CIA guys had no problem betraying one another. Some of them actually seemed to enjoy sticking the knife in the backs of their own colleagues. Loyalty had its limits. That was why Gerlach had worked alone for the past ten years.

A minute later, both men reappeared from the alley. His target walked out first. A younger man stepped out behind him. Both were in a hurry. Gerlach only saw the younger man's face for a fleeting moment, but it was a face permanently seared into his brain. A wry smile moved over his lips. Sam Callahan. He couldn't believe his luck. It was suddenly two-for-one night.

The Gray Wolf moved in quickly.

THIRTY-EIGHT

Sam spotted the man before Mack did. At first, Sam had to do a quick double take. Alger Gerlach? Could it really be the same man who had ruthlessly hunted him last month, first in New Orleans, then again in DC? An infamous assassin who had left Sam with a bullet scar in the back of his arm? A hunt that was fully funded by the CIA director? Sam didn't want to believe it, and yet there was the Gray Wolf, charging down the sidewalk straight toward them at twenty feet, looking like a man on a sinister mission.

"Mack! Wait!" Sam yelled, but it was too late.

Gerlach raised his right fist and fired off two muffled shots with his gun. Mack jerked twice, one bullet hitting him square in the chest, the other in the head, sending blood flying everywhere. Before Mack even hit the pavement in front of him, Sam darted dead left, straight through the propped open door of a pizza parlor, feeling a bullet whiz right by his head. Without slowing, he raced past a front counter, where two young girls were fiddling with menus and engaged in discussion. Sam heard both girls scream out behind him, probably at the sight of Gerlach rushing in with a gun. The small pizza parlor was half-full, with booths lining the outer walls and square tables in the middle. Sam threaded the patrons at the tables, headed toward the back kitchen as all eyes in the room turned to watch the crazy man running through the restaurant.

He then heard the panic set in behind him, knowing Gerlach was still right on his heels. He barged through the revolving door of the kitchen, crashed into an unsuspecting waiter on the other side, sending the man to the floor and a pizza tray flying through the air. The kitchen was loud, with music blaring and several of the staff scrambling all about. Following a map that had flashed through his mind, Sam ran straight toward a back kitchen hallway. As he rushed past, he reached up, grabbed one of the metal shelves, yanked it over behind him, sending it crashing down and cluttering the hallway. Spotting the exit door, Sam barreled into the alley behind the building, stumbled down to the dirty pavement, and quickly got himself up and running again.

The two-story building directly behind the pizza parlor was new construction and wide-open, with entrances at various points. Sam dashed straight onto the ground floor, nearly colliding with metal scaffolding in the dark. Because the construction was still in the beginning stages, there were few walls or hallways yet, only the framework of steel and concrete and cables. Finding a set of stairs in the center of the building, he ran up, his heart in his throat. The second floor was just like the first, only concrete and steel with all kinds of construction equipment and materials set everywhere. Because it was night, no one was working in the building.

Sam paused for the first time since he took off running, tried to listen above the sound of his own heartbeat pounding away in his eardrums. Sweat poured down his face. Where was Gerlach? Had he lost the Gray Wolf? He heard a clanking sound coming from the ground floor, as if someone had inadvertently kicked a bucket or something. Sam cursed. The assassin was nearby. Sam decided to stop running. He'd almost been killed trying to do that very thing a month ago while in Union Station, only to be saved at the last minute by a swarm of FBI agents. Instead, he'd rely on his uncanny ability to remain calm in a highly stressful situation. Gerlach would likely anticipate running. He would not expect Sam to remain still.

Spotting a thick bundle of cable hanging down from a metal beam over to his right, Sam noted the beam was up near the ceiling, at about twelve feet, and one of the darkest places on the entire floor. Taking careful steps so he wouldn't knock something over and expose his position, Sam put both hands on the cable bundle and tugged gently. It held firmly. Placing one hand on top of the other, he began climbing up the bundle as if he were on a rope back in gym class.

Sam paused in midclimb when he heard steps on the stairs. He needed to hurry. He reached the metal beam, maneuvered fully on top of it, and stared back down to the floor. Wrapping both arms and legs completely around the beam, he held it tightly to his body, trying not to move even an inch. He took a slow breath and let it out even slower, trying to summon whatever he possessed inside that kept him unusually calm. As he did, a warm sensation began to flow through him like a slow tide that gradually made his body settle and relax. This was why he'd never panicked when the cops came calling back when he was living on the streets and his buddies were all racing for the hills like idiots and getting caught. Perhaps he got this skill from his father.

Sam spotted a shadow of movement over by the stairs. The Gray Wolf had arrived on the second floor. The man held his gun out in both fists in front of him, moving about with careful precision, ready to aim and shoot at a split-second notice. Sam watched in silence from his twelve-foot perch. The assassin moved directly beneath him. Only six feet of dark space now separated them. One false move and Sam knew it would be over. He held his breath, not wanting his body to make a single sound. He only hoped that an unexpected drop of sweat wouldn't fall down onto Gerlach.

When Gerlach paused, Sam fought off a sudden voice inside that tried to convince him to drop right now, straight on top of the assassin, try his best to fight his way out of there. Although he'd taken some basic self-defense with Pelini's team, he knew he would be no match for someone like the German.

Gerlach eased forward, around a column, out of sight.

Again, Sam fought off an irrational voice that screamed for him to make a run for it right now. That's exactly what Gerlach wanted him to do. Sirens suddenly filled the air near the building and grew louder with each passing second. Someone had obviously called the authorities. A man had been shot dead on the sidewalk. A man with a gun had chased another man through a restaurant.

At the sound of the police arriving on the scene, Sam spotted Gerlach move back toward the stairs and quickly descend. Was the assassin bolting? Just to be sure, he waited another ten minutes without moving from his position on top of the beam. There was no reason to take chances. Finally, he climbed his way down the cable bundle and returned to the floor. Moving carefully down the stairs, he searched the ground floor, spotted no movement. Then he slipped back into the alley, found the sidewalk, and poked his head around the corner.

Several police cars and ambulances filled the street. Sam thought of Mack, again felt heavyhearted. But he didn't have time to mourn. Stepping out onto the sidewalk, he headed opposite the crowd, took off running, with several new questions now pushing their way into the front of his mind.

Why was the Gray Wolf in Milan?

More important, who sent him there to kill?

THIRTY-NINE

Stepping up to an ICU room at George Washington University Hospital, Lloyd looked inside to where Agent Michelle Blair was recovering from a bad car wreck the previous night. Michelle had fortunately been stabilized and was now alert. For some reason, she'd immediately called Lloyd and asked for him to personally come see her at the hospital. She said it was urgent. Because Lloyd didn't know Michelle other than through her role with the FBI, he found her request unusual. He hated hospitals and was having to spend way too much time inside them the past twenty-four hours.

Standing outside the door, he saw Michelle's head completely wrapped up in white bandages. What showed of her face was badly bruised. He didn't know the full extent of her injuries, but he'd spoken to a nurse before coming over to the room. The nurse said Michelle was in bad shape, but the doctors thought that in time, she'd make a full recovery. She was lucky to be alive.

Lloyd knocked gently on the door, poked his head inside the room. Michelle gingerly looked over, nodded for him to enter. Walking up to her bedside, he offered her a warm grin. "How're you doing, Michelle?"

She swallowed. "Okay, I think. Still in *a lot* of pain."

"You need me to get a doctor or something?"

"No, they've already got way too many pain meds pumping through me. Can't think clearly."

"Looks like you took a real beating out there."

"Yeah." She didn't elaborate.

Lloyd didn't know many details. It was a Metropolitan Police matter. He'd heard it was an apparent hit-and-run incident after some idiot stole a car. "Doctors are saying you're going to be okay," Lloyd mentioned, still unsure why he was standing there and feeling a bit awkward about it. "But I don't want you to feel like you have to rush back to work."

"That's not why I asked you here," Michelle clarified.

"Okay."

"I think something really bad has happened."

"I'll say."

"No, not just me in this bed. Something else. I was in the car last night with my friend, Natalie Foster, when all of this went down."

Lloyd perked up a bit. He immediately recognized Natalie's name through his investigation of Sam Callahan. The two were engaged and spent most of their time together. He was suddenly more curious about where all this was going.

"Is she also in the hospital?" he asked Michelle.

"No, she wasn't hurt as badly as me. They sent her home. But she's missing."

"Missing? Why do you say that?"

"As soon as I woke up after surgery today, I started calling her. She hasn't answered *or* returned any of my calls, either. And she knows I'm in serious condition here in the hospital. That's not at all like her. I've been trying her all day, with no response. I even called her editor, who said he hasn't heard from Natalie since last night—when she apparently left him an urgent voice mail—so he was also concerned. No one at her office knows where she is right now. I think something bad may have happened to her."

"Maybe she just needed a personal day, turned her phone off."

Michelle sighed, stared off for a moment. Lloyd could tell by the look on the young agent's face that something more was going on here.

"Start talking to me, Michelle. Not to be insensitive, but I don't have all day. Tell me what's going on."

"Okay, sorry." Michelle swallowed again, each time looking painful. "Natalie was working the Dowerson story yesterday and asked me to dig into it for her. She's a friend, so I try to help when I can—*if* it doesn't compromise my FBI work."

She hesitated. Lloyd understood why.

"Speak freely," he insisted. "What happened?"

"I discovered something disturbing independent of the Dowerson situation that involves her fiancé."

Lloyd inched closer. Now Michelle really had his attention. "What about him?"

"We came across a video intercept out of Moscow last night."

"We?"

"Lamar was assisting me."

Lloyd's eyes narrowed. Lamar worked on Russian matters. "What kind of video?"

Another painful swallow. "One that showed Sam standing in a room full of dead bodies who'd clearly been executed by someone."

"Are you sure?"

"Yes. Lamar thinks it was a CIA feed. He can show it to you. I immediately took the video to Natalie, and she confirmed it was indeed Sam. Natalie had no idea he was in Moscow—she thought he was in London on legal matters. She was confused and obviously horrified. A month ago, she'd asked me to look into something after she and Sam had been interviewed by FBI agents—only I discovered they were actually CIA agents. Natalie was suspicious."

"Suspicious of what?"

"She wasn't sure. She thought Sam was acting strange, maybe keeping something from her. Look, I don't know what to make of all of this, but not five minutes after I showed Natalie the video last night, a maniac drives a Suburban at high speed right into our vehicle and tries to take us both out."

"Metro says it's a hit-and-run," Lloyd challenged her.

She shook her head. "Last night was no hit-and-run. It was an assassination attempt. And it nearly worked. I'm fortunate to be having this conversation with you. But now Natalie is missing. I'm telling you, there's no way she wouldn't call me right back unless she's in big trouble. We need to find her."

"Who else knows about this video?"

"Just me, Natalie, and Lamar. I never told Lamar about Sam, so he doesn't know anything about any of this. He doesn't even know I took the video."

"Don't tell another soul about it," Lloyd ordered. "Not until I look further into this, you understand me?"

"Yes, sir."

Lloyd tried to soften, so he wouldn't put more stress on Michelle, even though his mind was exploding. Sam in Moscow? CIA? Dead bodies?

"Just get some rest, okay?" he urged Michelle, forced a grin. "I'll look into it."

"You'll let me know when you find Natalie?"

"Of course. I'm sure everything is fine."

He patted her on the arm, headed for the door. Walking down the hallway with renewed urgency, Lloyd immediately called Epps. He instructed him to get Lamar James into a conference room ASAP and for Epps to pull everything they had on Natalie Foster. Lloyd would be back at the office in ten minutes.

"One more thing, Michael," Lloyd added. "Send someone over here to keep watch over Michelle. I'll explain more when I get to the office."

FORTY

Natalie stood near the Vietnam Veterans Memorial. The DC sky was overcast and drizzling, with hints of more rain, but there were still plenty of tourists out on the sidewalks near the wall and over by the Lincoln Memorial. Earlier, she'd ditched the Redskins cap after purchasing a new black hoodie at Old Navy with cash. She wore the hoodie now with her head completely covered. Ms. Anonymous. She needed to keep mixing up her appearance, just to be safe, although she certainly hoped it would never come down to drastically changing her hair. Then again, she'd shave her head completely bald it if meant somehow getting Sam safely home.

She wasn't at the memorial wall to sightsee, of course; she was looking for someone. Her military contact, Levi, had found her a guy he thought could help her. She was appreciative of his quick work. She needed answers soon, both for her own safety as well as to find Sam. Natalie's desperation grew with each passing hour and no word from Sam. It had become increasingly difficult to guard her thoughts from drifting to the worst-case scenario—a life without Sam in it.

She spotted someone approaching who matched the description Levi had given her. Short and stocky, midthirties, buzz cut, walked with a slight limp because he'd caught shrapnel from an explosion in Afghanistan. Abe Dones. He wore military fatigue pants and a tight black T-shirt that showed off the muscles in his arms and chest. Stopping midpoint at the memorial wall, he looked around in both directions. Natalie did a last sweep of the area, checking for anyone suspicious that she might have missed. Then she made her move, hit the sidewalk, sidled up behind the guy.

"You Abe?" she whispered.

He turned, gave her a once-over. "Yeah."

"Will you walk with me?"

He gave her another up and down, grinned. "You bet."

They moved away from the memorial wall, farther up the sidewalk, steering clear of the mass of tourists. Natalie immediately spotted the Hell Dogs tattoo on the back of the man's right hand.

"Thanks for coming," she said. "Levi said you might be able to help me."

He shrugged. "I'll try. I owe Levi. He got me a good job with Centennial Security last year. Really saved my ass and got me back on my feet."

"How long you been out of the military?"

"Five years. Steady work has been a bit difficult to find."

"Afghanistan?"

"Three tours," he said proudly. He pointed down at his leg. "Would've kept on going if not for this damn thing."

She gave him a sad smile. "Sorry."

He shrugged. "Price of freedom."

"Can you tell me about the tattoo?"

He glanced down at his hand. "Well, no offense, ma'am, but that's kind of between me and my platoon."

"You keep in touch with the other guys?"

"A few. A lot of them didn't make it back, unfortunately. Who are you trying to find?"

Natalie pulled the Metro photo out of her pocket, handed it to Abe.

"You know him?" she asked.

He squinted at the photo, nodded. "He in some kind of trouble?"

Natalie wasn't sure how she wanted to answer that. Abe was protective of the guys from his platoon; otherwise, he would've just come out and told her the guy's name. She could simply lie, tell Abe she needed to find the guy for no consequential reasons, and hope he just gave up the name. Or go with the truth.

"He tried to kill me last night," she said, choosing the truth. "He chased me through the Metro with a gun."

Abe's eyes narrowed. "You serious?"

She nodded.

"Damn," Abe replied, looking at the photo again. "His name is Lenny Gregor. A real hell-raiser, always getting us into trouble. Was dishonorably discharged after hitting our commanding officer. I never really liked Lenny. But I never figured he'd pull something like this. Why was he chasing you?"

"I don't know yet. You know where he lives?"

Abe shook his head. "Haven't spoken with him in a few years. Although another buddy recently told me Lenny had started doing some shady odd-job security work. Nothing legitimate, like I do with Centennial. This was more gangster-type intimidation for poor man's debt collections and such. Doesn't surprise me. Lenny was always picking fights and busting people up."

"Any ideas how I can find him?"

Abe thought a moment. "Lenny used to hang out over at the Raven. Not sure if he does anymore."

"On Mount Pleasant?"

"Yeah, that's the place." He studied Natalie. "Hey, are the police involved?"

She nodded but didn't elaborate.

"Well, if you need my personal protection, I'll happily give it to you. If Lenny comes back around to mess with you again, I'd take great pleasure in kicking his ass."

"Thanks." She forced a smile. "You've been a tremendous help already."

FORTY-ONE

Sam stood near a curtain-drawn window inside a cramped first-floor room at Motel Flora, a rent-by-the-hour dump of a building two miles away from where he'd just watched Mack get gunned down by Alger Gerlach. And had barely escaped himself. Thankfully, Tommy was with him, sitting in a rickety chair at a tiny desk, laptop open in front of him. After fleeing the scene, Sam had made sure to sweep by, immediately grab Tommy, and get them both far enough away where Sam might actually be able to think clearly again.

Standing there, he wasn't sure that was possible, knowing the Gray Wolf was still in the same city, eager to put a bullet in him. He still couldn't believe he'd just had another face-to-face encounter with the infamous assassin. Had the CIA once again sent the Gray Wolf? Was a bigger cover-up going on than Sam had even imagined? Had they set Mack up with the proposed meeting place only to ambush him? Had they found Mack the same way Tommy had? By tracking his CIA alias? Sam's thoughts went to a darker place. Or was all this the sinister handiwork of a man they called the Lion?

He'd been pondering the last possibility ever since Mack mentioned that Pelini might have been planning to disappear after the operation. Had this all been one big setup so that Pelini could finally be paid and then vanish like a ghost? Would the gray-bearded man really hire an assassin like Gerlach to clean up his loose ends? Just the thought of it made Sam's stomach coil up into a fist-tight ball and sent a wave of chills down his spine. Somehow, he almost hoped the CIA was behind Gerlach and *not* Pelini. Because the second possibility would likely cripple Sam in such a way that not even God himself could ever help him recover.

Turning from the window, Sam looked over at Tommy, who was working on getting them both on a train to Paris tonight. From there, they'd travel to Le Tréport, where Mack had mentioned Lucinda was hiding out at a safe house. Sam only hoped they could somehow get to her before the Gray Wolf did.

"The CIA is now *officially* looking for you," Tommy mentioned.

"How do you know?"

"It's out in the open now on their internal channels. They're officially searching for you, Pelini, Lucinda, and Mack."

Sam shook his head. "I should call their hotline, inform them that Mack is now dead. Then again, there's a strong possibility they already know that if they hired Gerlach to hunt down each of us."

"I don't know. These are clearly 'find and detain' instructions."

Sam leaned in from behind Tommy, watched as he scrolled down to show profile photos of each of them, including Sam. "The omission of the others probably means they've already confirmed them all dead."

"Most likely," Tommy agreed. "Last known whereabouts for each of you is still listed as Moscow, but there's no mention of any details on why you were all there together."

"Nor any mention of our other aliases."

"Correct. Which seems odd."

"Unless Pelini put them together himself, off-line, for his own reasons."

Tommy looked up at Sam. "You still believe he might be behind it all?"

"So far, most of the bread crumbs lead back to one strong possibility, whether I want to believe it or not."

"Damn." Tommy sighed as if he also felt the weight of Sam's disappointment. "What do you want to do, man?"

"The only thing we can do. We hunt the Lion. And we don't stop until we find him."

FORTY-TWO

As instructed, Agent Epps had Lamar James waiting to meet with Lloyd inside a small conference room at FBI headquarters. Lamar sat upright in his seat when Lloyd barged through the glass doors. The young agent seemed uneasy about sitting there for undisclosed reasons—like a teenager who'd just been called down to the principal's office, unsure of why he was being busted. Lamar had a slender build, with a thick mop of fiery red hair. He was a good analyst who worked mostly on Russian affairs.

"Relax, Lamar," Lloyd suggested, getting situated. "I just need you to show me the video you pulled up last night when Michelle Blair was sitting with you."

Lamar's eyebrows pinched. "Moscow?"

"Correct." Lloyd pointed at the laptop sitting on the table. "Pull it up on the big screen for me, okay?"

"Yes, sir."

Lamar reached over, opened the laptop, began typing in his passwords. Standing near the head of the table, Epps used a remote to power up the digital screen on the wall of the conference room. Lloyd walked over, stood beside him, stared at the screen.

"What's this about?" Epps asked.

"Not sure yet. Let's just watch and see first."

Within thirty seconds, Lamar had the video up on the big screen. Lloyd's eyes narrowed as he took in the scene. It looked like surveillance footage from inside the living room of a small house. Lloyd immediately counted the bodies he could see within view of the camera. He could make out four of them: two on the floor, one slumped over a table, and a stone-faced man in his fifties who sat directly in front of the security camera, blood covering his neck.

"What the hell?" Epps said.

"Roll it, Lamar," Lloyd instructed.

The video played. Within seconds, a man walked into the living room. He wore black pants and a black jacket, began carefully stepping over and around the bodies until he stood directly in front of the camera—clearly oblivious to being recorded. Epps cursed, took a step toward the screen. Lloyd shook his head. Sam Callahan. Michelle was right. Callahan took a few things off some of the bodies, disappeared from camera view for a few seconds, reappeared with a black bag, then was gone from the room.

Lloyd turned to Lamar. "That's it?"

"Yes, sir. That's all that was intercepted."

"Where did we get it?"

"Not entirely sure. I believe it's a CIA feed, but I didn't try to track it. Should I?"

Lloyd shook his head. "No, leave it alone. You're certain this is Moscow?"

"Yes, sir. I can place a pin on a map for you."

"Not necessary. You can go back to your desk now."

Lamar stood from his chair, circled the table, headed for the glass doors.

Lloyd stopped him. "One more thing, Lamar. Not a word of this to anyone."

"Yes, sir."

Alone in the room, Epps and Lloyd huddled.

Epps said, "What the hell, Chief? Why's Callahan in Russia?"

Lloyd quickly filled him in on the story Michelle had told him from her hospital bed.

"Marcus Pelini?" Epps queried.

"That's my best guess."

"That's a lot of dead bodies. I'll have Krieger run whatever we can from this video through facial recognition, see if we can identify anyone else in this room."

"Do it. And let's go find Natalie Foster."

FORTY-THREE

Lloyd spent the drive on his cell phone, confirming everything Michelle Blair had just told him at the hospital. Natalie was indeed missing, at least from anyone who was close to her. Natalie's editor, Nick Montague, had not heard from her since late the previous night, in spite of his repeated calls to her all throughout the day. Montague told Lloyd this was after Natalie had left him an urgent voice mail to call her back. Natalie had been working on a *big* story, Montague suggested, so it was highly unusual for her not to check in with him at all. As a matter of fact, no one else at *PowerPlay* had heard from her all day, either. They were all seriously concerned, especially with the news that she'd been in a car crash. Montague said he knew through police sources about Natalie's claims of a goateed man with glasses and a gray ball cap—the same claims Michelle had made to Lloyd at the hospital. Montague and Lloyd agreed to keep each other posted if they got any word from Natalie.

Epps parked the Buick on the curb outside a row of colorful brownstones on a quiet street near Dupont Circle. According to the address they had on file, Natalie lived on the third floor of the red building in the middle. Lloyd followed Epps up the stairs. When they reached the door, Lloyd immediately suspected something was wrong. The door was cracked open. He could hear noise coming from somewhere inside the apartment. Epps gently pushed the door open a few inches. Looking inside, Lloyd could tell the place had been ransacked, just like his condo the previous night.

Lloyd and Epps shared a glance, both reaching for their guns. Epps pushed the door farther open, where it bumped up against something with a *thud*. The noise they heard from deeper inside the apartment suddenly stopped.

"FBI!" Epps shouted. "Come out with your hands in the air!"

No response. Epps slipped inside the apartment, Lloyd right behind him. Looking around, Lloyd found everything completely trashed. Whoever had been there—or was still there—left no stone unturned. Lloyd could only hope that Natalie Foster was not home. His pop had experienced the devastating ramifications of something like that.

Guns prepped for firing, they maneuvered farther into the apartment, entering the living room, searching for the noise. A kitchen was in front of them. A hallway to their right, likely leading back to the bedroom. Epps took the lead down the hallway. He poked his head into the bathroom, found it empty, kept moving to the bedroom, stepping over spilled boxes. The door was wide-open. Epps peered into the room, gun first. Lloyd also poked his head around. The window was open, the drapes fluttering in the breeze. Then they heard a banging noise from outside the window—shoes on a metal fire escape!

Racing to the window, Epps jumped out onto the fire escape, Lloyd right behind him. Peering down, Lloyd spotted a man in a black hood who had already made it to the bottom, where he jumped to the dirty pavement in the alley behind the building. Epps was in pursuit down the fire escape, but he was never going to catch the guy. Lloyd kept his eyes on the man, hoping for just one glance back.

When he got it, Lloyd cursed.

The same man who had put his pop in the hospital.

Mike Madrone. CIA shadow operative.

FORTY-FOUR

The Raven Grill was on the street level of a four-story condo building along a commercial strip that included a dry cleaner, a Laundromat, and a dollar store. Not exactly a high-end establishment. A neon martini glass was aglow in the front window. Night had just fallen on the city as Natalie grabbed a front booth all by herself. She wore a brown cap pulled low on her head with every strand of her hair tucked up beneath it, as well as newly purchased black-framed eyeglasses with no prescription that were just for show—and disguise. She couldn't afford to be recognized by *anyone* right now and felt confident she wouldn't be. Natalie had been to the Raven once before with two girlfriends to meet up with some guys. The dive bar had a certain old-time charm with its tabletop jukeboxes, nicotine-stained walls with peeling paint, and various portraits of entertainment icons like Elvis, John Lennon, and Bob Dylan.

Surveying the narrow dive bar, she took in the dozens of faces sitting at the other booths, tables, and at the bar in the back of the joint. No sign of Lenny Gregor—her infamous man with the goatee—and the man who seemed intent on taking her out. Lenny had checked out just as Abe Dones had suggested. Dishonorably discharged from the army several years back. Not much on public record of his employment anywhere for the last few years. Lenny was leasing a crummy apartment unit off Quincy Street, not far from the Raven. Natalie had been scoping out the apartment building for the past few hours, with no luck. No one had gone in or come out of his unit. So she'd now set her hopes on finding Lenny at the Raven tonight. It was a slim hope, but she had no other plans at this point. Lenny was her only current pathway toward getting to the truth, so she decided she'd sit there in the booth until the place closed, if necessary.

She didn't have to wait all night. Lenny walked inside about an hour into her visit. The goatee and glasses were in place on his stocky frame. He wore a black T-shirt with jeans and brown work boots. Natalie immediately felt a shiver of chills on her neck. She eased down into the booth as he passed by her without a second look and made a quick path toward the bar. He grabbed a stool, ordered a shot of something, quickly downed it, then ordered another. Natalie watched him intently through fingers laced together on the tabletop in front of her, hiding her face.

Sitting there for several minutes, Lenny kept checking his phone, then glancing back toward the front door. Was he meeting someone? Natalie wasn't sure what to do now that she'd actually put eyes on the guy. Under any other conditions, she would have turned Lenny right over to the police. Lock him up and keep herself safe from a lunatic with bad intentions. But these were not normal conditions. Locking Lenny up would not help her find the truth—whoever was behind his role in all this would only pull in ranks and perhaps disappear altogether. She needed to keep Lenny in play for now to monitor where he went and whom he talked with, if she had any chance of finding out what was really going on with Sam.

Still, it felt odd sitting there, not thirty feet away from a guy who'd just put Michelle in the hospital, and who twenty-four hours ago had chased her with a gun through the Metro terminal and out onto the sidewalks of the city. Using her burner phone, she took a few unsuspecting photos of Lenny sitting there at the bar. A half-drunk old man two barstools down tried to engage Lenny in conversation, but Lenny waved him off with a hard glare.

Natalie flinched slightly when the front door of the bar opened again. While pretending to mess with her phone in her hands, she watched as a thirtysomething man in a dark-blue business suit with slicked-back brown hair moved toward the bar. He didn't look like he belonged in a joint like the Raven. He sat down on a stool right next to Lenny. Animated but hushed discussion quickly ensued between the two men. Using her phone, Natalie again took several pictures. Who was this guy? She didn't recognize him.

The meeting lasted only a few minutes. The business-suit guy eased off his stool, slipped through the bar, and exited the Raven. Lenny stayed put, ordered another shot. Waiting only a few seconds, Natalie slipped out of the booth, moved toward the front door. Stepping outside, she followed the man in the suit up the sidewalk, leaving a twenty-foot gap of safe distance between them. He was already on his cell phone with someone—although Natalie was not close enough to make out the conversation.

Two blocks from the Raven, the guy stepped off the sidewalk and opened the driver's door of a sleek black Lexus sedan parked along the curb. Natalie cursed. The Dodge truck she'd borrowed from Levi earlier that day was parked two blocks in the opposite direction. She quickly spun around, searching for a taxi anywhere in the vicinity. She spotted one headed down the street toward her, tried to flag it down without looking like a crazy woman, but it passed without slowing. The business-suit guy started up the Lexus and began pulling off the curb.

Natalie cursed again, gave up on the taxi. She typed the license plate number of the Lexus into a notes app on her phone. Then she sent it along with a brief text message to one of her contacts with Metro police, hoping she might be able to ID the guy ASAP.

When she returned to the Raven a few minutes later, Lenny Gregor was gone.

FORTY-FIVE

Lloyd walked down a sidewalk next to the Tidal Basin near the Jefferson Memorial. It was dark and drizzling out, so the sidewalks were nearly empty. Only a couple of hard-core late-night joggers still appeared here and there along the water's running path. Most tourists were already tucked away in their hotel rooms. He found the rental dock with the paddleboats—which was currently closed—waited by a bench. Seconds later, a fiftysomething bald man with a neatly trimmed beard stepped out of the shadows directly behind Lloyd, sending a charge through him that almost made him reach for his gun.

"Why the hell do you always do that?" Lloyd said.

"Do what?" the man asked.

"Pop out from behind me. It's unnecessary, and creepy."

The man gave him a wry grin. "Old habits die hard, I guess."

Lloyd shook his head. Bruce Markson. A thirty-year man with the CIA, who in his thirties and forties had done hundreds of covert tours all over the world. After taking a bullet in the leg during an operation in Tehran three years ago—one that had left him unable to move at a pace beyond a slow walk—Markson had transitioned to a desk job. The man knew just about *everyone* and *everything* going on over at Langley. Last month, when Lloyd had been chasing down Alger Gerlach, Markson had been the source who had shared with him that a secret operation was indeed going on involving Sam Callahan and Natalie Foster. Lloyd had been unable to get much more out of him. Even if they were old friends, Markson was not quick to divulge the Agency's secrets, which Lloyd respected. But he needed the man to help him put some of the puzzle pieces together tonight.

"How's the leg?" Lloyd asked.

"Still gets me from A to B, but I won't be doing the Rock 'n' Roll Marathon this year."

"Me neither. But my excuse is I'm old."

"Age isn't how old you are but how old you feel, my friend."

"I feel like I'm a hundred. How's Marcia?"

Markson had married Marcia last year. His third wife. The CIA could be hard on marriages. So could the FBI, which was why Lloyd had never remarried after his divorce.

"What do you want, Spencer?" Markson asked, ignoring the question, lighting up a cigarette. "I don't think you invited me out here in the rain to talk about my wife."

"What can you tell me about the Lion?"

Markson took a slow drag but didn't respond right away.

"I'll get you started," Lloyd offered. "Marcus Pelini, a thirty-year man much like you. A ghost who has barely existed in any official channels for the past fifteen years. A guy who somehow recruited a fresh-faced rookie lawyer into a situation that left him standing in a room full of dead bodies inside Moscow last night."

Markson cursed. "How do you even know about Pelini?"

"I've been digging around for the past month—ever since I got my pants yanked down by the CIA. I placed Sam Callahan and Pelini together."

"Dammit, Spencer! Haven't I already warned you about going around and asking these kinds of questions? People are going to get hurt."

"My father's already in the hospital fighting for his life because of these questions."

Markson tilted his head, pulled the cigarette away. "You serious?"

"A man broke into my condo last night looking for something, whacked him good over the head, and put my old man into a coma. He might not make it."

"Damn. Sorry to hear that. But why do you think it's connected to Pelini?"

"I've ID'd the guy. He's one of yours. Guy named Madrone."

Markson's eyes narrowed. Dropping his cigarette to the sidewalk, he stomped it out with the toe of his shoe. Lloyd could almost see the wheels spinning in the man's head, contemplating what he could or should share right now.

"Tell me *something*," Lloyd urged him. "Hell, you owe it to my father. You've certainly taken enough money off him in our poker games over the years. My father nearly bled out on the carpet because of this guy Madrone, and whatever the hell is going on with Pelini."

Markson took another long moment before finally responding. "Fine. You're correct in that Pelini recruited Callahan last month for a covert operation called Black Heron. The operation took place in Moscow last night and went badly. The entire black-ops team was ambushed. Nearly everyone was taken out."

"By who? The Russians?"

"We don't think it was the Russians, although they're certainly in play."

"Someone else have reason to execute your team?"

"Maybe. We're searching."

"What can you tell me about Black Heron?"

"I can't share those details with you, I'm afraid."

"What about the kid? Was Callahan killed, too?"

Markson shrugged. "We're not sure yet. Haven't confirmed anything. But the kid has already proven to be a hell of a survivor."

"I don't get it. Why would Callahan sign up for this?"

Markson lit up another cigarette, took a puff. "Turns out Marcus Pelini is Callahan's real father. Info that was dropped on him last month and used to recruit him."

Lloyd's jaw dropped. "You kidding me?"

"Nope. And you and I both know how messy father-son relationships can be. Hell, I still do stupid things trying to please an old man who can never be pleased." Markson's eyes narrowed again. "Now it's your turn to talk. How the hell did you know Callahan was standing in a room full of dead bodies last night?"

"One of my agents intercepted a video feed from Moscow. She then shared it last night with Callahan's fiancée. Minutes later, a man in a Suburban tried to crush her Jeep into oblivion with both of them still inside. My agent is in ICU. Natalie walked away okay but is currently missing."

"You think Madrone did it?"

Lloyd shook his head. "He doesn't match the description of the driver. But we ID'd Madrone at my condo, *and* I found him ransacking Natalie's apartment a few hours ago. He fled out the fire escape before we could chat with him."

Markson took a long drag on his cigarette. "I honestly don't know what Madrone is doing."

Lloyd could feel his neck flush red. "Don't jerk me around, Bruce."

"I'm serious," Markson insisted. "He's not operating within any *official* CIA channels."

"So you're telling me it's just a coincidence that Madrone shows up right after your black-ops team gets sideswiped in Russia and starts wreaking havoc on any local players who might know more than they probably should?"

"Madrone got the shadow treatment earlier this year for special-assignment work. Pulled completely from the grid. Believe me, he's not a guy you want to mess around with. He's the guy you send into a cave all by himself to assassinate a Taliban leader."

"What kind of special-assignment work?"

"I shouldn't be telling you this. Few at the Agency even know. But we're hunting an intelligence mole. Someone has been sharing classified information. It got one of our top assets killed in Moscow earlier this year. She was a mistress to Vladimir Zolotov, one of our key Russian targets. Madrone is part of a select off-the-books special-ops team that's been hunting down the mole."

"You think it's someone inside the Agency?"

"We started there, of course. Nothing to show for it yet."

"Who's leading the hunt?"

"Bradley."

Dan Bradley was assistant deputy director for operations. He was quickly climbing the CIA ranks. Lloyd didn't know too much about him. The Agency didn't broadcast news about their people.

Markson suddenly cursed as if he was putting some things together in his own mind and the sky was starting to clear for him.

"What?" Lloyd asked him. "You think Bradley's involved?"

"I gotta go."

"Talk to me," Lloyd urged him.

"I need to look into something first."

"Dammit, man. Don't leave me hanging here."

"I'll call you in the morning, I swear."

A split second later, Lloyd knew he'd never receive that call. He heard the familiar crack and pop of a sniper rifle, followed by Markson's head snapping forward, spraying blood across Lloyd's shirt. On instinct, Lloyd dove to the ground, just as he heard another shot and felt a bullet hit something directly behind him. Lloyd looked over to Markson, who had fallen face-first to the sidewalk. He was a goner.

Lloyd army-crawled forward, pressed his back up against the nearest tree. Another sniper shot, and the bark of the tree exploded just inches above his head. Lloyd had to keep moving. The tree couldn't fully protect him. Five feet in front of him was a big green metal utility box. Pushing off the tree, he dove for the box just as he heard another sniper shot. The bullet hit the utility box with a loud pop. Lloyd pressed his back against it, pulled his gun out—not that he planned to fire it. The sniper was clearly on the other side of the Tidal Basin, taking shots across the water from a few hundred yards. Who was it? Madrone?

He took out his phone, called Epps. His heart pounded in his ears.

"Get to the Tidal Basin ASAP!" Lloyd ordered. "I'm under fire!"

FORTY-SIX

After sitting in the truck outside Lenny Gregor's apartment unit until two in the morning with still no sign of him, Natalie finally gave up waiting for him to return. She had no idea if Lenny would even come home tonight. For all she knew, the guy could be currently staking out her brownstone right now. Exhausted, she got a room at the Washington Court Hotel, mainly because it was on the same block as Sam's apartment building, and she just wanted to somehow feel close to him right now. With still no word from Sam, the full emotional weight of the past twenty-four hours was now hitting her hard.

Lying on the bed, she replayed the words from the note he'd left in his London hotel room for her in her head—*Natalie, if you're reading this, I fear the worst has happened to me*—until tears covered her cheeks. They'd already survived so much. Their first devastating breakup two years ago, his tracker assignment gone bad last fall, his mother's tragic death earlier this year that had sent them both down a difficult path, and his recent trip to Mexico last month. But could they survive this? Would they even get the chance?

Walking over to the window, she pulled back the curtains, where she had a view below of the well-lit Georgetown University Law School campus. The hotel clerk had found it an odd request for a room view—nearly *everyone* wanted a peek toward the Capitol Building a few blocks south—but Natalie had her reasons and didn't bother to explain.

Standing there, she could still envision Sam walking the landscaped grounds of the beautiful campus with his backpack slung over his shoulder. They'd shared many picnics on the perfectly green grass beneath the clock tower. Natalie would often show up after one of his late-morning classes with a bag from Ching Ching Cha, their favorite Chinese restaurant. She smiled at those memories. When they'd first started dating, Sam had just been a regular law student hoping a degree would allow him to one day help those who were less fortunate than he was. She'd been a budding investigative reporter still looking to make her mark on the city. They were simply two kids falling in love for the first time. She fiddled with her engagement ring. So much had transpired since those days.

The buzzing of her cell phone snapped her away from the window. She snagged it from the hotel nightstand, stared at the incoming text. *Bingo!* Her contact at Metro police suffered from insomnia, so she wasn't surprised to get a reply from him in the middle of the night, with a license plate trace of the Lexus sedan. It belonged to a man named Nathan Barnes of Capitol Hill. Natalie didn't recognize the name.

She did a quick Google search on her phone. A profile page popped up near the top from a DC law firm called Easton & Lanister—a big corporate firm she *did* recognize. Sitting there on her screen was a smiling head shot of the same man in a business suit who had just engaged in a clandestine bar meeting with the muscle-bound army reject who'd tried to kill her last night. Why was this lawyer meeting with Lenny? Was he a law firm client? Not likely. Easton & Lanister represented big companies, not lowlifes. They certainly weren't drinking buddies. What she monitored at the Raven was clearly a business meeting of sorts.

Natalie quickly skimmed through Barnes's lawyer profile. Born in New Jersey. College at Rutgers. Law school at NYU. Joined Easton & Lanister five years ago, where he specialized in corporate and securities practices. No mention of wife or kids. Natalie pondered the connection to her situation. There was nothing obvious.

She found a few articles from eight years ago, when Barnes had played college lacrosse at Rutgers. He wasn't a star or anything, but his name appeared in several different tournament write-ups. There was also a team photo, and she quickly scanned the names and faces of the other players. No one stood out as meaning anything to her. Moving forward, she found several articles on legal websites listing Barnes's name—where he was involved in various legal matters—but again, nothing that looked connected to her current situation in any overt way.

Continuing her search, Natalie finally came across something interesting that grabbed her attention. It was a political article from a DC blog featuring a group photo taken the previous year on the Hill. Barnes was not central to the photo. He was standing over to the side. The central player in the group photo was Senator Clark Harris of New Jersey. According to the photo credits, Nathan Barnes was the senator's nephew. Did that mean anything?

Of course she'd heard of Senator Harris, although, admittedly, she didn't know too much about him. Newly elected, he had not yet established a long record of success or conflict in DC. She did a quick search on Harris to refresh her memory. Five years ago, Harris had ridden a surprisingly strong grassroots movement and won New Jersey's open Senate seat. Prior to that, he'd served two terms in the US House of Representatives. Engineering degree back in the day from Boston University. Harris owned a small engineering firm for two decades before going into politics. A wife and two daughters around Natalie's age. Natalie skimmed the list of various Senate committees and subcommittees where Harris had served since his election. None of them really stood out as a point of real interest—*except* for one.

Senator Harris was a sitting member on the Senate Intelligence Committee.

FORTY-SEVEN

Sam tried and failed to sleep on the overnight train to Paris. Once they'd cleared the station in Milan with no sudden reappearance of his nemesis, Alger Gerlach, he allowed himself to settle down into the train seat next to Tommy and closed his eyes. But a disturbing reel of dark images kept scrolling through his mind and snapping him back awake. Mack being killed on the sidewalk right in front of him; Luis shot dead in Red Square; the others all ambushed in the Moscow safe house. During the past nine months, he'd probably seen more dead bodies, many of whom had taken their last breaths while standing right next to him, than most county morgue workers. He kept trying to find a way to reconcile the past year in his mind, in the same way that Pastor Isaiah had helped him to address and make some peace with the pain of his broken childhood. But the steadily growing body count all around him made it difficult to make sense of anything.

Staring out the train window, Sam thought about Pastor Isaiah. Sam had not mentioned anything to him about recently discovering his long-lost father. He regretted that now. Perhaps his wise mentor and friend would've advised him to walk away from all this when he'd first had the chance. A month ago, Sam had convinced himself that it was best, and safest, for everyone not to know the truth. Safer for Natalie.

Safer for Pastor Isaiah. Safer for his boss, David. But he now realized he simply didn't want anyone to talk him out of it. Because of that, dead bodies were everywhere. Each of them betrayed by power or money or politics—whatever the reason.

Sam had also been betrayed. And it was looking more and more like it was at the hands of his very own father. He would never be able to come to terms with it. What kind of evil would push a man to invite his own son into a dangerous situation with every intention of betraying him?

Tommy started mumbling in his sleep in the seat next to him. The train car was dark, and Sam assumed pretty much everyone on board was snoozing right now. Sam was grateful to have Tommy with him. They'd been through a hell of a lot together during the past year. Sam had never had a more loyal friend. Tommy was the only person on the planet right now whom Sam had told the complete truth to. After a month of keeping daily secrets, with lies at every turn, it felt liberating not to have to take great care with his words around Tommy. He longed to go back to that place with Natalie.

He stared out into the darkness of the French countryside. Natalie had to be worried. Given his absence, Sam wondered if David had asked hotel security to check inside his room. Most likely. David would've remained chill for most of the day, thinking Sam was still feeling the ugly effects of his stomach bug, but at some point, he would've also grown concerned.

Sam cursed when it dawned on him that David might have also discovered the note he'd left for Natalie, just in case he didn't make it back from Moscow. If David had found the note, would he have then shared it with her? Sam sighed, shook his head. If that exchange had happened, Natalie was probably in an all-out panic right now. This made him feel even sicker to his stomach.

He pulled out his phone, began typing in her phone number. Then he paused. What would he even say to her? How could he call his fiancée from an overnight train traveling through Europe and explain that he'd done nothing but lie to her for the past month? Not only that, but most of the members of the CIA covert-ops team that he'd secretly joined were now dead. He also currently had the Gray Wolf back on his tail, along with a new Russian assassin intent on killing him. That was not a conversation to have over a bad phone connection from more than four thousand miles away. Especially when the phone call could immediately put Natalie in grave danger. Sam cleared her number from his phone.

Whether he liked it or not, he could not make contact with Natalie until this was over. Not until he got the truth. Next time he spoke with Natalie, he had to tell her the full truth about *everything*. And never lie to her again. Would she even forgive him? He couldn't be sure. After all, he might never forgive himself.

FORTY-EIGHT

Standing outside the front door of FBI director Luther Stone's two-story redbrick colonial in Forest Hills, Lloyd knocked firmly. Most of the lights were off inside, so he knew he'd be waking up his boss. Not a smart move, but he had no choice. Stone was known for going to bed early but being at the office every morning by four thirty. It was common knowledge to not wake him in the middle of the night unless it was an all-out emergency. Lloyd thought that getting sniped at by an assassin in the middle of downtown qualified. Especially when he was standing right next to a top-level CIA officer who did not survive the attack. Lloyd still felt shaken by seeing his old friend take a bullet to the head and collapse like a falling tree right in front of him. All because he'd asked Markson to share info with him.

He knocked again, looked for signs of life.

Epps had arrived just in time to pull Lloyd to safety but not in time to find the shooter on the opposite side of the water. The sniper had disappeared. Lloyd had decided it was best for them to disappear as well instead of sticking around to deal with the fallout of a CIA agent shot dead on the banks of the Tidal Basin. They'd holed up in a cheap motel room for the past hour, where he and Epps began putting the pieces of the puzzle together. The news had not broken about Markson's death, but it was just a matter of time. One way or another, Lloyd had a feeling this thing was about to completely unravel. You don't start assassinating federal agents without being desperate. Which was why Lloyd was on Stone's doorstep right now.

Another knock and Lloyd finally saw a light come on in the hallway.

Seconds later, Stone was at the door wearing his brown bathrobe, looking like he wanted to bite Lloyd's head off. The man's hard scowl had a way of making even the toughest of men's knees shake. Short and stocky, Stone had a boxy head with a military haircut. He'd won the NCAA wrestling championship for the army back in his day and still looked like he could compete today.

"What the hell, Spencer?" Stone growled.

"Sorry to wake you, sir," Lloyd said. "I wouldn't be here if it wasn't urgent."

Another grunt. "Come in."

Stone led him into a study right off the foyer, turned on a few lights. The director sat behind a massive wooden desk. Lloyd stood awkwardly in front of it.

"What the hell is it?" Stone demanded.

"Markson with the CIA was shot by a sniper near the Tidal Basin earlier tonight."

Stone's wrinkled face bunched up even more. "How do you know that?"

"I was standing next to him. The sniper missed me by inches."

Stone cursed, leaned forward in his chair. "Start explaining."

Lloyd knew he had no choice but to tell Stone *everything*—including his admission that he'd disobeyed Stone's direct orders for him to leave the CIA matter involving Sam Callahan alone. Stone didn't look too happy at this revelation, but Lloyd powered through with all that had unfolded over the past two days. If Stone had any empathy that Lloyd's father was in a coma in the hospital, his face didn't show it. His beady eyes were glaring holes right through Lloyd.

To his credit, Stone didn't butcher him the moment he'd finished. "I assume you've already looked deeper into Bradley or you wouldn't be here right now?"

"Yes, sir, we did."

Lloyd took a moment to tell Stone about their findings on Dan Bradley, assistant deputy director of operations at the CIA, the man whom Markson claimed was leading the charge to find the intelligence mole while using Mike Madrone as a central player in their hunt. Although he couldn't prove it yet, Lloyd was convinced that Madrone had fired the sniper bullets earlier tonight. At fifty-two, Bradley was divorced with two adult kids. He went to college at Boston University, did five years with the Hartford PD, then joined the CIA more than twenty-five years ago. Bradley had spent most of his career overseas, where he'd held the position of chief of station at several important foreign posts.

"His last post was Moscow," Lloyd declared, finding that the most intriguing.

"So you think Bradley could be behind this?"

"I'm not ready to make that claim just yet. But Bradley purchased a 1920s row house in Columbia Heights last year for one-point-two million dollars. Pretty hefty price tag for a CIA lifer. I doubt he makes more than a hundred fifty a year, and there is no trace of any family money. Plus, when Markson mentioned Bradley earlier tonight, I could tell he was beginning to put two and two together."

"Markson said as much?"

"He didn't get the chance, sir. His head exploded seconds later."

"And you think Madrone pulled the trigger."

"Long-range marksmanship is part of his unique skill set."

That info seemed more interesting to Stone, as he eased back in his office chair, rubbed his clean-shaven square chin. "You're certain it was Madrone who was inside your condo two nights ago? And the man who broke into Natalie Foster's place?"

"One hundred percent."

Stone cursed, not looking happy. "I knew about Black Heron," he admitted. "Director Barton shared that info with me last month, which is why I was willing to grant the favor and pull you off this deal with Callahan. By the way, I'm still pissed at you for disregarding my orders."

"Yes, sir. My apologies."

Stone continued to ponder tonight's new info. "Okay, so let's say Bradley is as shady as you propose. There's no way he's doing it alone. The Russians aren't wiring money straight into his account. If everything you say is true, another big player has to be involved. Bradley would know it's too risky to turn over classified info himself."

Lloyd nodded. "We're searching."

"You have to find me that player, Spencer. Because I'm not jumping on the phone with Barton and shoving a stick of dynamite like this in his face without having something more concrete in my hands."

"I understand, sir."

Stone stood from his chair, walked Lloyd back to the front door. "Listen, I want you to completely close ranks on this for now. No one else can know what you're doing. I don't want anything leaking back to Bradley this morning. Call me hourly with updates. I won't be sleeping the rest of the night, anyway. And don't get yourself killed."

FORTY-NINE

They switched trains without incident at a station in Paris and finally arrived in the coastal town of Le Tréport just as the sun was peeking up over the cliffs along the English Channel. The train dropped them at a picturesque station near the water's edge, with an easy walk to Avenue du Maréchal Foch, the main strip for shopping, restaurants, and hotels. They'd used the train ride from Paris to do their research on the resort town. Sam and Tommy ducked into a café to grab some coffee and pastries, as well as to plan their next move in finding Lucinda.

Sam didn't know where she was hiding—just that, according to Mack, she was there somewhere. However, they did have a good lead. Tommy had been able to trace Mack's communication with Lucinda through their use of the secure website to an IP address that belonged to a bookstore along the town's main strip called La Librairie Pittoresque. The bookstore sat directly across the street from them on the ground level of a three-story redbrick building. It was closed but would likely open soon, as the sidewalks were already growing busy with tourist traffic. The early plan was to go inside once the bookstore opened, describe Lucinda with a cover story, and find out if anyone knew where she was.

It was a long shot, but it was all they had.

Tommy had his laptop open in front of him, as usual. "We've got about two dozen hotels all within easy walking distance from the bookstore."

"Two dozen, huh?" Sam said, sighing. "That should make this easy. And still no alerts yet on Lucinda using her CIA alias at any of them?"

Tommy shook his head. "Still nothing."

"So how's she paying for her stay here?"

"She must have a third alias. Or she's got a stack of euros."

Sam stared out the window at the sidewalks, sipped his hot coffee. He needed a gallon of it right now, his body dripped with so much fatigue. "I don't know, Tommy. This feels like an odd hideout for a member of my crew. Can't be more than five thousand people here. Not exactly where I would go to get *lost in the crowd*."

"Beats me. But I don't think like a spook."

"There's more to it," Sam insisted, taking a bite of pastry. "Still nothing on Pelini?"

"Nope. That man is a ghost."

After fifteen minutes of drinking coffee, Sam noticed a man in a black cardigan approach the bookstore, unlock the front door, and go inside. Moments later, the **FERMÉ** sign in the window flipped to **OUVERT**.

"We're in business," Sam mentioned. "Stay here."

"Roger that."

Sam slid off his chair, trotted across the street to the bookstore. An older couple had entered right before him. Stepping inside, Sam noticed the fortysomething man who unlocked the store standing behind a checkout counter, sorting paperwork. Sam did a quick scan of the store. Not much to it. Only a few rows of books, some new, some used. A wooden desk in the corner had a desktop computer on it. Sam wondered if that was where Lucinda had sat to communicate with Mack.

Walking over to the counter, Sam got the attention of the store clerk, a man with a thick brown mustache and an easy smile.

"Puis-je vous aider?" the clerk asked him.

"Do you speak English?"

"Yes, of course. How can I help you?"

"I'm looking for my sister, actually. I was scheduled to arrive in Le Tréport tomorrow, but I came a day early to surprise her on her birthday. She's midthirties, slender, straight black hair just past the shoulders. My sister loves bookstores, so I thought she might have come in here recently."

The clerk pondered the description. "There was someone in here yesterday who matches your description." He grinned. "A very attractive woman, I must admit."

Sam matched his grin. "Did you get her name?"

The clerk's eyes narrowed on Sam. "I thought you said she was your sister."

Sam tried to be casual. "Yes, she is, but she's also a popular actress, and oftentimes uses different names when she's staying at hotels and such. Just for anonymity. Which is why I need help finding her, *if* I don't want to call her up and spoil the big surprise."

Sam's explanation must've seemed logical to the clerk, as his face relaxed. "I didn't get the name she was using, unfortunately. Your sister didn't buy anything; she just browsed a bit and then used the public computer over there."

Sam sighed. "Okay, thanks."

"But I did see her again last night on my stroll home," the clerk added.

Sam perked up. "Where?"

"She was walking into the Yvonnette. A villa off rue Sadi Carnot, a couple of blocks from here."

"Merci!"

FIFTY

Jacket hood up over his head, Sam stood on a busy sidewalk across the street from the Villa Yvonnette, a four-story redbrick building with bright blue doors and blue balconies. The Yvonnette sat in the middle of a long row of attached redbrick buildings, all with different shades of vibrant trim. In many ways, he felt the place was appropriate for someone hiding out. It was not one of the resort hotels, with their massive lobbies and lots of people around. Instead, the Yvonnette was tucked away on a quiet street. According to Tommy's research, there were only six units available, which were actually more like small apartments than hotel rooms. All the units had full-size kitchens with separate washers and dryers.

Sam wondered if Lucinda had plans to stay in Le Tréport for a while. He wondered if she'd bolted London at the same time he'd jumped on the middle-of-the-night plane ride to Moscow. He wondered if she'd had any contact with Pelini since all hell had broken loose. He hoped that he wouldn't have to keep wondering for long. After an hour, Sam noticed Lucinda step out the main blue door of the Yvonnette. Wearing a tan coat with a scarf around her neck and big sunglasses covering her eyes, she walked purposefully down the sidewalk in a crowd of others.

Her steps were measured, as she was clearly keeping close tabs on her surroundings.

Hands in pockets, Sam moved briskly across the street, followed her up the sidewalk. He didn't want to jump out in front of her and spook her. When he'd done that with Mack, Mack had put him into a headlock, and he'd almost caught a bullet. Sam had no idea what Lucinda would do. The woman could certainly hold her own. Instead, he wanted to choose his moment wisely and look for a less abrupt way to engage her properly.

Lucinda turned the street corner, headed to a busier part of the main strip. Sam hustled up to the corner behind her. It was midmorning now, and the coastal town had sprung fully to life. The sidewalks were busy with foot traffic, the streets with cars zipping past. He trailed Lucinda at thirty feet, waiting for her to peel off somewhere, like a café or a gift shop, where he could more easily slip in and talk to her quietly outside the mass of crowds. She casually coasted up the sidewalk for a bit, window watching, easing in and out of the people traffic.

Sam did the same, keeping slow pace with her. *Come on, Lucinda.* Glancing across the street at the opposite sidewalk, Sam suddenly froze in his tracks. He spotted a familiar-looking man briskly walking up the opposite sidewalk. Sam couldn't believe his eyes. The Russian assassin. The tall man wore the same jacket he'd had on yesterday when chasing Sam and Tommy through Salzburg. How had the assassin found Sam? Had he tracked their train ride from Milan? Was he working with Gerlach?

But then Sam noticed that the Russian wasn't focusing on him; instead, the assassin's eyes locked on Lucinda forty feet ahead of Sam. The Russian didn't even seem to register that Sam was trailing behind her. He was going after Lucinda. How had the Russians found her?

When the Russian reached into his jacket and discreetly slipped out his gun, panic gripped Sam. He was going to take her out right there on the street? Sam had to do something immediately. But what?

He couldn't just scream her name—the assassin might start firing his weapon.

Lucinda paused up ahead to look into a storefront window. In that moment, Sam noticed the Russian begin making a path across the street straight toward her. Cursing, Sam glanced directly to his right, where he noticed a young man parking his motorcycle at the curb. On instinct, Sam stepped off the curb, shoved the guy straight off the motorcycle, causing him to tumble into the street. With the motorcycle still running, Sam jumped on the back of it, grabbed the handlebars, and revved the engine. The bike exploded forward, hitting the curb with its front tire, bouncing up onto the sidewalk, and causing people to dart out of the way and yell at him. He didn't slow down as he threaded through the bystanders. Lucinda turned to look back at the ruckus going on behind her on the sidewalk. Sam nearly crushed her up against the building as he skidded the bike to a sliding stop. He clumsily hit the brakes, nearly flipped off himself.

Pulling off his hood, he yelled, "Get on right now! They know you're here!"

Wide-eyed, Lucinda glanced toward the street, where she spotted the assassin rushing forward, his gun now fully exposed. She quickly climbed on the back of the motorcycle, grabbed Sam tightly around the waist. He jumped the bike forward, navigated it back into the street. Peeking behind him, Sam watched as the Russian stood there in the middle of the street. The assassin seemed stuck between a rock and hard place, unsure if he wanted to start shooting at them in front of a gawking crowd.

The Russian's hesitancy was all Sam needed.

He took his first right, gunned the bike.

FIFTY-ONE

Creating plenty of safe distance between them and the Russian, Sam finally parked the stolen motorcycle by a remote lighthouse tucked way up on a cliff overlooking the water. No one else could be spotted for a mile. Climbing off the bike, Lucinda walked over to a short stone wall. She took off her sunglasses, rubbed her eyes, and looked like she was trying to gather herself after their dangerous encounter back in town. Sam told her he needed to make a quick phone call. He stepped down a gravel walking path, rang up Tommy on his burner phone, and informed him about the Russian assassin's unexpected appearance and his dramatic escape with Lucinda. Tommy agreed to get to a safe place until he heard back from Sam.

Hanging up, Sam returned to Lucinda, the same woman who had run point on his dramatic flight out of Mexico City last month. "You okay?" he asked.

She turned to look at him. "Who was the man with the gun?"

"A Russian assassin."

"How do you know that?"

"The same guy tried to kill me in Moscow and again in Salzburg yesterday."

"Did he follow you here?"

"No, he was clearly here for you."

"How? I've been careful. I've covered all my tracks."

Sam shrugged. "I don't know."

"Okay, then how the hell did *you* find me here, Sam?"

"You don't seem happy to see me."

She exhaled. "Sorry. Believe me, I am. I'm just freaked out right now."

"I talked to Mack in Milan last night. He said you were here."

She nodded. "Is he okay? He hasn't returned my last message."

Sam pressed his lips firmly together. "He was killed last night. I got away."

A measure of sadness fell on Lucinda. "By the same Russian?"

Sam shook his head. "Alger Gerlach."

"What?" Lucinda tilted her head, aghast. "I don't understand any of this."

"That makes two of us. Someone brought the Gray Wolf back into play."

"Who? Who did all of this?"

"I was hoping you might know."

She stared at the ground, thinking hard. "Unfortunately, I don't."

"Let's start at the beginning," he suggested.

Sam took a few minutes to share everything that had happened from the moment he'd left his dinner with Lucinda and his boss, David, in London two nights ago to the point of him standing there with her this morning. Midway, Lucinda sat on the edge of the stone wall, as if she was on shaky legs. She'd clearly been in the dark about so much of what had tragically taken place the past two days.

"I'm sorry, Sam," she offered. "I'm so sorry you were dragged into this."

"I signed up on my own. No one dragged me."

"Still, it wasn't supposed to go down like this."

"What can you tell me about what happened in Moscow?"

"Nothing. I wasn't even there."

"Then why are you here hiding out in Le Tréport? That wasn't in our exit plan."

She looked away, didn't respond. But she clearly knew something more.

"You have to talk to me," Sam insisted. "I've had two assassins relentlessly hunting me for the past thirty hours. Nearly everyone who was a part of this operation has been killed, including two of your friends, who were standing right in front of me when it happened. You'd probably be dead yourself right now had I not been there to grab you off the street. I think I've earned the right to hear the damn truth. They're after all of us—whoever *they* are!"

She turned back. "I don't know what the truth is anymore."

"Have you had contact with Marcus?"

He watched her closely. Her hesitancy gave him the answer.

Sam cursed. "Where the hell is he? Tell me!"

"London," she finally relented.

"Why do you know that when *no one* else does?"

She looked up at him with wet eyes, catching him off guard. "Because he's supposed to be here with me right now, okay? We were going to leave all of this behind us—the covert operations, the lies, this silly game of death we play every day as part of our jobs. We were done with it. We were going to start a brand-new life together. That's what was *supposed* to happen!"

When she finished, a couple of tears rolled down her cheeks. Mack had been right. Pelini was indeed planning to disappear. But Sam was stunned to hear that it was *with* Lucinda. He'd never caught any hint of their relationship back in DC while training with them.

"Who else knew about you guys?" he asked.

"No one. We made sure of it. When this was all done, we were going to meet here, in Le Tréport, then slip away together. Find ourselves a private beach on the other side of the world and never be heard from again. But then everything fell apart. Marcus instructed me to wait here until he could tie off loose ends."

"Loose ends?" Sam asked, flushing red. "Like eliminating everyone on our team?"

Her eyes turned to slits. "Marcus would *never* do that!"

"Then tell me who's behind this."

"I don't know!" she yelled. "But he would never sacrifice his own team members."

"What about the list, Lucinda? He stole it right out from under us."

"He didn't steal the list."

"Come on! I have the video—he's on the property. Perhaps he has even you fooled."

"He didn't steal the list," she repeated, looking even more adamant.

"Then why the hell are the Russians still coming after us?"

"They don't want the list, Sam. They want the boy."

Sam's brow bunched. "What . . . boy?"

"Charlie."

He stared at her for a long moment, his mind reeling. "Wait . . . What are you talking about? You mean the little boy I encountered while inside Zolotov's town house?"

"Yes, that boy."

"Why would the Russians think we have Charlie?"

"We do. Marcus took him."

Sam's mouth fell open, shocked. "You're telling me Marcus came onto the property behind me to abduct a *child*? Why the hell would he do that?"

"Because Charlie is his son."

This time Sam was speechless. *His son?*

"I promise I don't know anything more than that," Lucinda insisted. "Marcus kept me in the dark for my own protection, he always said. He told me he would explain everything about Charlie when he got back here to Le Tréport—*after* the operation was a success. Except now I don't know if he'll ever make it here to me."

More tears ran down Lucinda's cheeks, but Sam was unable to console her. Not with the way his head was swirling around this new revelation. He suddenly felt light-headed, and took his turn to sit on the short wall beside her. Charlie was Pelini's son? If true, that meant Sam had—a brother! He suddenly flashed back to his brief encounter with the boy the other night, remembering the scraggly brown hair, the similar blue eyes, and the feeling that the boy reminded him *a lot* of himself as a child. Could it really be? Could he really have a brother? Or was this all just another one of the gray-bearded man's sick mind games? Had he played Lucinda in the same sinister way he'd played everyone else in his life? Sam couldn't be sure of anything until he had the chance to look Pelini square in the eyes.

"He has the boy with him?" Sam asked, looking over at Lucinda.

She shrugged, wiped away the tears. "I don't know. We've had only one brief message exchange, where he let me know he was okay, in London, and he insisted we not make contact again. Not until he'd finished what he called necessary business."

"What do you think he meant?"

"I think he's also trying to find out who's behind what happened."

"How do I find him?" Sam asked, feeling more determined than ever.

"*No one* can find Marcus, unless he wants you to find him."

"I have to try, Lucinda," Sam pleaded. "Don't forget, I'm also his son."

She nodded, slowly exhaled. "We once stayed at the Milestone, a small private hotel tucked away in the center of London."

FIFTY-TWO

Sam dropped Lucinda on a sidewalk in Dieppe, another small town thirty miles down the coast. She couldn't return to Le Tréport. Not with the Russian, and whoever else, closely on her tail. Whether she wanted to or not, Lucinda had to immediately begin a new journey toward getting herself *lost* again. A journey that unfortunately did not include Marcus Pelini, as she'd previously planned. Sam could tell this absolutely crushed her. Lucinda clearly loved the man deeply. In her fragile state, Sam worried she might make a mistake that would eventually get her killed. Other than Pelini, Lucinda was the only person still left standing from his group—a sobering thought. He desperately wanted to keep it that way.

Because Lucinda had nothing on her other than the clothes on her back, Sam gave her his entire roll of euro bills. Standing on the sidewalk together, they shared a brief hug. It was time for them to separate.

"You sure I can't ask Tommy to help you?" he said. "The guy is known for pulling rabbits out of his hat."

She shook her head. "I've done this many times. Don't worry about me—just take care of yourself, okay?"

"Okay."

She turned, took a few steps down the sidewalk, but then pivoted back to him. "I do hope you finally find what you're looking for, Sam. You deserve it."

He nodded, swallowed. He knew Lucinda was talking about more than surviving all of this. She was talking about deserving something more from his relationship with his father. Sam had resisted the urge to ask her if she had any deeper insight into how Pelini might actually feel about him. He was afraid her answer might crush his spirit right now. Moments later, Lucinda turned a street corner and disappeared behind a block of buildings. Sam wondered if he would ever see her again.

Starting the motorcycle, he drove back toward Le Tréport. Midway, he ditched the bike in a parking lot behind a business complex. The motorcycle had probably been reported stolen, so he couldn't chance driving it back through town right now. Besides, he needed a car. He had to get to London as fast as possible. He was unwilling to wait for a train ride, and he wasn't going to travel more than four hours on a motorcycle with Tommy's skinny arms wrapped around his waist.

He quickly searched the parking lot for prospects. About thirty cars were parked up and down four rows. At the edge of the lot, he spotted an older black Honda Civic with the driver's window slightly cracked, which piqued his interest. First, he doubted the old Civic had a fancy alarm system. Second, the driver had given him an easy entry point. Making sure no one was watching, he stuck his hands in the crack of the window. The driver had left just enough room for him to slip his fingers over the edge of the glass. He grabbed the glass window in both hands and began slowly but firmly rocking it back and forth. Within ten seconds, the car window came loose from its tracks, allowing Sam just enough space to reach his right arm all the way inside and unlock the door.

Another peek around the parking lot. Still no eyes on him. He dropped into the driver's seat, did a quick search for a hidden spare key. Back in his days as a teenage car thief whiz kid, Sam had found some people would lock their doors and feel secure enough to keep an extra key hidden in the glove box or inside the console. As a car thief, there was no better feeling in the world than stumbling upon a hidden spare key. It saved him a lot of effort and trouble. Digging through the clutter of the glove box, Sam felt that same familiar rush move through him. He found a single car key.

He stuck the key in the ignition, and the Civic's engine fired right up. Sam put the car into drive, peeled out of the parking lot, and pressed his foot down to the floor.

First stop, snag Tommy back in Le Tréport.

Second stop, go after his father in London.

FIFTY-THREE

Nathan Barnes owned a gray two-story Victorian town house near Lincoln Park on Capitol Hill. Around four in the morning, Natalie parked her borrowed truck across the street from his place and began walking the sidewalks. Although it was no longer raining, a sticky-wet humidity still hung in the air. If Barnes was an early riser, she wanted to be ready to follow him. Maybe he'd head straight to his law firm office—or maybe he wouldn't. She couldn't sleep right now, anyway. She just tossed and turned in her hotel bed. She had the feeling she might finally be getting closer to the truth. And she was tired of seeing Sam standing in a room full of dead bodies, a look of fear on his face, every time she closed her eyes.

Circling the block, she spotted the narrow alley drive to the back of the town houses. She walked down it until she found the black Lexus sedan sitting in a one-car paver driveway, letting her know that Barnes was indeed home. Returning to the truck, she started it and moved it over for a clearer view of the alley drive, where she'd be certain to notice if Barnes was leaving in his Lexus.

Sitting there inside the truck, she again pondered whether Barnes's connection to Senator Harris had something to do with all of this. As a member of the Senate Intelligence Committee, Harris had critical inside access to top-secret information involving US–Russian intelligence matters. He might even know what the hell Sam was doing in Moscow. Could it really be a coincidence that his nephew was meeting with the same guy who put Michelle in the hospital and tried to take her out on the Metro? She doubted it. And her gut was usually spot-on. There was a connection there, and she was determined to find it.

She eased down into the truck seat, waited.

At five, Barnes was on the move, making Natalie glad she came early. She followed him closely. There was other traffic, so it was easy for her to trail him without standing out. Barnes navigated through downtown until he finally pulled the Lexus to a stop at the curb in front of the historic Saint Patrick's Catholic Church. Up the block, Natalie also pulled to the curb. She checked the time on her phone. Five fifteen. *A little early for morning Mass,* she thought. So what was he doing there?

Getting out of his vehicle, Barnes walked the sidewalk toward the ornate church building. He was again wearing a sharp dark suit. Natalie also got out, trailed him quickly up the sidewalk. Instead of trotting up the steps toward the main entrance of Saint Patrick's, Barnes followed a sidewalk around the side of the massive old building, opened a wrought-iron gate, then walked down a path into a big interior courtyard. Natalie paused by the wrought-iron gate, wondering if she should follow Barnes inside. She felt exposed and vulnerable. Taking a deep breath, she decided she had no choice and carefully followed the dark path after him.

The courtyard had a big water fountain in the middle, with several benches situated among an expansive garden. Barnes was standing by himself in the middle of the courtyard, as if he was waiting on someone else to arrive. Natalie hung back in the shadows near the edge of the courtyard, where she hugged one side of the church building and stayed out of sight. Who was Barnes meeting? This didn't feel like a place where he would meet a lowlife like Lenny Gregor. It was someone more important.

Five minutes later, another man also wearing a suit entered from the same courtyard path and joined Barnes. She didn't immediately recognize the man, although there was a vague familiarity about him. He looked to be in his midfifties, with short brown hair and a slender build. The two men quickly shook hands but didn't immediately dive into a discussion. They just loitered there for a moment. That told Natalie someone else was still joining them. She resisted the urge to snap a few photos with her phone—she didn't want to do anything right now that might alert them to her presence inside the courtyard.

A few minutes later, a third man joined the party. This time, Natalie did recognize him and perked way up. Senator Harris. Natalie felt a charge of adrenaline race through her. She'd been right. Harris didn't bother shaking hands with either man. He also didn't look too happy to be standing there. Animated discussion quickly ensued, mostly led by Harris. Natalie was unfortunately too far away to make out any of it. She had to get closer, and quickly. Easing off the building, she slipped along the edge of the courtyard. She still couldn't make out anything they were saying, although Harris was definitely raising his voice and seemed to be arguing with the third unidentified man. Who was he?

Frustrated, Natalie looked for a way to somehow get even closer to them, see if she could make out *anything* they were talking about. It felt like a critical moment. She carved out a path with her eyes, one that would take her around the courtyard and behind a set of benches, where she thought she might have a clearer hearing space.

Moving again, her foot hit a small potted-plant feature, knocking it over, making a clanking noise. Natalie cursed. All eyes from the three-man group turned, glanced over in her general direction. She remained perfectly still, unsure if the men could see her. When they started talking again, she exhaled.

But before she could even take another step, Natalie felt a big hand suddenly reach around and grab her mouth while a second arm wrapped fully around her waist, lifting her up, and quickly yanking her backward into the darkness of the outer courtyard. She instantly had panicked visions of Lenny Gregor snapping her neck and finishing the job he'd started two days ago. But no neck snapping followed.

Instead, she heard urgent words whispered into her ear.

"FBI. Don't scream. Don't move."

FIFTY-FOUR

They huddled inside a first-floor motel room, a quick drive from Saint Patrick's Catholic Church. Folders, papers, and photos were spread out across the bed, a whiteboard situated on a stand in one corner with writing all over it—as if they'd already had this place set up as their makeshift war room. The strong man who'd snatched her from behind called himself Agent Epps. Natalie had recognized the second man hiding behind him—Assistant Director in Charge Spencer Lloyd.

Together, the three of them had remained silent and hidden in the shadows of the outer courtyard until the meeting among Senator Harris, Nathan Barnes, and the third as-yet-unidentified man had finally ended a brief ten minutes after it had started. Natalie was unable to hear most of the heated discussion, but it was clear none of the three men were happy to be standing there. After the men had left, Natalie was quickly escorted to a Buick and immediately transported to the motel room, where—based on the current expression on Lloyd's face—she was about to be interrogated as if she was at the top of their Most Wanted list.

Lloyd shut all the curtains, offered her a firm hand toward two wooden chairs sitting next to a lamp in the corner. "Please sit down, Ms. Foster."

"I'd rather stand. Thanks."

Lloyd glared at her. "Please."

She reluctantly took a seat, immediately felt the heat of the lamp on her face. Epps lingered by the door.

Standing directly in front of her, his arms crossed, Lloyd said, "Please explain to me what you were doing inside that courtyard."

Natalie shrugged. "Probably the same as you, Agent Lloyd. Looking for answers."

"Did you follow one of the men there?"

"Did you?"

Lloyd exhaled in frustration. "We don't have time for these games, Natalie. We're racing the clock here. And you nearly blew things up for us just now."

"How do you even know who I am?" Natalie countered, glowering.

She refused to be intimidated and was still a bit miffed about being grabbed in the courtyard. Afterward, neither agent had even asked for her name or identification. They just seemed to know who she was and acted as if they were not altogether surprised to find her there. Why?

"We've been looking for you," Lloyd admitted. "I spoke with Michelle Blair in the hospital yesterday morning. She told me about showing you the CIA video of your fiancé in Moscow—a video I've now seen—and the car wreck that followed shortly thereafter. Michelle called it an assassination attempt. She was concerned you were still in serious trouble because she's been unable to reach you."

Natalie softened at the mention of her friend. "Is Michelle okay?"

"She's tough. She has a long road to recovery, but she'll be fine."

"What about Sam?" she pleaded. "Do you know *anything*?"

"Are we *finally* ready to start talking?" Lloyd asked her.

She nodded and nearly held her breath while awaiting his answer. For the past thirty-six hours, she'd lived with the constant dread that at any moment, she might get devastating news about Sam. Would Lloyd be the one to deliver it?

"Sam was involved in a covert CIA operation in Moscow two nights ago that went off the rails and left many from his team dead. But I've been told *nothing* has been confirmed about Sam just yet. The CIA is actively searching for him. That's all I know, I'm sorry—I wish I could tell you more," said Lloyd.

Natalie felt some small sense of relief. "Thank you."

"Did you know about Sam's involvement with the CIA?" Epps asked.

Natalie shook her head. "Not until two nights ago, when I found out about something called Black Heron. Then I stumbled upon the warehouse where they must've trained for this operation. I went underground shortly thereafter."

"Why'd you go underground?" Lloyd asked.

"When you find out your fiancé has been lying to you for over a month about some secret CIA mission, then a thug shows up and takes two different cracks at your life, you tend to not know who to trust anymore. Better to lay low."

"Believe me, I understand. I dodged bullets myself last night."

Her forehead wrinkled. "Who's trying to kill *you*?"

"I'm working to figure that out. Could be the same people who are behind your thug. So how about we help each other out?"

"What do you want to know?" Natalie asked, ready to embrace whatever help she could get right now.

"Tell me everything that happened after Michelle first showed you the video."

Natalie explained her path toward identifying Lenny Gregor—the tattoo on his right hand, connecting the dots through two different military sources, and how she'd finally tracked him down at the Raven last night. She then talked about his meet-up with a lawyer named Nathan Barnes, whom she followed to the meeting this morning with Senator Harris and the other man.

"Barnes is Senator Harris's nephew," she clarified. "I don't know the identity of the third man. Do you?"

"Dan Bradley, assistant deputy director with the CIA."

Natalie cursed. "You serious? So you're telling me the CIA is behind trying to take us both out?"

"I don't think so," Lloyd said, shaking his head. "At least, not officially. I found out last night that Bradley has been leading a covert hunt for an intelligence mole. The same night that Black Heron went south in Russia, one of the black-ops agents on Bradley's secret team, a man named Mike Madrone, broke into my condo and ended up putting my father in the hospital. We found the same guy ransacking your place yesterday. I also believe Madrone was the one who shot and killed my CIA contact last night while trying to execute me in the process."

"You think a CIA agent assassinated another CIA agent?"

"Yes. And it's all connected to what went down with Sam in Moscow."

"How so?"

"I've been following your fiancé for the past month, ever since my uneasy encounter with him at Union Station, where my boss was specifically asked by the director of the CIA to let Sam walk right out of there—no questions asked. I now believe word of my off-the-books investigation into Callahan somehow made it back to the wrong person at the CIA, which put me personally at risk two nights ago."

"And you think that wrong person is Bradley?"

"Yes, for many reasons. But I don't understand the connection to Senator Harris."

"They were college roommates."

Lloyd's eyes narrowed. "How the hell do you know that?"

Natalie was starting to put it together in her mind. "After finding out the lawyer was Senator Harris's nephew, I was up all night researching *everything* I could possibly find about Harris. I now remember reading a profile piece from a publication called *Bostonia*—BU's alumni magazine—where it specifically mentioned Senator Harris and Dan Bradley, onetime college roommates who were now both working high in the government."

Lloyd considered that for a moment. "Okay, but that still doesn't explain *how* or *why* Harris would be involved in Black Heron."

Natalie stood, paced slowly around the motel room, processing all the information flashing through her mind. Then a moment of clarity struck her, and she turned sharply back to Lloyd. "Unless Senator Harris *is* the mole."

"Harris?"

"You said yourself that Bradley *had* to be working with a bigger player."

"I did, but . . ."

"Think about it. We know that Harris sits on the Senate Intelligence Committee. The man has direct access to highly classified intelligence info that could be very valuable if put into the wrong hands. Harris also has motive. He's currently in a tight battle to keep his Senate seat in next year's election. His opponent is a rich real estate mogul who's already poured tens of millions of dollars of his own money into his campaign to beat the sitting senator. Harris can't compete on his own—his net worth is under two million—*unless* he somehow gets resources from the outside. Harris is also in a position to help Bradley advance more quickly up the CIA ranks. Perhaps two college buddies worked up this whole scheme over a couple of beers."

Lloyd was processing. "Damn. So instead of hunting the mole, Bradley has actually been protecting him."

Natalie jumped in again. "But *something* happened in Moscow two nights ago that threatened to jeopardize everything. So Harris and Bradley panicked and began trying to tie off every possible loose end to prevent from being exposed."

Lloyd and Epps shared a wide-eyed glance. For a moment, all three of them stood there in silence, as if the heavy weight of the truth had finally rested on them.

"What do you think?" Lloyd asked Epps.

"I think Natalie is right, Chief," Epps admitted. "All the threads are right there."

"Which means we need to move quickly. Call Krieger and have him start pulling everything he can on Senator Harris. His financials, his travel records, his phone records—all of it. Do the same with Nathan Barnes, and go get that lowlife Lenny Gregor off the streets."

"What about Bradley?"

Lloyd considered it a moment. "Put a team on him, but be careful. I don't want to spook him and send him running. We already know he's a dangerous man. Not until we talk to Stone."

"I'm on it."

Epps marched out the motel room door, phone already to his ear.

Lloyd turned his attention back to her. "Under the circumstances, Natalie, you've done some incredible investigative work."

"We'll see. I hope I'm right. I just want this to be over. That's the only chance I think I have to get Sam home—*if* he's even still alive."

"If there's one thing I've learned about Callahan, he's a hard man to take down. I think he'll make it home. And I'll do everything in my power to help make that happen."

"Thank you. What's next for me?"

"You're coming with me right now to meet with Stone."

Natalie nodded. The last time she'd stood face-to-face with Director Stone was when she'd just hammered out a story last fall exposing the dark conspiracy between congressional candidate Lucas McCallister and Victor Larsen, the powerful and sinister CEO of Redrock Security. Watching Lloyd pull everything from the bed and stuff it into a brown satchel, she noticed an eight-by-ten photograph fall out of a manila folder. She picked it up, examined it. It was a surveillance image of

Sam standing beside a park bench next to a familiar-looking older man with a gray beard.

"I know this man," Natalie stated, eyes stuck on the photo.

Lloyd looked over. "Marcus Pelini. CIA."

"Why do you have a picture of Sam standing with *him*?"

"Pelini is the one who recruited Sam to Black Heron in the first place. He ran point on the whole operation."

Natalie felt shocked by this news. She immediately flashed back to sitting in a hotel suite last November with Marcus Pelini, Lisa McCallister, and Sam, where they'd finally discovered that Pelini was the manipulative man who'd played puppet master with Sam's life and had sent him on the run from deadly assassins. Staring at the photo, she couldn't make any sense of this new revelation. In the aftermath of Redrock, they'd both agreed they hoped never to see the gray-bearded man again.

And yet Sam secretly had agreed to join him for Black Heron?

"Why would he do it?" Natalie asked, almost to herself.

"Do what?" Lloyd asked.

"Why would Sam join Marcus Pelini?"

Lloyd stopped what he was doing. "You really don't know, do you?"

"Know what?"

"Marcus Pelini is Sam's father."

FIFTY-FIVE

Alger Gerlach exited a cab near Kensington Palace, stepped out into a gray London day with steady rain. Pulling the collar up on his jacket, he quickly paid the driver, grabbed his bag, and trotted up the front steps of the Royal Garden Hotel. Shaking off the wet, he did a swift scan of the lobby, as he usually did upon entering any place where he'd be staying the night. He felt extra cautious today. The last time he was in London, he'd been forced to execute two MI5 agents. Studying the faces around him, he found no one that gave him any reason to be overly alarmed.

Walking up to the front check-in counter, he offered the woman behind the desk one of his many aliases. She typed into her computer, smiled.

"Welcome to the Royal Garden, Mr. Munchin."

"Thank you."

She set a card key on the counter. "Do you need help with your bags?"

He gave her a quick smile. "I'm fine."

"We have a package waiting here for you."

Gerlach tilted his head. He wasn't expecting a package. That made him a bit uneasy. The clerk turned, searched a console behind her, then returned with a thin manila folder with the name Jonas Munchin written in black marker on the front.

"Enjoy your stay with us," the clerk said.

Once inside his hotel room, Gerlach dropped his bag on the carpet and tore open the manila envelope. Inside, he found half a dozen surveillance photos of a gray-bearded man in a black trench coat walking out the front doors of the Milestone Hotel. Gerlach immediately recognized the man—Marcus Pelini—the *reason* he was in London in the first place. His client must have already done some legwork. That could make the job very easy for him today.

Setting his bag on the bed, he quickly found the silver case with his gun inside. He pulled the gun out of the foam and screwed on the suppressor. Removing his jacket, he slid his arms into his chest holster, placed the gun in its pocket, and put the jacket back on.

Gerlach stared at himself in the mirror over the dresser and felt a jolt of adrenaline push through him. Marcus Pelini. For as long as Gerlach could remember, Pelini had been a powerful force in their shadow world. A man who inspired fear in even the best contract operatives. Many of the top assassins on the planet had ultimately met their demise over the years at the hands of the legendary CIA agent.

It would be a great thrill to take him out today.

Gerlach smiled, headed for the door. There was no time to waste.

The Gray Wolf was about to prey on the Lion.

FIFTY-SIX

Sam ditched the stolen Civic and huddled with Tommy at a small table near the front window of a coffeehouse a few blocks from the Milestone Hotel—the *only* lead they currently had on Marcus Pelini. They'd made the drive from Le Tréport to London with no hiccups—which was nice, for once. But Sam still had no idea how he was supposed to find his father. Lucinda was probably right. Pelini couldn't be found unless he wanted to be found. Still, Tommy was doing his best to assist, including hacking a full list of people currently booked at the Milestone. Sam was skimming through every name on that long list and feeling more hopeless with each passing minute.

"Anything?" Tommy asked him.

"Nothing," Sam said, staring at the laptop screen. "None of these names mean *anything* to me. He could be any of these people—or none of them."

Turning the laptop back over to Tommy, Sam stared out the window and watched the rain continue to fall over London. It had been a steady drizzle ever since they'd arrived this afternoon that soaked the sidewalks and streets, and seemed to put a cold damper on everyone who stepped into the coffeehouse with them.

"What about the CIA boards?" Sam asked.

Tommy shook his head. "Nothing. There's been no chatter about him *anywhere*."

"You check Lucinda's private account again?"

"Yeah, dude. For the tenth time already."

"And you still can't trace his only message to her back to an IP address around here somewhere, like you did with Lucinda?"

"I tried, believe me. Nothing but dead ends."

Sam grunted in frustration. "Maybe I should just go hang out in the lobby of the damn hotel. See if he happens to step out of an elevator or walk in from the outside. Because I'm never going to find him by sitting in this coffee shop all afternoon."

"Be patient, man."

"I'm out of patience, Tommy."

"I hear you."

"Even if I get lucky—which is a long shot—what would I even say to the man?"

"What do you mean?"

"He's never shot straight with me. It's been nothing but smoke and mirrors with my father from the first moment we met. Why should I expect anything different?"

"I don't know. But you have to try. He may be your only way out."

Sam nodded, sighed again. Tommy was right—and that sucked. Sam again thought about the boy. Could Charlie really be his brother? If he was truly Pelini's son, why the hell would he be living in Zolotov's palatial residence? The boy seemed to be full-blooded Russian and quite comfortable in his bedroom there. It didn't make sense. Sam still had so many questions for Pelini and wasn't sure if he'd ever get the truth.

He rubbed his face with both hands, feeling exhausted. He needed to sleep for a week. He tried not to think about what Natalie was doing right now, and what had to be an escalating amount of worry building up in her at his complete disappearance. Every few hours, he fought the temptation to ring her up on his burner phone. He longed to hear her voice. And yet he knew he couldn't do that. He was desperate to finish this and get back to her. To beg her forgiveness and to start all over—again. But that might never happen if finding Pelini was his *only* chance.

"Damn," Tommy suddenly muttered, eyes popping wide-open while staring at his laptop.

"What?" Sam asked.

"It's him."

"Who?"

"Pelini. He just sent me an email clearly meant for you."

Tommy turned his laptop to face him. Sam leaned in for a closer look. In the center of the laptop screen was an email with a message that damn near took his breath away.

His father *wanted* to be found.

> Sam,
>
> Science Museum. Ground floor. Making the Modern World. Thirty minutes.
>
> —Marcus

FIFTY-SEVEN

Sam hustled the eight blocks from the coffeehouse over to the Science Museum, his shoes splashing rainwater the entire way. In the brief time they had, Tommy did his best to try to trace the message in reverse—and somehow verify it actually came from Pelini—but he hit nothing but dead ends. Whoever sent the message knew how to cover his tracks, even from someone as brilliant as Tommy. There was no way for Sam to know for sure it was Pelini unless he simply showed up. He could only hope it wasn't all a trap sent to draw him out, with a deadly assassin waiting to greet him at the other end.

He was certainly willing to take that risk.

One way or another, this had to end.

The Science Museum was a massive old building with an impressive row of columns at the front. Sam paused half a block away, surveyed the landscape directly in front of the building, searching for anything or anyone suspicious—or maybe even an early sign of the gray-bearded man. The rain was coming down harder now, making it difficult to see the many faces hidden behind umbrellas, hats, and coats with collars flipped up. He checked the time, moved his position to the opposite end of the block, hung out there for a few minutes. He still spotted nothing that alerted him to any danger.

Finally, Sam stepped out from beneath a building overhang, hustled over to the front glass doors of the museum, then entered with a small group of other visitors. Inside the spacious lobby, Sam left his jacket hood up over his head, even though most other tourists were busy removing caps and coats and shaking off the rain. The museum was bustling with activity. He followed a vast hallway to the left, slowly navigating through crowds of people, eyes keenly taking in every face within his vicinity. He grabbed a map from a guest counter, noted that the Making the Modern World section was at the opposite end of the ground floor.

Moving deeper into the museum, he stepped into a wide-open corridor. He felt completely exposed—there were hundreds of people everywhere. He walked through a section called Energy Hall with a true-to-life display of an old steam engine. Sam spotted the back of a man with a black trench coat ahead of him who looked like he could be Pelini. He briskly darted through a group of people, noticed the man stop near the entrance to Exploring Space. Cautiously stepping around for a better look, Sam exhaled in disappointment. It was not Pelini. Just another man with a beard.

Checking the time on his phone, Sam noted he still had eight minutes left from the time stamp when he'd first received the message. Did Pelini know they were in the coffee shop? Had he been watching them the whole time? He moved into Exploring Space, found an even larger crowd awaiting him, all of them finding fascination in the old rockets and satellite displays. Sam kept moving, passing through the space section, until he finally found himself at the entrance of Making the Modern World.

Pausing there, he took another deep breath, actually said a prayer.

He checked the phone again—three minutes. His heart began to race.

Stepping into the spacious hall, Sam found displays for old locomotives, planes, cars, computers—everything a person could think of that had modernized the world over the past hundred years. It was also the most packed section of the museum. Standing in the center, Sam wondered how the hell he was going to find Pelini in this mass of people. Or had Pelini already found him? Was he watching Sam right now?

Sam kept moving. He couldn't just stand there. He maneuvered in and around the hundreds of different displays, paying them little attention while closely studying every single person who crossed in front of him. He did this for nearly ten minutes without ever spotting the gray-bearded man. That's when he started to get worried.

Was this a trap? Did an assassin already have him locked down and was now just waiting for him to leave the museum so he could take Sam out? That same thing had happened to Mack back in Milan.

Ten more minutes of anxious walking around. Feeling desperate, Sam considered going back to the front of the building. Then he spotted Pelini standing across the hall from him at about a hundred feet. Sam froze, locked eyes. The gray-bearded man was staring right at him, wearing a black trench coat with his hands stuffed in the pockets.

Sam wasn't sure what to do next. Should he walk over there? Would Pelini approach him? Why was the man just standing there without doing something?

Sam took a step toward him. When he did, Pelini turned, began briskly walking away. *What the hell?* He followed, not willing to let the gray-bearded man out of his sight for even a second. Was he trying to lose Sam? This didn't make any sense. He's the one who wanted to meet. But Pelini was clearly trying to get away.

The man swiftly threaded through different groups of people, exited the hall for Making the Modern World, then entered an equally busy section of the museum called Welcome Wing. Sam could barely keep up with him. He wanted to take off at a dead sprint but knew that would only draw unwanted attention to himself.

Hustling into Welcome Wing, Sam peered all around. Where the hell was Pelini? He then spotted him circling behind a crowded diner in the corner and headed straight for a rear museum exit. Sam cursed. This time he did start running. Ahead of him, Pelini pushed through the exit doors, where Sam momentarily lost sight, sending a cold panic through him. He had not come this far only to miss his chance to talk to the man.

Spilling out onto the sidewalk, Sam jerked his head left and right. The rain came down in droves, making it difficult to see. *There!* He spotted Pelini rushing across a busy street, dodging car traffic, and trotting up the opposite sidewalk. Sam hustled forward into the same street as Pelini ducked into an alley between two apartment buildings. Sam was nearly crushed by a bus, jumped out of the way, then stumbled into the same alley as Pelini. Fifty feet up ahead, he spotted the back of the man.

"Marcus! Wait!" Sam yelled, feeling desperate.

His father never slowed; instead, the man darted right, following a path into yet another alley. Sam sprinted forward, splashing water up onto the legs of his jeans, his heart in his throat. He reached the next alley just in time to watch Pelini enter through a back door into what looked like an old warehouse building. Sam didn't understand any of this. Why was the man running away from him?

Reaching the same back door within seconds, he pulled it open, stepped into a damp and dark warehouse room with tall shelves stuffed full of wooden crates. It was eerily quiet inside. Standing there, he peered in both directions but couldn't find Pelini anywhere. Where the hell had the man gone? Hearing a noise over to his left, he hustled in that direction, his wet shoes squeaking on the concrete floor.

Sam spun around a row of shelves, nearly lost his footing. Squinting down the long row, he thought he saw a shadow of movement up ahead. Taking slow steps forward, Sam listened closely. He wiped moisture from his face, a mix of rain and sweat. He could feel his heartbeat thumping in his chest. He slowed, tried to calm down his breathing so he could better hear any movement around him. Nothing. Had the man managed to vanish on him?

"Marcus!" he yelled at the top of his lungs, his voice echoing through the rafters.

Just then, Alger Gerlach stepped out of the shadows ten feet in front of him, a gun raised in his right hand, pointed directly at his head. Sam was stunned. He was standing face-to-face with an assassin he'd somehow managed to evade on multiple occasions. But his luck had finally run out. Sam had nowhere to run. Not even his own unique mental gifts could get him out of this.

To make things worse, his own father had clearly led him to this slaughter. His father had lured him into this warehouse so that the Gray Wolf could end his life. The wicked smile forming on Gerlach's face told Sam the assassin was going to enjoy this moment.

Two shots suddenly rang out from directly behind Sam, both hitting the assassin in the chest, causing the man to stagger backward. Sam spun around, spotted Pelini, who used his arm to shove Sam out of the way while he continued to charge forward. More shots rang out. Gerlach dropped to his knees, his gun hanging limply in his hand. Pelini put two more muffled bullets straight into the guy, who finally collapsed altogether. Pelini stood over him for a long moment to make sure he was dead.

Walking up behind Pelini, Sam stared down at the man, Alger Gerlach—the Gray Wolf. Sam had been wrong. His father hadn't lured him out of the museum to harm him—he did it to protect him. He must have known Gerlach was nearby.

Pelini finally looked Sam in the eyes. "You okay, son?"

Sam nodded. Standing there, he didn't even know what to say. After everything he'd been through the past two days, it felt surreal to finally be face-to-face with his father again. Sam swallowed, tried to find the words.

Then he watched Pelini suddenly groan, clutch his chest, drop to a knee. That's when Sam realized his father had also been shot in the exchange of gunfire with Gerlach.

FIFTY-EIGHT

Pelini pushed himself up against a metal shelf, sat there on the concrete floor, breathing heavily, both hands pressed up firmly to his chest. Sam noticed the blood now seeping through his father's shirt and covering his hands. He wasn't sure what to do. He didn't have time to process any of his complex feelings at the moment. His father was bleeding to death right in front of him.

Kneeling next to him, Sam said, "We need to get you to a hospital."

Pelini shook his head. "No."

"What are you talking about? You've been shot. You'll die if we don't get moving."

"There's no time for the hospital," his father insisted. "You have to go get the boy and take him to the safe house."

"Charlie?"

"Yes. He's in my hotel room."

Pelini didn't expound or seem surprised that Sam knew about Charlie. Sam could only presume that his father had somehow renewed contact with Lucinda over the past few hours, and she'd filled him in on Sam's encounter with her in Le Tréport. It would also explain how Pelini knew to make contact with Sam through Tommy.

"What safe house?" Sam asked.

"Outside the city," Pelini said, coughing up blood. "They're waiting for me. You have to take Charlie there."

"Who's waiting for you?"

"People you can trust, Sam. I promise."

Pelini recited an address. Sam committed it to memory.

"Is he really . . . my brother?" Sam asked, still finding the question surreal.

Pelini nodded. "Yes."

"I don't understand . . . how?"

Pelini coughed several more times. "The boy's mother was one of my best assets in Moscow because she was a mistress to Vladimir Zolotov. Natalia regularly gave us valuable intel and risked *a lot* to get it. We began a courtship several years back that lasted longer than it ever should have, considering the circumstances. She got pregnant."

"So Zolotov thinks the boy is his?"

"Yes."

"Where's Charlie's mother?"

"Zolotov had her killed two months ago. The mole we've been hunting leaked information to him that she was a CIA asset. I knew I had to get the boy out of harm's way. If Zolotov ever got suspicious and discovered the truth about Charlie, there's no telling what that monster might do with him."

"So Black Heron was all a ruse created by you to get the boy?"

Pelini shook his head. "No, the operation was real. The list exists. I only planned to get the boy in addition to everything else. None of this was supposed to happen. I underestimated the level of betrayal I was really facing."

"So then, where the hell is the list?"

Reaching into his coat pocket with his bloody right hand, Pelini pulled out a small flash drive, held it up for Sam to see.

Sam cursed. "You did steal it out from under us?"

"Nonsense. The list was stolen from our safe house when they ambushed the team. I've spent the past two days hunting it back down, which is why I'm here in London instead of with Lucinda right now. I couldn't let them get away with it. Someone has to pay for the deaths of my friends."

"And you know who that *someone* is?" Sam asked.

"I do now." He nodded at the flash drive. "It's all on here. You have to get this to Director Barton. Take it with you to the CIA safe house. Protect it at all costs, Sam, or many more people will surely die."

He held it out in his bloody palm. Sam reached over, took it.

Pelini wiped his mouth with blood-soaked fingers. "I want to thank you for what you did for Lucinda. She's still alive only because of you. That means something to me, son."

"I only did what I had to do to survive."

"That's not true. You have something deeper inside that drives you. Something that makes you a better man than me. Don't ever lose it."

Sam was finding this all a bit overwhelming. Why did it take a bullet to the chest for his father to be finally willing to have a real conversation with him? Realizing he was working with limited time, Sam asked Pelini the question that had torn him up inside from the moment Lucinda had told him he had a brother.

"Why did you go to all this trouble to get the boy?" he asked, swallowing.

There was clearly a second unspoken question, but he couldn't get himself to say it. Why would Pelini go get *this* son when he'd never made any effort to rescue his *first* son? Even with his father lying there dying, Sam felt a renewed surge of anger push up his spine that made him grit his teeth.

Pelini seemed to sense it, reached over, put his hand on top of Sam's hand. "I'm truly sorry, Sam. For everything. More than you'll ever know. I knew I couldn't make the same mistake I made with you. I was absent once, and it caused a tremendous amount of pain and suffering. I wasn't going to let that happen to Charlie."

Sam felt his chest tighten, his eyes growing wet. He fought with everything he had to hold back his shaky emotions. "It's not too late," he pleaded with his father. "We can still get you to a hospital. You can still make it through this."

"No!" Pelini shook his head. "I won't risk the lives of both of my sons to try to save my own. I've made my bed. I refuse to let either of you die in it with me."

This time tears did start falling down Sam's cheeks.

"You have to get moving now," Pelini urged him. He pulled out a card key. "This is to my hotel room. Get Charlie to the safe house. Take care of your brother."

Sam took the key, nodded.

He wanted to argue with his father, to beg him not to die right then and there. But he knew it was pointless—this was the end. Another explosive coughing fit. This time it continued for several seconds, until his father spit a load of blood out on his chest. Then his face went completely pale, and he stopped breathing.

His father was dead.

FIFTY-NINE

Sam raced down the streets of London in the pouring rain.

He possessed a flash drive in his pocket that supposedly contained the CIA asset list *and* identified the traitors who were behind the intelligence leaks that had left a long wake of dead people—including his father—and had put Sam on the run for the past two days. Buried in his other pocket was a hotel key that opened the door to the only family he still had left.

The small hotel was about a mile away. Even running through the rain, Sam covered the distance in less than seven minutes. Soaking wet, he hustled up the front steps of the hotel and dipped into a small lobby. A clerk behind the front desk turned to stare at him. Sam didn't even bother to slow down. Hustling through the lobby, he was inside an elevator carriage five seconds later, ascending to the third floor, his heart in his throat. What would he say to Charlie? Would he tell him he was his brother?

Down the third-floor hallway, Sam found the door to Pelini's room. He paused a moment to catch his breath and tried to wipe the moisture from his face. He noticed he still had some of his father's blood on his hands, so he used his shirtsleeves to wipe away as much as possible. Ear to the door, he listened, thought he could hear a kids' cartoon playing loudly on a TV inside the room.

One more deep breath. Then Sam stuck the card key in the slot, opened the door. It was more than a simple hotel room. Pelini had booked a suite with two separate bedrooms and a full-size living space. That's where Sam found Charlie, sitting cross-legged on the carpet only four feet away from a large flat-screen TV inside a cabinet. The boy was wearing a blue T-shirt, jeans, red athletic shoes. Charlie was so glued to the TV that he didn't even notice Sam had walked into the room.

Sam approached the boy cautiously so he wouldn't alarm him.

Within five feet, he knelt, grabbed the boy's attention. "Hey, Charlie."

Charlie finally turned, stared at Sam, his forehead wrinkling. In that moment, Sam felt it was as clear as day, as if he were staring directly at a younger photo of himself. The boy looked exactly like him. There was no question they were brothers.

"Leo?" the boy asked, surprised.

Sam smiled. The boy was sharp. Even though he had been half-asleep the other night, Charlie remembered his brief encounter with Sam and the fake name he'd used while pretending to be a security guard.

"You can call me Sam now," he told the boy in English. "What're you watching?"

"Batman," Charlie replied, eyes back on the TV.

"Cool. I love Batman."

He sat with the boy for a few minutes, just trying to allow Charlie to get comfortable with his presence. It didn't seem to be a problem. Charlie was lost in the cartoon and immediately began telling him all about what was happening in the TV episode—the good guys, the bad guys, and how Batman was going to save the day. He said he'd seen this cartoon a thousand times already. While cloaked with a Russian accent, Charlie's English was nearly perfect. Sam complimented him on it. The boy smiled shyly, again mentioned that he had a private English tutor, as well as tutors for Chinese, French, and Arabic. Sam wasn't surprised, since he'd been living in such affluence. Charlie said English was his favorite because all the best superheroes were from America.

With Charlie continuing to watch the cartoon, Sam got up, walked into the first bedroom. There was a small bag on the floor filled with brand-new boys' clothes. Shirts, pants, shoes, jacket—the works. Pelini had gone shopping for him. The bed was disheveled on one side where Charlie must have slept. Zipping up the bag, Sam grabbed it and moved into the second bedroom, where he found another unmade bed and a small leather bag filled with Pelini's clothes. He searched inside the bag to see if there were any items worth taking with him—cash and so forth—but found nothing. Pelini was obviously traveling light. Sam had no idea how Pelini had managed to hunt down info on the intelligence mole and recapture the CIA asset list while having a five-year-old boy at his side. It was an impressive feat, even for someone like the gray-bearded man.

Returning to the living room, Sam again knelt in front of the boy.

"We have to go now, Charlie," Sam said to him.

Charlie turned, wrinkles in his forehead. "Go where?"

Sam gave him a reassuring grin. "On a big adventure."

"Really?" Charlie smiled wide. "What kind of adventure?"

"Well, we have to avoid the bad guys and make it back to the Batcave."

"But what about Uncle Marcus? He said he was getting doughnuts."

Sam pressed his lips together, swallowed hard. Pelini had clearly not told the boy he was his real father yet. The boy should probably never know that information—or at least not for a very long time. Eventually, Charlie needed to know *everything*. Sam knew firsthand how damaging it was never to know who you really are in life.

"Uncle Marcus asked me to take you on this adventure."

"Oh, okay. Will I be going home soon?"

Sam swallowed. "Yes, but the adventure first, okay?"

"Okay!" Charlie jumped up, ready to go.

Sam smiled, put his hand on the boy's head, tousled his hair. A brother. It felt like a dream, not real. And yet, standing there, Sam knew he'd do just about *anything* right now to protect Charlie. The boy deserved a chance at a normal life—a chance that Sam had never been given.

After helping Charlie get his jacket on, they headed for the door. Sam let the boy punch all the right buttons on the elevator down. Once in the lobby, Sam asked the front-desk clerk if he could call them a taxi. They waited for a few minutes on a sofa in the corner of the lobby—mostly talking about superheroes—until the clerk alerted them that a taxi had arrived for them.

Stepping outside, Sam noted the rain was still coming down hard. A hotel valet held a big umbrella for them while the taxi driver opened the car door. Sam and Charlie climbed into the back of the taxi together. Sam was now eager to get to the CIA safe house and turn over whatever Pelini had placed on the flash drive.

He was ready for this to be over.

He was ready to get back home to Natalie.

Unfortunately, someone else was not yet ready.

Glancing a hundred feet down the sidewalk, Sam felt sideswiped by a surge of panic.

The man was swiftly closing the gap, eyes already locked in on Sam.

The Russian assassin.

SIXTY

Sam felt trapped. If he was by himself, he might have been able to dart straight back out of the taxi and get away. But he had the boy. That changed everything. He tried to quickly sort out his next move. They couldn't just sit there in the back of the car. The Russian would be on them in seconds. Sam noticed the assassin reach inside his jacket. It was now or never. He had to do *something*, or he was dead.

And possibly Charlie, too, if the boy was returned to Zolotov.

Slipping between the front and back seats, Sam jumped into the driver's seat, shoved the gear into drive, and punched the gas pedal to the floor with his foot. The car bolted forward. The taxi driver, who had just circled the back of his vehicle, tried to grab his door handle in a mad scramble, but it was too late—Sam already had the car away from the curb and speeding down the street.

"What's happening?" yelled Charlie in Russian, alarmed.

Directly in front of them, the Russian assassin stepped off the curb into the wet street, boldly pointed his gun at Sam through the windshield.

"Get down, Charlie!" Sam yelled, reaching around with one hand, grabbing the boy's jacket collar, yanking him to the floor.

Four consecutive gunshot punches hit the windshield. With only one hand on the steering wheel, Sam swerved, barely able to keep the taxi from spinning out of control on the rain-soaked street. He regained control of the wheel and sped straight toward the assassin, who dived out of the way but wasn't finished yet. As the taxi raced past him, he raised his fist again, fired his weapon. Sam continued to hold Charlie down with one hand as the back window completely shattered, sending glass everywhere. This time the taxi did spin wildly, the tires slipping on the wet pavement, sending the car sliding straight into a sedan that was parked on the opposite side of the street. The taxi collided with the vehicle, side to side, as metal crushed and more glass shattered.

"You okay?" Sam asked, peering down at Charlie in the back seat.

"I'm scared."

"Don't be scared, Charlie," Sam assured the boy, with a forced smile. "This is all part of your adventure. It's just fun and games."

"Really?"

"Sure! But the only way for us to get you to the Batcave safely is for you to stay on the floor, okay?"

Charlie nodded but still looked terrified.

Sam noticed the Russian sprinting after them down the center of the wet street. He turned the key in the ignition. The taxi sputtered but didn't start. *Come on!* The assassin was quickly gaining ground. A desperate prayer, another turn of the wrist—the taxi engine finally roared back to life. Both hands now on the steering wheel, Sam punched the gas pedal down again. As the tires spun, the car scraped away from the crushed sedan. Checking his rearview mirror, Sam saw the Russian stop running, take dead aim.

Sam whipped the steering wheel right, kept the gas pedal to the floor as the taxi skidded across slippery lanes. This time, he didn't lose control.

Seconds later, he'd lost the assassin behind a block of buildings.

SIXTY-ONE

The taxi eased up a long hill about twenty miles outside of London and finally pulled to a stop fifty yards from an isolated bungalow. In the back seat, Sam wrapped his arm around Charlie, who couldn't stop talking about his wild *adventure* back in the city. With Sam's continued reassurance, the boy believed the whole experience with the Russian assassin outside the hotel had been created just for him—which was fine with Sam. He didn't want Charlie to be further traumatized. The boy had been through too much already. The sudden death of his mother. What had to have been a frightening abduction from his own bedroom, where a man who'd called himself Uncle Marcus had somehow escaped Russia with him overnight.

And now Charlie sat next to yet another stranger in Sam. Although he didn't want to be a stranger for long. So far, the boy seemed to be handling it all like a champ. But Sam didn't know what was truly going on in the recesses of the boy's mind and heart. Sam still felt haunted by traumatic events that had happened to him when he was the same age as Charlie. If these kinds of events were addressed poorly—or never addressed at all—Sam knew they could scar for a lifetime. Sam knew the right man to walk Charlie through all of this in a healthy way, if given the chance, but he wasn't sure at this point what was next for either one of them. They'd soon find out.

Tommy sat on the other side of the boy. Once they'd escaped, Sam had immediately ditched the stolen beat-up taxi. Not only was the car barely drivable but it had surely been reported stolen to the police. They needed new travel arrangements. Taking Charlie by the hand, they'd hustled four blocks over, hailed a different taxi, then snatched up Tommy on their way out of the city.

The rain had stopped, leaving the lush hillside glistening under a sun that was finally peeking out. They all got out of the taxi. Sam peered over toward the bungalow, noticed two identical black Ford Explorers parked out front. The address matched what Pelini had given him—the CIA safe house. They'd made it. But he had no idea what awaited them on the inside. Pelini only told him to get to the safe house with the boy and turn over the flash drive. Everything else was still up in the air.

Sam encouraged Charlie to go play near a pile of rocks next to the gravel road. He happily obliged and began picking up rocks and tossing them as far as he could. Sam turned to Tommy. It was time to part ways with his good friend. Tommy insisted he had no desire whatsoever to get involved with the CIA. He'd helped keep Sam alive—again. His job was now done. Time to go.

Sam put a warm hand on Tommy's shoulder. "I don't know what to say to you that I haven't already said ten times over during the past year."

"So save it," Tommy replied, grinning. "Don't get all mushy right now, okay?"

Sam smiled. "Okay. Where will you go?"

Tommy stared out over the English countryside. "Not sure yet. Thinking maybe the coast of Italy. Almost went there instead of Salzburg. There's a place on the coast called Manarola—they say it's the most colorful town in the world."

"Send me a postcard, okay?"

Tommy laughed. "I don't know, Duke. The last postcard I sent you ended up getting me into big trouble."

"I'm done with all of that now."

"Yeah, sure."

They shared a brief hug. Moments later, the taxi turned around with Tommy inside and headed back down the hill. Sam walked over, corralled Charlie. Then the two of them covered the remaining fifty yards up to the bungalow. Before knocking, Sam took a deep breath, unsure how everything would play out from here. But this time he trusted that Pelini had steered him in the right direction. He knocked twice, waited. Seconds later, a buff guy with a buzz cut wearing a black polo and jeans answered the door. Sam noted two more men playing cards at a table in the background.

"Who are you?" the buff guy asked, clearly not expecting to find Sam or the boy standing outside the door.

"Marcus Pelini sent me."

The guy's eyes narrowed, then he cursed. "You're Callahan, aren't you?"

Sam nodded. "Please watch your mouth around the boy."

He was already playing the role of brotherly protector.

"Sorry. But we've been looking *everywhere* for you."

"Here I am."

"Where's Marcus?"

Sam glanced down at Charlie, who was busy kicking dirt around with the toe of his sneaker and barely paying attention.

Quietly, Sam said, "He's dead."

The buff guy seemed stunned at this news, as if Sam had just told him their tribe's great warrior had met his demise.

Sam pulled the flash drive out of his pocket. "He told me to get this to Barton ASAP."

"Come inside," the guy said, quickly ushering them into the bungalow.

He introduced himself as Agent Berg but told Sam to call him Manuel. Then he introduced the other two agents. Manuel said all three of them had been waiting several hours for Pelini to arrive. They all seemed shocked at the news that the man they referred to as the Lion was dead. Sam was having a hard time believing it himself.

The agent who called himself Shane took the flash drive from Sam. He immediately started uploading the contents onto a high-powered laptop where he said Director Barton could have instant access to whatever Pelini had promised him was there. Sam told Shane he didn't know what was on the flash drive and didn't want to know, either.

While Charlie played with a set of Jenga blocks on the floor in the next room, Manuel formally interviewed Sam about everything he'd been through over the past two days.

"Damn, Sam," Manuel said. "Hell of a job surviving out there."

"Well, the Russian is still on the hunt," Sam mentioned.

"You guys are safe here," Manuel reassured him. "This place is a fortress."

Sam exhaled, felt a newfound wave of exhaustion. Was it really over?

"What's next?" he asked Manuel.

"Barton is already on his way. So we sit tight."

SIXTY-TWO

Two hours later, Manuel and the two other agents closed down the safe house and ushered Sam and Charlie into the back of one of the black Explorers. Manuel drove their vehicle and followed the other SUV down the long hill. Shane had given Charlie a tablet to play on and even downloaded several apps that were suitable for a five-year-old boy. Not surprisingly, Charlie's favorite was a superhero game. The boy seemed delighted with his new toy and at ease sitting with Sam.

Watching the boy carefully, Sam noticed they shared several of the same physical mannerisms. They both fiddled with the back of their hair when concentrating. They both squinted and grunted slightly when they became frustrated about something—Charlie while playing the game on the tablet. Sam had lost so much this past year—first his mother, then his father—so it felt strangely comforting to have gained something as significant as a brother.

Staring out the window, he thought of Natalie. He was so desperate to call her, to begin to pour his whole heart out to her, but Manuel wouldn't allow it without Sam having first spoken with Barton. Sam's situation involved high-stakes geopolitical matters, so there was a proper protocol they all needed to follow right now. Manuel insisted it wouldn't be much longer.

Twenty minutes into the drive, Manuel pulled the Explorer through an open gate and down a long road that Sam realized was a private airstrip out in the middle of nowhere. They followed the airstrip all the way to the end, where he spotted a hangar that was probably big enough to store two private planes. Both SUVs entered the hangar and parked over to the side.

Getting out, Manuel opened the back door. "Barton will be here any minute."

Sam stepped out of the vehicle but let Charlie stay in the back seat, playing on the tablet. Within seconds, he noticed a plane descending out of the late-afternoon sky. It touched ground at the end of the airstrip, where it throttled to an easy speed and eventually came to a rolling stop right outside of the hangar. Manuel hustled over to the plane. The door popped open, and the stairs descended. Two men in dark suits exited first, met Manuel at the bottom.

Then Sam watched as Director Barton stepped out of the plane and joined them on the ground. It felt surreal that he was about to sit down with the director of the CIA. Wearing a tan jacket over blue jeans and what looked like work boots, the powerful man was tall and lean, with a thick head of dark hair. Several decades ago, Barton had starred as a basketball player at Kansas. He even spent a few short years bouncing around the NBA as a journeyman before eventually going into law enforcement.

Sam shifted awkwardly as Barton placed eyes on him. Then the director charged right over and stuck out his hand.

"Good to finally meet you, Sam," Barton said.

Sam shook his hand. "Director."

"Call me Cliff." Barton's eyes went over to a door that looked like it might lead to a small room. "Let's go over here and talk. Agent Berg will watch the boy."

Before following Barton, Sam made sure he told Charlie he'd be nearby if the boy needed anything. The room had a sofa and two brown leather chairs, along with a circular table in the corner surrounded by four chairs.

"Please have a seat." Barton offered a hand toward the sofa.

Sam sat, and Barton joined him in one of the leather chairs.

"First off," Barton began, "I want to offer you my sincerest condolences on the loss of your father. We hated to get this news."

Sam shrugged it off. "I hardly knew the man."

He had no real desire to share a heartfelt moment with Barton. After all, according to Pelini, Barton was the same man who had contracted Gerlach to put Sam through the *ultimate* test last month. Even though he was glad to be sitting there, Sam didn't exactly have a lot of warm and fuzzies about Barton.

Barton continued. "You never got the chance to know him, and for that, I'm very sorry. As complicated as your relationship might have been, Sam, you should know that your father was one of the most distinguished agents of my generation. No one was more respected than Marcus Pelini. His work over the years literally saved thousands of American lives. We've already recovered his body, thanks to you, and we'll make sure he's honored with a proper memorial. Marcus will be greatly missed by all of us who knew him and had the pleasure of working with him."

Sam was having a hard time envisioning his father as some kind of hero. The man had caused him an insufferable measure of pain. "He also jeopardized our entire operation in Moscow for his own agenda," Sam mentioned.

"True. And we'll get to that. But you've gained a brother."

Sam tilted his head. He had not told Manuel that Charlie was his brother. He'd just said the boy was fallout from an operation that went badly.

"I know *everything*, Sam," Barton assured him. "Marcus detailed all of it on the flash drive he gave you. My deepest gratitude to you for delivering it. Because of that flash drive, we're working with the FBI back home to make several significant arrests at this very moment."

"So who betrayed us?"

"One of my own, I'm sorry to admit. Dan Bradley, one of my assistant deputy directors, put together an off-the-books special-ops team to take out the members of Black Heron. He tried to make it look like the work of the Russians. He might have succeeded had you not survived."

"Bradley also hired Gerlach?"

"Correct. He sent a man to find him."

"What about the Russian assassins who've been chasing me?"

"They work for Zolotov."

"They still out there?"

"Yes. But we're doing our best to remedy that."

Sam sighed. "My father really knew how to make my life miserable."

"Because of your father, we've been able to protect hundreds of valuable assets whose lives have been in serious jeopardy for the past two months."

"You also lost some really good people," Sam countered, thinking of Roger, Mack, Luis, and the others.

"True. And we mourn those losses deeply, I assure you. However, you should know that each of them knew exactly what they were walking into and signed up for it, anyway. This is the dangerous nature of the high-stakes world we work in day in and day out, where thousands of lives are always on the line."

"I guess."

Barton leaned forward on his knees, seemed sympathetic. "Look, you were worked over and manipulated by your father on this thing. I get it. That would be a tough pill for me to swallow, too. For that, I'm sorry. I allowed it to happen on my watch."

"No one twisted my arm. I knew what I was doing."

Barton leaned back again, took a moment. "You did know what you were doing. You were everything Marcus believed you were, Sam.

There was a reason he put you through so much to recruit you. You're truly a remarkable talent. Much like your father. Without you, we'd be looking at the deaths of countless people over these next few months. You saved their lives by putting your own life on the line. I hope you can take some satisfaction in that."

"Maybe someday. What happens to Charlie?"

"That's tricky," Barton admitted. "The smartest thing we can do is send him back to Russia and protect the relational dynamics we already have in place."

"You can't do that!" Sam blurted, bolting off the sofa.

The door to the room opened at his outburst. One of the suited agents peered inside, ready to pounce on Sam, but Barton told him everything was fine. He shut the door again.

"Calm down," Barton told Sam. "I didn't say that's what we're going to do."

Sam slowly sat again. "What, then? Charlie can stay with me."

"You can't keep the boy," Barton said, shaking his head. "At least not right away. If the boy is out in the open with you, it'll be a mess for us. As you well know, the Russians are all over this because of Zolotov. And, like it or not, you're at the center. At this point, it's best if the Russians believe the boy disappeared with Marcus."

"You're going to make my father disappear?"

Barton gave him a tight smile. "Your father disappeared more than a decade ago."

Sam knew what he meant by that. "So then, what will you do with Charlie? I need to be able to see him, even if he's not living with me. I know someone who I think would take Charlie into his family. A good man and a good family."

"Isaiah Washington?" Barton queried.

Sam again tilted his head. How did he know about Pastor Isaiah?

"I told you, I know everything," Barton said, filling in the gap. "I can make that happen. We can give Charlie a new identity, place him in Denver, and even offer him some discreet protection. At least until this thing settles down. But you'd have to understand that I'd be doing you a personal favor. Like I said, the smartest move for us is to send him back to Russia."

Sam studied Barton. Where was he going with this *favor* talk? When someone called something a favor, it usually meant a return favor was expected. It didn't take Barton long to reveal his cards.

"I'd like you to consider something," Barton said. "As I mentioned earlier, you have the most unique of skill sets. Mental abilities that most of us don't possess. Hell, I think I could count on one hand the men under my command who might have been able to survive everything you've been through the past month. Believe me, the list is short."

Sam cut him off. "I'm not going to be one of your covert special-ops guys, if that's what you're suggesting. No, thanks. I've already seen enough death for one lifetime. I just want to get back home and start helping normal people with real problems. It's the reason I went to law school in the first place. Screw all of this."

"It's actually that moral compass I want from you, Sam. I assure you, I already have enough highly trained special-ops agents who have no problem walking into a dark room and putting a bullet into a really bad guy. With you, I'm talking about something different. An opportunity to help innocent people all over the world."

"What innocent people?" Sam asked, although he couldn't believe he was even remotely engaging with Barton on this matter.

"Good people caught in the middle of complex geopolitical firestorms. Some held hostage and used as bargaining chips for political reasons. Many who've been swept up in hostile situations, where their governments, including ours, have been forced to publicly orphan them. Some are just kids, like Charlie. Innocent children who, by no fault of their own, find themselves being used as pawns in dangerous international games among sinister people."

Sam thought of Charlie. "What would I do?"

"Use your unique skill sets, both as a street survivor and as a lawyer, to help these people find their way out. I've created a special unit to carry out these missions. Sometimes they're able to resolve these matters diplomatically. Sometimes they have to find other ways. As a personal favor to me, I'd like you to think about joining the unit."

Sam's eyes narrowed. "If I don't, you send Charlie back to Russia?"

"Of course not. The favor is in the consideration. That's all."

Sitting there, Sam felt shocked by the proposition. Never in a million years had he expected Barton to invite him to stay on with the Agency in some capacity. He expected to be put on a plane, sent home, and told to keep his mouth shut. Which would've been just fine with him. He didn't want to talk about this stuff. But he also felt shocked by his own curiosity over such a proposal.

"How do I know this isn't another one of the CIA's tricks to pull me into something very *unlike* what you're describing?"

"You have my word. I'll get you real cases to review."

"Would I have to keep secrets?"

"From Natalie?"

Sam nodded. "I'm done lying to her."

"You don't have to lie to her. She can know what you're doing. Although you may not be able to share mission specifics, of course. Some of what you'll be seeing is the most classified intel on the planet."

"What about others? Friends? Family? Can they know what I'm doing?"

"In a roundabout way, yes. You'd simply tell them you took a State Department job working as an analyst on diplomatic matters. Not lying—just not giving full disclosure."

Sam rubbed his forehead, not sure how to process it all right now. Barton seemed to sense he was overloaded.

"Just think about it, Sam. I don't need an answer today."

"Can I call Natalie now?"

Barton grinned. "No need to call. I brought her with me."

SIXTY-THREE

Sam bolted out the door of the small room, raced over to the private plane, his heart in his throat. The stairs were still down, and one of the agents had just walked up them to enter the cabin. A moment later, Natalie appeared at the top of the stairs, causing Sam to fall to his knees on the tarmac, tears filling his eyes. She looked like a vision. Seeing Sam, she rushed down the stairs. He stood to embrace her, but she paused before letting him, her eyes narrow, her face stern. Then she slapped him hard across the cheek, stunning him.

"Don't ever lie to me again, Sam," she demanded with wet eyes.

He swallowed, rubbed his cheek, realizing in that moment that Natalie already knew a lot more than he'd imagined. "I'm so sorry, Natalie. I deserved that. I deserve a thousand slaps. I promise I will never lie to you again."

She continued to glare at him.

"Have I already lost you?" he asked.

Her face softened. "Would I be standing here if you'd lost me?"

"I just need you to say it," he begged.

She stepped forward, wrapped her arms around his neck, pulled him in for a kiss. He pulled her even closer, damn near squeezing the life out of her, the tears falling more freely now from both of them.

Sam didn't even care that several CIA agents were staring at them. He saw nothing but her.

She held his face in her hands a moment. "You could never lose me, Sam. But you've got a hell of a lot of work ahead of you to regain my full trust."

He nodded. "I'm willing to do that work."

"Good."

"How are you even standing here?" he asked her.

"Oh, Sam," she replied, sighing, "there's so much you don't know. So much that has happened back in DC while you were away."

He noticed cuts and scrapes on her face. "What happened? Tell me!"

"I will. On the plane. Let's just go home."

"I'm ready to go home. But I'm bringing someone else with me."

She tilted her head. "Who?"

"My brother."

Her mouth dropped open. Clearly, Barton had not yet shared everything with her. Probably because the director wanted the bargaining chip in his private discussion with Sam without complicating matters by telling Natalie in advance. Sam quickly explained about Charlie, leaving her further stunned.

"The boy doesn't know I'm his brother yet," Sam mentioned. "I'll address that at some point down the road. You want to meet him?"

"Of course!"

Holding Natalie by the hand, he led her over to the black Explorer, where Charlie was still in the back seat, playing on the tablet.

"Hey, Charlie, I want you to meet Natalie."

The boy looked up at her, grinned. "You're pretty."

Natalie smiled wide. "Thank you."

"I agree, Charlie," Sam added. "Hey, you want to go on that jet over there?"

"For real?" Charlie asked, wide-eyed.

"Yes, for real. How about you, me, and Natalie go climb into that plane over there and go on another adventure?"

Charlie beamed. "Cool!"

Minutes later, they all sat in the back of the plane, along with Barton. The other two agents sat near the front. Charlie had his face pressed to one of the glass windows as the plane rocketed down the runway and lifted up into the sky. Sam held Natalie's hand so tightly, he thought he might cut off her circulation. But she didn't seem to mind.

Staring out the window, Sam slowly exhaled—a breath filled with relief.

SIXTY-FOUR

Lloyd hustled down the hospital hallway toward the ICU.

His swift pace was driven not by fear but by exhilaration. Pop was finally awake and alert. He'd just gotten the call ten minutes ago. And according to the nurses, not only was his father awake but he was already acting as ornery as ever. While that would have usually frustrated him, Lloyd felt pretty damn happy to hear it today.

He arrived at Pop's room just in time to see a nurse walk out in an angry huff. His father was propped up in the bed. While he still looked fragile, the blood had returned to his face. And the fighting spirit was certainly back, as his father started yelling at him the moment he placed eyes on Lloyd.

"Dammit, Spencer! Get these damn tubes out of me and get me out of this place."

Lloyd laughed, as two days of tension finally released from his chest. He walked over and hugged his father, who tried to push him away. But that only made Lloyd squeeze him even harder.

"Enough of that already," his father continued. "Are you listening to me? I said get me out of here."

"You need to be patient, Pop. You've been through quite the ordeal."

"I feel fine. This is all nonsense."

Lloyd couldn't stop smiling. It had been a damn fine day. With Stone and Barton working closely together, all the key players in this sinister conspiracy had already been apprehended without any further incident. Lloyd had made sure he was standing there when a swarm of federal agents had actually tackled an unsuspecting Mike Madrone to the pavement the moment he'd stepped out of an apartment building. The man who put his father in this bed in the first place—among many other more serious sins—would now suffer severe consequences for it.

"Why're you standing there and grinning like an idiot?" his father scolded him. "You like seeing me this way?"

Lloyd patted his father's arm. "Look, I can't get you out of here today, Pop, but how about I run to the store and pick us up the biggest carton of Oreo cookies I can find?"

His father glared at him. "Double stuffed?"

"Of course."

His father grumbled a bit more, then finally said, "Okay, fine."

SIXTY-FIVE

Natalie began working on her story for *PowerPlay* while on the plane ride home with Sam from London. Focusing on her story seemed to be a healthy way for both of them to share their versions of events because it allowed them to somewhat detach from the heavy emotions of everything they'd been through over the past two days. Although with each new revelation she shared with Sam of what she'd had to endure to stay alive and get to the truth, he seemed to get angrier with himself. He kept saying he was just trying to protect her, but all he really did was put her in even more danger. He'd never be able to forgive himself.

Natalie offered little to help soften his blows—he deserved it. She was okay with Sam treating himself like a bit of a punching bag right now, even if she could understand how the shock of discovering Marcus Pelini was his real father might have clouded his decision-making. Still, she would not let him off easy. If they had any future together, she had to draw a hard line. Trust was *everything* in a relationship. To his credit, Sam accepted her cold-shoulder approach. He was not letting himself off easy, either.

Upon landing in DC, Natalie headed straight to her office at *PowerPlay* to finalize her story while Sam took Charlie back to her apartment. Natalie couldn't imagine what was going through that sweet boy's head right now. Charlie had a long road ahead of him.

The office was abuzz when she arrived. Her editor, Nick Montague, was waiting for her, along with several other reporters and staff who had been working her story nonstop since Natalie had called in the cavalry earlier that day. Although the FBI had already apprehended Senator Harris hours earlier, creating a serious DC buzz, no news outlet had been able to give many details on the reasons behind his arrest. With a press of a button on her keyboard, Natalie would be changing that shortly.

Although the arrest of Senator Harris understandably created the most excitement around town, several other arrests had also taken place across the city in what had officially become a joint FBI–CIA investigative effort. With Stone's blessing, Natalie had made sure members of her team were there to document each of the arrests in person with their high-powered cameras.

Lenny Gregor—the thug who had relentlessly hunted her.

Nathan Barnes—the attorney who had likely contracted Lenny on behalf of his uncle, Senator Harris.

Dan Bradley—the assistant deputy director with the CIA who had been in cahoots with Harris from the beginning.

A dark political conspiracy with far-reaching international repercussions.

And another serious notch on Natalie's investigative-reporter belt.

Sitting at her desk, Natalie felt half a dozen sets of eyes on her from behind. Everyone on her team was waiting for her to press Enter. To upload her full story to the website and set Twitter on fire. They all lived for these moments. The air was thick with anticipation.

Natalie hesitated a moment. There was only one source of tension for her: Sam. Once again, she'd been placed in the precarious position of having to leave out key components of a dynamic story in order to protect the man she loved. Would that ever end?

Sam had told her on the plane about the proposition Director Barton had put in front of him in London. She had to admit, it seemed right up Sam's alley—*if* everything Barton was saying about helping the most vulnerable was true. Sam seemed open to it but insisted he would never take a step forward without Natalie's full blessing.

Could she give Sam that blessing?

Natalie already felt the emotional tug-of-war happening inside.

On one side, the man she loved; on the other, her journalistic integrity.

What kind of future was that? Could they survive that constant tension?

What kind of journalist would she become?

Still—she loved Sam deeply. More than anything.

Reaching over, she pressed Enter, as the office erupted in cheers.

SIXTY-SIX

With Charlie standing by his side, hugging on his leg, Sam knocked firmly on the door. A moment later, Pastor Isaiah opened the front door of his home with the brightest of smiles. Sam exchanged a warm embrace with the man. Then Pastor Isaiah knelt before the boy, where he could look him eye to eye.

"You must be Charlie," Pastor Isaiah said.

Charlie nodded, shifted awkwardly.

"My name's Isaiah. It's wonderful to meet you."

Charlie grinned shyly, hugged Sam's leg a bit harder.

The boy knew he'd be living with a new family in a city called Denver. But it was clearly difficult for him to step into yet another unfamiliar situation. Sam had done his best to prepare Charlie for a new life in the States. Up until they had left London, the boy clearly thought he'd be returning to his home in Moscow at some point. That had created some bumps in the road. To ensure the transition went smoothly, Director Barton had allowed Charlie to stay with Sam for a full week in a remote DC location, where they'd bonded over games, movies, and every sort of fun adventure Sam and Natalie could possibly dream up for the boy. Sam had done his very best to pour everything he had into Charlie during that short time frame in an effort to help the boy feel as safe and secure as possible. Now it was up to Pastor Isaiah and Alisha, who had immediately agreed to take him into their home for however long it took.

"We're so glad to have you here," Pastor Isaiah continued with Charlie, his voice filled with the same gentle warmth that had first embraced Sam ten years ago, when he'd been a listless sixteen-year-old street kid.

Pastor Isaiah led them inside the home. Alisha had everything decorated to the nines, as usual, and Sam could smell something amazing brewing over in the kitchen. Sam hugged Alisha, who then also knelt in front of Charlie and introduced herself in a way that seemed to make the boy more at ease. Pastor Isaiah had suspected Charlie might warm more quickly to Alisha, considering the boy had had some major dysfunction with the male figures in his life.

Pastor Isaiah's three kids were also in the living room, looking prim and proper and ready to meet their new houseguest. The twin boys, Myles and Kevin, were the same age as Charlie, which Sam felt would be hugely beneficial. Grace was eight, and every bit the hostess, just like her mother. After Sam hugged each of them, Grace took Charlie by the hand and walked him down a hallway to show him his bedroom. The boys followed closely behind.

"They're all very excited," Alisha told Sam.

"I can't thank you enough," he said, looking at both of them.

"We're honored to do it, Sam," Alisha reassured him.

"After all, he's family," Pastor Isaiah added.

Sam grinned, hugged them both again.

"I hope you're hungry," Alisha said. "I made your favorite."

She winked at him. Homemade lasagna. He'd breathed in the indescribable aroma the moment Pastor Isaiah had opened the front door. Sam could've eaten Alisha's lasagna for every meal during the year he'd lived with them as a teenager. His stomach had actually begun craving it as soon as the plane had touched down at the Denver airport.

"Yes, ma'am!" Sam replied, smiling wide.

Alisha returned to the kitchen. Sam and Pastor Isaiah walked down the hallway to check in on the kids. Sam was pleased to see Charlie sitting on the carpet in the boys' bedroom, all of them playing a fun board game together. They were already laughing about something. Charlie looked like he was having fun. Sam's eyes grew wet at the sight. While it would be difficult to get back on a plane to DC without him, Charlie was in such good hands with this family. Sam's family.

Pastor Isaiah wrapped his arm around Sam's shoulder. "Let's go for a walk."

They shuffled down the quiet sidewalk of the cozy neighborhood. There was so much Sam wanted to tell Pastor Isaiah—especially about his father—but he could share none of it with the man. *Everything* was classified, Barton had instructed. He was allowed to inform Pastor Isaiah he'd been involved with the CIA during the past month, so not everything was clouded in complete mystery. His mentor seemed to understand that Sam could only dance around certain topics.

"How are you, Sam?" Pastor Isaiah asked, always getting to the heart.

"I'm not sure, to be honest. Everything's a bit of a blur right now."

"Seems that way. Are you and Natalie doing okay?"

"Yes, I think. It's complicated."

"She's an amazing woman."

"More than I deserve."

"Well, you've become a remarkable man," Pastor Isaiah added.

"I appreciate that."

In the past, Sam would have quickly dismissed that comment. But Pastor Isaiah had worked so hard over the years to help him build renewed confidence in who he was because of the redemptive work God had done in Sam's life.

"So what do you think is next for you?" Pastor Isaiah asked. "Will you be continuing your work for David at the law firm?"

Sam sighed. "I actually wanted to talk to you about that. I've been given a unique opportunity to be involved with something where I might be able to help some of the most vulnerable and desperate people on the planet."

"Sounds like a good fit for you."

"Maybe."

"What's the hesitation?"

"Well, this type of work would likely place me deep in an underground world of sorts, if you know what I mean."

Pastor Isaiah looked over at him, seemed to register what Sam was implying. "I see. Would you have to keep it from Natalie?"

"No, sir. I've been assured of that."

"Is it the kind of work you feel is suited to your God-given skills and experience?"

"That's the thing. It almost feels like everything I've been through in my life, all my past experiences, even the most painful ones, have led me to this moment. Is that possible? Does God even work that way?"

Pastor Isaiah smiled. "That's exactly how God works, Sam."

SIXTY-SEVEN

Two months later

Sam stood on fresh-cut grass under a beautiful wooden arch that Natalie's father had handcrafted for this very moment—his only daughter's wedding day. There had never been a question about where Sam and Natalie would get married. Ever since she was a little girl, Natalie had dreamed of a backyard wedding at Foster Farms, her childhood home in Glendale, Missouri. Fifty of the most beautiful acres anywhere.

Sam wore a simple black suit and black tie. Tommy stood next to him, donning a similar black suit and tie, and looking awkward as hell. Sam was so glad to have him there—although Sam had to ask Director Barton for help in finding Tommy and getting him news of the wedding. Tommy had given him a lot of grief about that. But Sam couldn't have imagined this day without him.

Sam peered out over the small crowd. Natalie's expansive family and friends filled about fifty white chairs. All four brothers were there, along with their wives—each of whom stood up front and across the aisle from him—and more than a dozen of Natalie's nephews and nieces. After today, Sam guessed they would also be *his* nephews and nieces. That realization blew him away. In a matter of minutes, Sam would go from a family of two, just him and Charlie, to a family of more than twenty.

David Benoltz sat in the second row. Because their relationship was protected by legal privilege, Barton had allowed Sam to share almost everything with his boss. It felt good to come clean. David had taken such good care of him.

Charlie sat in the front row, next to Alisha and her kids, wearing a cute little blue suit and bow tie. As expected, the boy had blossomed in his two short months with Pastor Isaiah's family. Sam had spent a good amount of time flying back and forth from DC. He was fully committed to being a regular presence in the boy's life.

Sam winked and smiled at Charlie, who gave him the biggest grin back.

A string quartet began playing over to his left. It made butterflies flutter in his stomach. It also brought on a small wave of sadness. There was one person who was not there that he'd have given just about anything to see sitting in the front row. His mother. She'd loved Natalie dearly. Barely a day went by when she hadn't scolded Sam for not marrying Natalie immediately. She had, of course, been right all along. Reaching into his pants pocket, Sam put his fingers around the cross necklace she'd worn up until her very last breath. He could only hope that God would now part the clouds and allow his mother to take in this moment with him.

"Go time," Tommy whispered in his ear.

Pastor Isaiah, wearing his usual sharp black suit and tie, stepped out from around a set of bushes in the back. Then he began a slow path down the grass aisle. Reaching the front, he gave Sam a subtle fist bump and a thousand-watt smile, then turned to face the expectant crowd. The moment had finally arrived.

After taking a brief pause, the string quartet began playing the wedding march.

When Natalie appeared, holding the arm of her sharp-dressed father, Sam felt a tear roll down his cheek. She looked as beautiful as ever in her mother's classic wedding dress. Sam wasn't the only one who'd had to grieve about a loved one who couldn't be there to celebrate this day. They connected eyes. Sam felt another tear pop out. He quickly wiped it away. Natalie had warned him—no tears!—or she might also become a blubbering mess. But it was too damn hard for him to stop. How could he not cry right now as he watched this woman pledge her life to him? This woman who had believed in him when no one else had. This woman who had brought so much healing into his life and had offered him so much undeserved grace. This woman who had already forgiven more than a lifetime should probably allow. This woman who had risked her own life, on more than one occasion, to try to save his. This woman was everything to him.

Waiting to take her hand, Sam had never felt more sure about anything in his life.

SIXTY-EIGHT

Sam again checked the address on the crumpled piece of notepad paper in his hand. Looking up, he found the numbers on the side of the old brick building. This was the place. It sure as hell didn't look like much. As instructed, he bypassed the building's front entrance and instead stepped into an alley between two buildings. After circling a red metal dumpster, Sam found the gray unmarked door. On the outside wall right next to the door was a small black box.

Sam lifted the lid off the box and noted the keypad inside.

Taking a deep breath, he pressed in the numbers he'd been given.

He heard the door click open.

Pulling on the door handle, he stepped inside and found himself walking into a large open room with big digital screens along the outer walls. One of the screens was showing a global map. Desks filled the middle of the room, where a small group of people were working and carrying on. Sam immediately felt a certain energy coming from the room that appealed to him.

He noticed a black woman in her sixties in a dark suit standing in the middle of it all. She had distinctive gray streaks in her hair and carried herself with a certain authority. After spotting Sam standing there, she set down a folder and walked straight over to him with the kind of smile that let him know she could be both friend and foe.

"Good morning, Sam. Welcome to the Orphan Unit."

ACKNOWLEDGMENTS

Readers, your enthusiasm inspires me to write every day. Thank you!

I wouldn't be here without the incredible support of Liz Pearsons, the best editor on the planet and such a delightful and caring person to work with every day, as well as the rest of my amazing publishing team at Thomas & Mercer. I've been blessed beyond measure to be part of the T&M family. Thank you!

A big thanks to Bryon Quertermous, who is a master at seeing the holes in a manuscript and bringing my best story to the surface. Thanks, BQ!

Thanks to David Hale Smith, a rock star of an agent and an all-around great guy. It's been fun to travel these early roads with you, DHS. I really appreciate the way you keep steadily moving my career down the publishing tracks. We have even more exciting days ahead!

I'm fortunate to have an unbelievably supportive group of family and friends who continue to encourage me at every turn. I've enjoyed taking this adventure with all of you. Your outpouring of emails, texts, and social media messages mean everything to me. Thank you!

The most important support starts in my home. Anna, Madison, and Lexi, thank you for giving Daddy the space to write and proudly telling all your teachers about my books. I know you really want to read your father's books soon—but let's get out of elementary school first!

This book, and all of my dreams, would not be possible without the tireless support of my incredible wife, Katie, who sacrifices so much every day and works so hard to make this all possible for our family. I wouldn't want to be in the bunker with anyone else.

ABOUT THE AUTHOR

Photo © 2017 Amy Melsa

Chad Zunker studied journalism at the University of Texas, where he was also on the football team. He's worked for some of the most powerful law firms in the country and has invented baby products that are now sold all over the world. He is the author of two previous Sam Callahan thrillers, *The Tracker* and *Shadow Shepherd*; lives in Austin with his wife, Katie, and their three daughters; and is hard at work on the next novel in the Sam Callahan series. For more on the author and his writing, visit www.chadzunker.com.

Made in United States
Cleveland, OH
07 April 2025